"*Such a Lonely, Lovely Road* is at once fascinating and unforgettable. Set in the new South Africa slowly recovering from decades of apartheid, it tells the complex story of Kabelo and Sediba, two men finding love and navigating the difficult terrain of race, homophobia in the black community and family ties. Molope writes a riveting tale of finding self and finding love in this gripping story of men in love in post-independence South Africa."

—JUDE DIBIA, author of *Blackbird*

Such a Lonely, Lovely Road

A NOVEL

Kagiso Lesego Molope

MAWEN ZI
HOUSE

We acknowledge the support of the Canada Council for the Arts for our publishing program. We also acknowledge support from the Government of Ontario through the Ontario Arts Council.

Cover design by JD&J Design LLC

Library and Archives Canada Cataloguing in Publication

Molope, Kagiso Lesego, 1976-, author
    Such a lonely, lovely road : a novel / Kagiso Lesego Molope.

Issued in print and electronic formats.

ISBN 978-1-988449-44-9 (softcover).--ISBN 978-1-988449-45-6 (HTML).--ISBN 978-1-988449-64-7(PDF)

    I. Title.

PS8576.O45165S83 2018   C813'.6   C2018-904117-X
                                         C2018-904118-8

Printed and bound in Canada by Coach House Printing

Mawenzi House Publishers Ltd.
39 Woburn Avenue (B)
Toronto, Ontario M5M 1K5
Canada
www.mawenzihouse.com

For Motsumi: Be anything. Be everything. Be the best of you.

Contents

Prologue

IT'S CONFUSING, YOU KNOW, to feel on the one hand sad and sorry that someone you love is dead, and then on the other hand utterly relieved. Since I am many different things, many different men, I suppose there's bound to be confusion here and there. So, sorry and relieved is what I felt when, that cold morning in May, Sediba, my former lover, phoned to tell me that my father had died suddenly, without warning.

I had been dreaming about him—my lover, not my father—and longing for him more than my body could stand. One minute he was in the dream with me and the next I was crawling across the bed on my stomach to pick up the phone, pushing back the pain when I noticed as I did every morning that the bed was too large and too empty.

Before I could say, "Hello," he was launching into it, starting and stopping as though he dreaded getting to the point. He told me my father had not had the chance to see his first patient that morning. His secretary had found him lying on the floor near the door, right hand clutching his left arm . . . and so on.

I let him speak, the details becoming less important as he carried on.

"Kabza," he whispered, as if to soften the blow. "*Eish! Eish, Jo. Askies.*" You know how everyone mixes languages. He and I had always done this, except when we were alone we'd pour in a lot more English. We'd never do it around our friends in Kasi because the way we spoke to each other was as much a secret as we were. I wondered if I might still be dreaming, because even as his voice came from the other end of the line, my flat carried the familiar scent of his skin. I could feel my tongue moving to taste something that was not there.

I knew I was supposed to be thinking about my father but my mind raced back, sifting through time and details, calculating. How long had it been since the caller and I had last spoken to each other? Had it been months? How many months? I wanted to ask, but first I had to find my voice.

I made my way to the kitchen to fetch myself some water, phone in hand, hoping to clear my throat. As I walked I got a bit panicked because he sounded so distant, even in offering his condolences. He kept calling me *Jo*, like he were only speaking to an old friend, just one of the guys back home. My heart ached. I started wondering if he might not remember loving me.

Above the fridge, the clock carried on at its usual languid pace, unaffected by the news. My feet tapped the floor for the warm spot just to the left of the sink. Winter seemed to have come early because lately I needed an extra blanket in bed and the floor was always cold, nearly numbing my toes.

"Kabza," I heard him say just as I found that spot, "Shorty came and fetched him . . . "

Shorty. Our impossibly tall childhood friend who worked at the mortuary. Shorty, the one who came in the night and carried out the dead? Then I stopped, thinking: Wait. Hao! My father at the mortuary? I couldn't imagine it, that he'd drop dead in the middle of the day and have his body carried out for all to see. For children playing on the streets to see. Not my quiet, private, dignified father.

I started thinking that maybe there had been a mistake. I could call the surgery, and as always the receptionist Neo would answer and hand him the phone. He'd pick up, pleased that it was his son and no one else disrupting a busy day. Then I could ask him professionally if he thought it was a myocardial infarction that he suffered. Would he need a bypass or would a stent be enough? He liked being the doctor even as a patient and we often joked about how he never trusted another physician to be as thorough as he was.

For a while my mind went on like this, until I became more than a little concerned that if I did phone he might in fact pick up and answer.

Yes, of course, I wanted my father to be alive but it's also true that I very much wanted him to be dead.

When the phone slipped and fell into the sink I made no attempt to pick it up and reconnect us. Now I felt a kind of energy I had not felt in years. That tightness in my neck behind my left ear, the knot that came from nights of staying on one side of the bed with my back to his side because I did not want to remember —that tightness seemed to ease. Even with tearful eyes, I found myself humming to the tune of "Summertime" that was coming through the walls from my neighbour's radio. I mean the rap, not the melancholy jazz song.

It's not that I wasn't devastated, because there's no question that I was. I never had siblings and now with both my parents gone, I was the only living member of my family. Just a few months before, as I saw it, I had killed my mother in that way we all fear killing our parents: I had failed to become what was expected of me. But my father was a different story. He and I had been in close touch since my mother's death and I cherished our now-adult friendship, calling him every Friday to hear about his week and to ask him for advice about my work. The two of us talked now like children who hadn't been allowed to be friends growing up—like we were just discovering one another. I held his opinion in very high esteem and he in turn told me how proud he was of me. His gift to me (or was it mine to him?) was to never speak of the thing that had ended my mother's life. I had, I thought, managed not to kill him as well. His death was squarely on him.

Still, that is not what had me humming a happy tune.

It sounds absurd and crass, but knowing that my father's death threatened to turn my life upside down made it the best news I had heard in months. I would have to leave everything I had established: four months into my year of community service, I would have to resign from my job at a township clinic, sell my flat, go back home to start running my father's surgery, and probably never return to Durban. Up until that moment I had been insisting that Durban was

great, unlike Cape Town it was peaceful and suited me quite well—
and there was truth in there somewhere, but as with other important
things in my life, I had found a half-plausible line to explain away
something I needed to hide.

The thing was, I had come to Durban under difficult circumstances
to begin with and sought in it a refuge from my life before, from what I
secretly called my "Cape Town mistakes." It probably never works to
try and make a home in the place you find in the immediate aftermath
of a youthful blunder. It helps to know first what you're looking for.
I'd had to escape Cape Town and Durban was the first place I could
think of, just far enough from home. By the time that phone call came,
I had given it a solid try. I had thrown myself into the place, thinking
that if I insisted, negotiated, coaxed the city long enough I could make
it my own. But Durban had refused to embrace me, and the phone call
about my father's death offered an escape.

So what I did almost immediately was to get on with the business
of peeling myself away, packing my bags with the anticipation of a
person going on a trip he'd been meaning to take all his life. A whole
new world awaited me, filled with things I had been longing for probably since I had left home at eighteen.

Home

I HAVEN'T KNOWN SEDIBA ALL my life but I feel as if he's always been there. He appears in my earliest memories. We grew up on the same street, his family having come to live there only a week after we moved up the hill to the new developments, called Zone Ex. Not X, but ex for extension. I remember the day his family moved in. They were taking the six-room across the street that had previously belonged to my friend Sesi's family. Her father had painted it a dark grey colour only a month before they moved.

Sediba's family arrived on a Saturday afternoon, one day after Sesi and her parents had driven off in a brown raggedy station wagon, its bottom threatening to collapse from the weight of all their belongings. Their clothes and furniture had filled up most of the car, so that all three of them rode together in the front, Sesi sat in the middle, reaching her hand across her mother's chest and waving goodbye to us. A flimsy rubber cord ran the length of the car, securing the fridge on the roof and a mattress that hung precariously out of the trunk. Sesi's father had decided to take the principal's job in Krugersdorp, his childhood home, after all. When he started painting I had been convinced it was a sign that they were deciding to stay, but they moved anyway, leaving me heartbroken without one of my oldest friends.

For years she had been my favourite person on the street, the best story-teller by far, knowing how to weave each saga from beginning to end so cleverly that I had been known to miss food and play just to find out how it would end. She told stories about boys who wanted dolls and girls who played football. She stopped moving the stones she used as characters on the ground and turned her chin up to demonstrate how someone chewed, or she would stand up to show how someone's leg dragged as they walked. I loved her so much that I spent the weeks before she left trying to convince my parents to let her live with us until the end of the school year. When I brought this idea to Sesi's parents, her father had looked down at me with a sweet, pitying smile and rubbed my head playfully.

"We're taking her with us," he said. "Your parents have you and who would we have if she lived with you?" I stared with teary eyes at his paint-stained blue overalls and the uneven, overgrown hair on his chin and decided that I hated him.

When we waved them away on the street, I saw the car stop and its left side collapse and my heart lifted with hope, but there were too many people around who knew how to tinker with cars for that feeling to last. They were up and running in a minute and we all waved again, pushing back useless tears.

I can recall what day it was when Sediba's family arrived because on Saturdays my mother's shop closed early and that day she had come home long before sunset. We had been playing soccer and had had to rush to move our bricks—our goal posts—out of the way whenever a car came down the street. We were annoyed that we had to make way for her car, and it seemed like only a few minutes had passed before we had to do it again for a lorry, which sprayed us with a cloud of dust and parked in front of Sesi's old house.

I stood across the street from Sesi's six-room holding the ball, which felt perfectly firm because Lelo's father had just pumped it. I cradled it for comfort as I watched the new family move in, feeling both sad and suspicious. To me it would always be Sesi's house and I didn't understand how I was meant to welcome these strangers, who in my view were invading someone else's space. First, the man stepped—no, jumped—out from the front seat and happily slammed the door shut. I could sense his enthusiasm and excitement from across the street as he gleefully rubbed his hands. He was a very tall man with a beard and no hair on his head, and he wore paint-stained overalls like Sesi's father, leaving me to wonder if he were taking both Sesi's father's house and his old job. I decided right there and then that I didn't like him. He was too animated: waving his hands in the air, grinning from ear to ear. No sign of being sorry for moving into someone else's home. I clenched my teeth and shifted my weight with the helplessness of childhood.

The woman, on the other hand, looked like a dream. She had the longest, straightest hair I had ever seen on anyone. Her white dress came just above her knees and was cinched at the waist with a shiny red vinyl belt, which matched her shiny red shoes and the red and white bag that hung in the crook of her elbow. I was mesmerized as I watched her step carefully out of the lorry, careful not to touch anything that might dirty her clothes.

"Ah! Oh-ho. They don't have a child," I heard one of my friends say behind me, regretfully sucking her teeth.

Someone else said: "No, they do. Look!" And there, out from the back seat, strode the best-dressed boy our age that we had ever seen.

"Is that a *tie*?" someone yelled and everyone giggled but I didn't join in. I was enthralled. He wore navy blue shorts, a white t-shirt and a blue scarf with white dots that was carefully tied around his neck, a little bit to the side. My first thought was that he looked like someone from a magazine. I forgave him right away because he was the only one who looked doubtful about stepping through those gates.

In a rather rare moment of leadership I turned to my friends and said: "Let's go and help," and we all leapt across the street to greet the new family. All I wanted was to get closer to the mother, so I walked up to her and ever so politely said: "Dumelang."

She turned around from giving her husband instructions about where to place the large, square mirror he was holding and looked down at me with the stretch of her lips, revealing perfectly straight, white teeth.

"Ao! Hallo," she said and held out her hand. It was a really sweet and sincere hallo, not the amused, pitying kind that most adults gave children. She took the tips of my fingers, a gentle and delicate handshake, and asked my name.

"Kabelo," I said eagerly and pointed behind me without turning: "I live in the big white house." It was unlike me to point out my parents' large and long house and mention that it was big. I had until then been quite embarrassed of the obvious disparities between my family and most of the others on our street, but I suppose at that moment I was eager to impress.

"Ah, Kabelo, I'm Aus' Bonolo. I'm happy to meet you. Do you want to help?" she asked, barely glancing at the house and handing me a blue vase. Her Setswana was pure and refined. I suspected that they were from Mafikeng or maybe even Botswana. She curled her g and her k stayed in her throat a little longer. She sounded like my mother.

Suddenly feeling important, I carried the vase as if it were the most valuable thing I had ever had in my hands. I stepped carefully past her and then turned around to ask where to put it, but before I could say anything I saw that her attention was already on someone else: her impeccably dressed son. She picked something off his t-shirt with her finger and her thumb and then gently cupped his chin with her hand. The boy was speaking too softly for me to hear what he was saying but I could tell from the way his shoulders drooped and his neck pushed forward that he was aware of the ridicule from the street kids. He was probably already wondering how he would fit in and his mother appeared to be soothing and reassuring him.

I was caught between my eagerness to impress her and my curiosity about her and her boy, so I walked towards the house, vase in both hands, looking behind to see what would happen.

After she had rubbed his head, giving him a kiss on the forehead, the boy—whose name we hadn't yet learned—turned to the pile of boxes on the lawn, picked up one marked 'kitchen', turned up his chin and strode confidently past us. All eyes were on him as he headed for the front door without looking at any of us. I think we all parted to make room for him because the change in him and the way he carried himself were so startling. My eyes went from his walk to his mother's handbag. Behind him I noticed the father's broad shoulders and realized that his stride was similar to the boy's. He walked as if he were in a suit instead of overalls. I couldn't help thinking the three of them seemed to be the kind of people who made you want to fix your shirt and check to make sure your shoes were shining.

When I stepped inside their house to put the vase down, I noticed that there was already a long credenza under the living room window. My friend Lelo stood at my side as we stared at the polished piece of furniture with its top lid opened to reveal a record player.

"That's where Sesi's mother had put the other sofa," I recalled aloud.

Lelo said: "So they don't have a TV?"

I guess our minds were on different things. We may as well have been talking to our own reflections. It was irritating.

The mother walked in just then and smiled down at both of us as she put her bag down on top of the credenza. She asked, her hands clasped delicately in front of her, "Do you boys want orange juice?"

We nodded, our legs unable to keep still, and stepped outside to sit on the stoep and wait. I noticed the lawn was freshly cut and flowers lined the fence. It was a typical hot day in Kasi. Everyone was outside in shorts and t-shirts but all I wondered about was the new boy in our midst, who seemed to have disappeared somewhere inside the house. I admired with a little bit of envy that he was wearing a scarf. Lelo and I sat looking towards the lorry, where other men from the street were helping unpack. The street was feeling more chaotic now, with all the neighbours having come to greet and help.

"They're getting Sesi's mother's roses," I said to Lelo, who responded, "You think she forgot about the orange juice?"

I remembered Sesi's mother wearing garden gloves, trimming her rose bushes and humming a church song. They had gone to church every Sunday, attending the Lutheran church that shared a building with the Early Learning Centre. I wondered now if this new family would also be going to the same church, if the mother would be trimming the rose bush while humming church songs, if in fact they would be taking over Sesi's family life as well. The thought made me feel the

way I did sometimes when I watched Aus' Tselane set the table for us
and then disappear to her room that was attached to the garage outside
our house. The feeling was heavy in my chest. It was like hearing a sad
song or visiting someone in the hospital.

When the mother finally appeared, it was clear that she had gone to
great pains to make a beautiful presentation. She stepped lightly, going
sideways across the threshold, holding a tray with two tall glasses
and a plate of biscuits. The glasses had yellow sunflowers on them,
matching the sunflowers on the tray. A white apron hung over her
neck with the words: *You pour the wine / I'll cut the cheese.*

We stood up quickly to help but smiled and said: "Take a glass and
sit."

When we did, the boy appeared behind us, carrying his own glass
of orange juice.

He was about the same height as I was—both of us shorter than
Lelo, who was by then already quite tall for his age—and his skin was
a darker shade than mine. His lips were fuller and his eyes larger. I
thought he was pretty, in a way that girls are, not handsome in the
way boys are. Both Lelo and I looked up at him curiously. He was
such a strange bird, his every move fascinating. We waited to see what
he would do next, if he would come and talk to us or go back in the
house. He looked around as if he were searching for something, his
eyes never meeting ours.

In a moment his mother said: "Diba, come and say hello," his
mother reached out her hand but he didn't take it. Instead he went
back into the house and re-emerged with a stool.

"Diba, this is Kabelo and Lelo," she introduced us when he had put
the stool down. "Boys this is Sediba."

Around him his mother was fussing, I thought, and looked suddenly uneasy the way people seemed when they were new in school.
The boy's eyes went to the stool he had set down in front of us while
his mother smiled nervously. Her lips parted and we thought she'd
say something but then she decided against it and went back into the
house. Now it was just the three of us, looking down at the ground. I

wanted to ask if he'd be sleeping in Sesi's room but thought he might find me too strange. But then he did the most unusual thing. Right there in front of me and Lelo, he sat down and crossed his legs.

I had never seen a boy sit like that. Lelo and I were still, our hands clutching the cold glasses in our hands. I suddenly got very worried that Lelo would laugh. It would be just like him to laugh out loud and make the boy feel embarrassed. I clenched my teeth and wished I could give him a sign, tell him to keep still, but I couldn't think of anything. When it seemed like a very long time had passed and none of us even sipped from our glass or said anything, I looked over at Lelo and to my surprise found him seeming annoyed instead of amused. This was not someone about to laugh, like I had expected. I couldn't say why but this made me panic even more. I said to Sediba: "We're going to play now, do you want to come with us?" I wasn't even sure if I wanted him to come, I couldn't see him fitting in on our dusty street, but I thought asking was the friendly thing to do and I needed Lelo and I to leave.

I was stunned and downright mortified when Lelo spoke before Sediba had a chance to answer. His voice made me cringe as it sounded out contempt for the boy we had only just met.

He said, "Why do you sit like a woman?"

I was afraid the boy would disappear back into the house and tell his mother, who would then come out and admonish us in her impeccable, refined Setswana, but he didn't.

The most astonishing thing to me was—and this is what I thought of a lot throughout the next few years—that instead of uncrossing his legs, Sediba shrugged, stayed in the same position, turned up his chin like he had done earlier and took sips of his juice.

Later when we were walking home, after we had politely thanked Sediba's mother and carefully placed our glasses into their empty sink, I wondered if Sediba would want to be our friend. I wondered what sorts of games he liked to play and couldn't quite see him getting dirty the way the rest of us did.

Lelo said, "I heard she is a hairdresser. She does hair in her house.

Where do you think she'll do it? In her bathroom?"

I shrugged and kicked a small stone, regretting immediately the dust that covered my shoe. Without answering him, I kicked another stone, this time out of some inexplicable anger that kept rising and rising inside me. Lelo continued talking. "He's like a girl, neh? Why is he dressed like that and why does he sit like that? Maybe he spends too much time around women." I noted that he said "women" instead of "girls" and I could see that Lelo had been just as unsettled by Sediba, because he was using words that made him sound older, more sophisticated. He was as uneasy as I was, but for different reasons. I didn't care if she did hair. My thoughts were more on the boy than his mother. Why had he stridden past us like that, his head held high? And why hadn't he cried? Why hadn't he run back into the house sobbing? I had never known anyone who didn't dissolve into tears when Lelo was irritated with them.

I didn't understand anything going on in my body; there was this overwhelming need to *hide*.

Now I wanted it to be the week before, when Sesi was still there. There was something about Sediba that I wished I hadn't known, that made me want to go back in time and not see it again. When we reached the middle of the street my friends were lining the bricks back up, getting ready to restart the soccer game. I stood there watching them, suddenly feeling too tired.

"I'm going home," I announced and turned around and went to lie on the sofa in our sitting room where I watched boring daytime TV where people did nothing but talk, speaking English with American accents and declaring their love for each other. My mother was standing at the dining room window when I walked in, one hand on her hip. He nails were freshly painted a solemn burgundy. She didn't turn around but told me to "close the door." then pulled her lips in and folded both arms as if to shield herself from a cold drought.

"Who are they?"

"The mother is called Bonolo, the boy is called Sediba. I don't know about the father."

"She's dressed like she's going somewhere important. Who wears a bright dress in a truck?"

I didn't know.

After months of dreading it, I was all of a sudden looking forward to moving up the hill, farther away from this new family, especially the boy.

———

In the following years Sediba remained somewhere in the background or right in front of me, but whenever we were at the same party or with the same two or three friends, we avoided each other. At first I thought it went one way, that I was dodging him, but then one day we went on a Boxing Day picnic with the same group of friends and I noticed him also turning his back to me or looking away whenever I started talking. We had the same friends, so why didn't we even speak? I grew very busy working at being as macho as possible, and he continued wearing fashionable yet not quite manly clothes so that I didn't like the look of him—or told myself that I didn't. Every now and then I would catch myself looking at his muscular legs when he was wearing shorts, or the way his jeans hugged his bum. Once I saw him lift his shirt and rub his stomach and caught sight of his navel. A little round dip above a startlingly smooth trail of black hair. That night, alone in my room, I couldn't be rid of the image—my hand down and under my boxers just before I fell asleep.

And then it all seemed to go in a different direction between us.

In the middle of December, a little less than two months before leaving for varsity, two things happened to solidify my suspicions that a) I wanted more than anything to be a doctor and b) I was only attracted to boys.

I got early acceptance from UCT. My father ran in one afternoon—too early for him to be finished with his work—and waved his keys and a long white envelope in his right hand. On TV, Cliff Huxtable was complaining about his son eating all their food when he was not even living at home. I was bored. None of my friends had been at their houses when I called on them, so I was watching Bop TV, the satellite station with the American shows that showed black people. Black people laughing, black people reminiscing about Dr Martin Luther King. Black people talking about segregation—something that would never appear on the government-regulated South African TV stations. Bop TV was like an illegal secret. You had to hold the antenna just right to get it going.

My father was not someone who raised his voice very much but that day I had heard him shouting as he burst through the door, "You're in! You're in, Doctor Mosala!" He'd already opened the envelope and read the letter. It would be months into my first year in medical school before it occurred to me that I had never actually read that letter.

My mother's car came hooting through the gate. She had often taken my school report down to old friends to brag, and I expected her to do the same with the letter.

"You're in, my son! Another Doctor Mosala!" she pronounced and then, ululating, she danced through the door.

I was in, and at the historically white university too, where they admitted their first Black medical student only four years previously. My father, in his time, had gone to a Black university. So this was new and seen as a breakthrough of sorts. I watched my parents' awkward embrace, their bodies coming apart too soon for the amount of exhilaration they had both just displayed. Neither came over to give me a hug. They reveled in their own pride only a few steps from where I stood.

I was in. I planned to go and never come back.

I had always been the child who was interested in illness and injury. I would follow my friends into their homes to watch as their mothers took care of a scrape or a bad cut, asking if I could help. The thrill that rushed through me when I saw a wound or looked through a microscope in biology class was matched by nothing else in my life at that time.

And so on a chaotic afternoon in December, when my friends and I were stuck at a music festival trying to find a way to get home after Sediba had just been cut with the sharp edge of a beer bottle, everyone knew who would volunteer to take him to get help. It wasn't an especially gruesome cut, but I could tell it was would need stitches. My suggestion that I take him to my father brought everyone great relief. All we had to do was find a lift since the guy with whom we had come to the festival had disappeared.

Finally one of Trunka's friends offered us a lift in the back of his van. I was the first one to climb in and held my hand out to Sediba to help him jump in. I remember even in that moment I didn't look at him, keeping my eyes on the wounded hand, which was now wrapped in his t-shirt soaked with blood. Sediba had in fact been pulling Lelo away from a fight with someone who had smashed his beer bottle against a rock and was using it as a weapon when it had caught and sliced across Sediba's palm.

I sat across from him on the truck floor, elbows on my knees and eyes looking in his direction but not right at him. I had never liked to look at him too closely or for too long, unable to see in him what I couldn't see in myself. By then he had lived in Kasi for about six years, and we had managed to be very good about avoiding each other, crossing the road and looking the other way when the other came along. Even as we continued to run in the same circles, holding on to the same friends. Now here we were facing a forty-minute journey on the back of a bakkie with no one else to speak to.

"Do you know how to do stitches?" he eventually asked, his voice rising effortlessly above the noise of cars on the road. He looked rather calm, considering that he was shirtless and bleeding through a very nice piece of clothing around his hand.

I squinted against the sun, clenching my bum, trying not to show my nerves.

"Heh?" I was pretending to be deep in thought, acting like his question had just reached me. "Uh . . . no. No, I don't."

"Don't you watch your father do it all the time?"

I thought: *Actually with a little trust from him and some opportunity I would have you stitched up in no time,* but I only chuckled at the thought.

Sediba, looking puzzled, shrugged and looked away.

When the silence started to feel like too much I cleared my throat. *Now*, I thought, *I should say something.*

"Does it hurt?" I tried.

Sediba shrugged and then slowly looked up at me, his mouth spreading into the most endearing smile I had ever seen, his eyes firmly on me and twinkling from the light.

"It hurts a lot, *Jo!*"

We both laughed. I felt the back of my neck go hot and I rubbed it with one hand.

"You look brave. You didn't scream or anything, just pulled off your shirt and wrapped it around your hand." As I spoke I mimicked him pulling off his shirt and wrapping it, and saw that the look on his face showed curiosity and intrigue. He'd thought I hated him and now realized he had been wrong.

His eyes were so gentle, his face carried so much kindness that I couldn't help but fall into it.

After a brief moment of contemplation, he said, "You can't cry around those guys."

I shifted, looked him in the eye a bit longer now and smiled. We both knew what we were talking about and that none of our friends could find out that we were having this exchange. It was like huddling against the cold, this acknowledgement. I felt at ease, comforted.

We rode the rest of the trip talking about our friends—their ambitions, our admiration of Trunka's hard work and how we could easily see him taking over his father's tuck shop; we joked about Base sounding like that guy in Boyz II Men with the startlingly deep voice. But all that time, neither one of us brought up about Lelo.

We laughed a fair bit and by the time we reached our house I was sorry I had avoided him all those years and was only getting to chat with him now, weeks before I would leave for Cape Town and he for Tukkies.

Our driver held out his hand as if we'd had an agreement and I handed him ten rand out of my pocket before he zoomed off.

I sat on the edge of the bath and Sediba sat on a chair I had brought for him, his hand held over the sink, the blood dripping into it. I had my father's brown leather bag on my lap, biting my top lip as I watched intently. My job was to hand my father his instruments as he meticulously worked his way through the cut, which looked much deeper than I had initially thought. My father had come to his door upon hearing me knock, wearing a t-shirt and having quickly pulled up a pair of jeans. By then I had already fetched his bag from the hook behind the door, its usual place in the spare room.

My father's eyes stayed squarely on his work while Sediba's were closed, his head resting against the wall. I gave myself full permission to look at Sediba's body. He was being brave, trying not to wince with every prick of the needle. His lips were pressed together and his other hand gripped his knee, his nails digging into it. I noticed another scar above his navel, a smooth bean-shaped burn mark with slightly wrinkly edges and was embarrassed to note that it hadn't been there about a year previously, the last time I had looked. Obviously he worked out—I had been with guys on the rugby field and had rarely seen such a toned torso. It took my attention away from the stitching and I was staring without knowing it. In my mind I traced my finger along the ridges of his defined biceps.

"Kabi?" my father was saying.

Startled, I looked up to find him holding out his hand. "I said cut the thread."

Sediba opened one eye and smiled at me knowingly and I bit my lip, feeling mortified.

The day after Sediba was cut the two of us walked out of Trunka's house at the same time but not actually together. As soon as we were out of sight from the guys he caught up to me quietly, looking behind him as though to make sure no one would notice. Hands in his pockets, he lowered his voice and said, "So . . . your father says the stitches can come out in two weeks."

It took a lot of effort to look at him. I said, "Two weeks is a long time."

"Yah, I can't help my mother so much but . . . "

"But it will heal."

"It will, yah."

When it was time for me to turn the corner and go up the hill he didn't turn back, continuing alongside me. The sun had gone down by then but all of Kasi was up, drunken men mulling about, everyone's attention on their music, their lovers, and their drink. As long as it was not our friends noticing us together, I thought, then it was fine.

There was nothing wrong with it, just two guys walking, chatting, but still I was glad it was dark, that people were too drunk to look, and that no one could see my hands go in and out of my pockets, my shoulders up as if it were cold when it was the middle of December. I was worried and convinced that if anyone saw us together, they'd know about me.

When I crossed the road he didn't turn back, walking me all the way up the hill.

He said: "Your father . . . he doesn't smile very much."

I laughed. All people ever said about my father was that he was a good doctor, respectable, admirable. I was surprised to feel relief when Sediba spoke about him the way I saw him. It was true, my father could be aloof. At that time, right before I left for varsity, I was spending more time with him at his surgery. Always busy and focused, he was a man married to his work. I thought it was lucky that I wanted the same career; or I'm not sure I'd have had a chance to know him at all.

"He's strict, neh?" Sediba said, chuckling with me. "He's not like my father."

"No," I said. "Your father whistles."

"He what?"

"He whistles! He sings and he dances. Look, even when listening to his favourite song, my father is quiet."

"Yah, my parents are good-times people. They used to wake me up in the middle of the night to go home, after I had slept on the bed at their friends' houses." They were so unlike my parents, I thought. I had seen his father with his hand sliding around his wife's waist. I had seen his mother rub her hand up and down her husband's beard.

The conversation was so smooth, so easy. We kept stopping and laughing all along the way, me forgetting about being seen, and then we were at my gate before I knew it.

I wanted him to linger or come inside, but he said, "I'll see you, *Jo*," with a wide grin. Before I could say anything in reply he was walking backwards down the hill, waving. And I was sorry he hadn't hesitated.

The next night, after an evening with our friends, I left them a little early, and before I reached the street corner, there he was at my side again, this time holding up a plastic bag. "New tapes," he said. Then we sat in his backyard, listening to new kwaito songs, sipping Coke and eating biscuits on the back lawn just behind the house, where no one could see.

Sediba was a keen listener. He liked to ask questions and then sit back and listen as I replied without stopping, going far beyond the actual answer. With my parents and friends, conversation was guarded. Always afraid that I might say something that could land me into a trap, I chose my words carefully. People called me things they call you when you're too afraid to talk: quiet, thoughtful, shy. I was just scared.

While Lelo, Trunka, and Base had always been my closest childhood friends, starting around fourteen they had had nothing but girls on their minds and talk of sex had taken over our conversations. I laughed at their jokes and once in a while pretended to know what they were talking about, but it was becoming tedious. Sediba had learned to evade the big issues in his life by finding plenty of other things to talk about. Whenever I heard him say something in a group it was safe but interesting. He had mastered the art of sidestepping without showing it. He seemed friendly and unguarded, but he still had that thing about him: the thing that stopped people from asking too much for fear of sounding too familiar.

When he talked about himself, he let you think he was opening up, but I knew he stayed very quiet about what could get him into trouble. "I want my own line of hair products, *Jo*. There are guys doing it for themselves. I want shampoos and oils that smell of peppermint, lilac, sage, and lavender." He was intrigued by scents. While the rest of us were constantly spraying ourselves with something so strong that you could almost smell it from a across the street, he was the only guy I knew who preferred a grapefruit body cream to strong men's cologne. He wanted his own house as soon as he finished varsity and he wanted to stay close to home, where he hoped more than anything to open his own salon. I didn't understand that part. I didn't understand not wanting to run away from here.

He said, "My mother has been working out of that back room for so long, I think this might be the year we finally open something. But she says no, I have to go to varsity first, I have to study business and then we'll talk about me opening a salon. So that's where I'm going next year."

On these secret evenings we'd lie side by side on the lawn almost— just almost—touching. I had to stop my body moving towards him, his shape, his scent; his words and his skin so inviting that staying still was nearly impossible and leaving him always a arduous process of lifting and pulling myself away. Every morning I couldn't wait for the day to end so that I could be with him.

We fell into a routine over the next few weeks, our time together lulled by summer's easy passing. Both of us worked in the day—I helped my mother at her shop, working at the till or stocking up shelves—and if my father needed me at the reception desk in his clinic I would be there. Sediba also helped both his parents at their work places. As soon as I was finished, I'd run home and wash, spray cologne and put in an appearance at Trunka, Lelo, or Base's then finally, either Sediba would go home and I'd follow afterwards or I'd leave first. Some nights he'd climb over our high gate and come to my backyard, where I would be sitting with cold drinks waiting for him. My parents, pleased with my performance in school and excited by my early acceptance into UCT, were now making some allowances. Beer was, in my mother's words, "OK in moderation." Sometimes we took the beer that my mother bought for my father, though he was never home long enough to sit and drink it. We'd sip from the same beer because neither one of us could finish an entire bottle alone. At least that's what we said to each other. That was the reason we agreed on.

My parents didn't mind him coming and going, and they said nothing about me spending long hours out some nights. Until the matric results were out, they would each fuss in their own way, my father calling me to the surgery all the time, trying to convince me that medicine was the right thing for me as if not wanting me to forget though all I did there was greet people, answer the phone, and write down messages. Maybe it was his way of having me close to him just one last time. Or maybe he noticed changes in me and wanted to be sure it was not my love for medicine that was slipping away. Then there was my mother, saying, "I'll come down to Cape Town a few times a year. I've always loved Cape Town," making my heart sink. On the nights my father was not home for supper, the two of us sat eating alone and she'd say something like, "Maybe you could consider staying close. Maybe then we could see you more often." I would pick up my glass of water and smile, thinking, *never*.

I would tell her, "UCT's the best, Ma. And you always say you'd love to come to Cape Town."

But then because summer has that mollifying effect on people, settles their nerves, by the end of December they were much more relaxed about me.

I came to look forward to seeing Sediba a lot more than to sitting around Trunka's house listening to vivid descriptions of women's bodies, cringing but also curious about what it was they found so irresistible. I went to see my friends less and less. Some evenings I'd go straight home after my work at the shop or the surgery, and wait for Sediba to come after finishing at his mother's salon. My growing affection for him was the first thing that had ever rivalled my love for medicine.

"Are you excited to leave?" he asked me towards the end, looking me in the eye in that way that sometimes felt a little bit sad and desperate—his face carrying more than his words could convey.

"I was—I mean, I am. I am excited." My throat felt dry.

"Won't you miss home?"

It took everything in me to stay still and keep my eyes on him.

"I will, *Jo*. I'll miss home a lot."

It was one of many fleeting moments when I saw us stopping, no longer dodging each other.

But then very quickly he said, "I've heard about guys taking their time getting to Cape Town, getting up to no good on the way," and like that we had shifted to safer ground.

There were two things we were aware of: First, my father had sewn stitches on the foreheads of comrades after prison stints, and his mother had hidden rioters in the back room of her salon. Our desires were strong but we knew we would never be seen as manly or African enough. What we wanted, the things we longed for in silence, were seen by our people as white and un-African. And second, being the only children to our parents, Sediba and I were star sons, model citizens. We had been groomed to be the boys who would come back and be our fathers' sons. "Don't bring all eyes on us" was one of my mother's favourite sayings. *O sa re tsenyetsa matlho.*

As my departure drew near, my parents decided to throw me a going-away party. A braai in our backyard.

I had expected it, of course; it is the ceremony that naturally follows when you've done well. A party for my mother to show everyone I was everything she had always said I was. See? All those school reports, all those science and biology trophies displayed in our dining room led to this moment. So just about everyone we knew was going to be invited to our house on my last Friday afternoon, the day before I was scheduled to leave, to eat and drink to their hearts' content.

Alone in my room, every night after Sediba left I would wonder what it would be like for me to be open and honest with him, imagining us letting go and giving in to our feelings. What would that be like? What would I say? Every time I was near him, I felt parts of me tugging, suppressed longings being pulled out from their safe hiding spaces and called to life. I'd watch him climb up the wall and the gate and jump down, his arm muscles bulging with his every move, shirt riding up to reveal more of him, and I could hardly breathe. Every time he left I had the unsettling urge to beg him to stay, to risk the scorn and the disappointment that would surely come tumbling down upon us, to put everything out in the open. I never did that. I could sometimes see his step slowing, his arms folding as if to stop himself from touching me, his eyes staying on me a bit longer. He never said anything either and I worried that we'd go on like this and then leave and go our separate ways—possibly never to have the chance again.

So that day, when my mother came home in the afternoon and announced, while taking count of the liquor bottles in the house, that there would be a party, I felt the end approaching. I thought: now or never.

There was a lot of sadness in the house on the day of the party. I had found my mother crying in her bedroom that morning, her chin trembling, palm pressed against her cheek. When I asked her what was wrong, she said, "I'm going to miss you so much," but I had the feeling that there was much more to her crying than that. "The good news is," she started, blotting her tears with a tissue, "I invited Tiny and she's bringing her niece." Her smile was genuine. I bit my lip.

Then, mysteriously—because neither one of my parents would say why—Aus' Tselane was not there the whole day and my mother brought in two of her employees from the shop to help with setting up. I ran around all day packing my bags and buying last-minute things, not entirely looking forward to the evening. My friends from school—Beast, Mohale, Dave and Elliot—who were also coming to UCT—had phoned several times asking questions like, "Should we bring pillows or do you think they provide them at the res?" and "There's enough beer in the cooler but not enough wine. Can you bring more?" We were all frantic, trying to make the transition from home to varsity as smooth and tolerable as we could. The phone calls were merely a sort of handholding we needed from each other. I was getting more excited until someone said, "Can you imagine the number of chicks we'll suddenly be surrounded by?" Then I felt like no one was holding my hand.

My spirits lifted when evening came, and then dropped again. Sediba was especially handsome in a crisp white short-sleeve shirt and a pair of dark blue jeans that looked new. He arrived with our other friends: Lelo, Trunka and Base, who were all wearing nice clothes for the occasion. Dark blue jeans and their shirts bright, crisp, and new. But Sediba stayed in the background and looked more nervous and less self-assured than I was used to seeing. The other guys were in top form. No Kasi boy ever misses an opportunity to dress up. They liked labels, called their shoes things like Kurt Geiger instead of just shoes and their shirts had to be Lacoste and not just a shirt. Trunka wore a rather dapper golf hat that he had turned slightly to the side and Lelo had very shiny black Kurt Geiger shoes. I was being given a proper send-off.

Sediba and I behaved as we usually did, barely acknowledging each other and skillfully keeping our distance, never sitting or standing next to each other at any moment. That party was the first time it occurred to me that for all the time we had spent together no one actually knew we had become close friends. We hadn't done anything that anyone would disapprove of, but it was as if the mere knowledge that we enjoyed each other's company might tip people off about what else we had in common.

As the hours passed the party became more and more torturous for me. Aus' Tiny, my mother's friend, arrived as expected with her husband and niece, whose name was Tshidi. The girl was tall and slim, strode in with confidence and (thankfully) set her eyes on Lelo. Girls usually did.

Sediba was fully aware of what was happening. He had been keeping his distance before but still stealing glances and giving me knowing looks. Now he was just plain ignoring me. It stung. I suppose it was hard to ignore my mother hurrying around in high heels and a glass of wine—one glass too many—saying, "Kabi! Kabi! See what Tshidi needs. Get Tshidi something to eat. Sit next to Tshidi, she doesn't know anyone." This was my mother: Other people's parents would only show an interest in girls they brought home. My mother took initiative and brought me a girl.

I'd once heard her tell her friends, "He's just shy, my baby. He's not like your sons. He just needs a little push."

Lelo rose to the occasion. As soon as he saw Tshidi's eyes on him the two of them were off in a corner. He was bringing her a plate of food, giving her a chair to sit on. He wasn't really interested, but that's always been irrelevant with Lelo. If there's a girl and she's interested you go over, you talk, you seduce. It's the principle of the thing: be a man, no matter what. He was the guy who had learned how to break into a car and steal the sound system. "Everything plus the speakers," he'd told us. Because "a man has to learn these things." He said he dragged himself up the hill every day to UNISA to get a law degree for the same reason. A man has to learn these things.

My mother walked over and pulled me aside: "Why do you leave her alone with him?" I shrugged—which, I realized, only worked to convince her that I needed her help.

"He's not better than you, you know. None of those boys are." I went to help my father with the meat on the braai stand.

Seeing Sediba so assiduously avoiding me, I became more and more restless and agitated. I was gripped by the fear that I might never see him again and thought: and this would be how it ends? What if I never again have the chance to see what it's like to kiss someone I actually really like? I so badly wanted us to have a little time to ourselves after everyone was gone. But even as the thought frightened me I wondered if and how that goodbye could be prolonged.

But what was prolonged was the party. My friends showed no signs of wanting to leave, which was exactly the way I might have like it, had I not had anything else on my mind.

They stayed late to help clean up the mess around the yard and even in the house. Then, just as I thought they'd leave, they sat down on the lawn, legs stretched out, reminiscing in that way that we all tend to do when getting ready to say goodbye. We watched Lelo walk Tshidi to Aus' Tiny's car, her smile wide and content. Lelo said something in her ear and she shrugged one shoulder, the smile not leaving her face. This was his show.

We'd all seen it countless times. He'd make no attempt to see her again after this, and you felt sorry for her even as some part of you was in awe of his skill. That thing that holds a girl's attention: I'd never had that. To be fair, I'd never wanted it, not with girls anyway, but skill is skill and you can't help but marvel and admire when someone excels.

Then he was back and lounging with us on the lawn, a satisfied smirk all over his face. It was what my mother couldn't stand about Lelo, this smirking, the confidence she saw as insolence. She didn't understand his self-assured manner, his refusal to act as if he didn't belong, while I needed a push and a shove just to speak to people. She didn't know how he saw the scene with Tshidi. He had won at a man's game. And he had won against me.

I don't know why he and I kept at it all those years, why I always wanted to measure up, because if he was always winning then it wasn't much of a competition, but it did go on much longer than it should have. When we settled down I turned up the music. Old R&B was now on, songs that were the soundtrack to our childhood. We wound down the evening with stories going back to the time before Sediba came, and when we talked about the day he arrived we graciously left out the embarrassing bits.

Lelo said, "We were all thinking: Hao! Who is this guy dressed like it's Sunday?" And we all laughed, pretending we hadn't minded him then, that we had welcomed him with open arms from the very beginning.

But there was a part of me—the part that remembered what Lelo had said after that first time we met Sediba—that cringed at hearing him reminisce. "*Eish, Jo.* All of us covered in dust because we had been playing soccer and your moving van had come barreling down the street!" And Trunka said, "Seriously *Jo*, how did you go that long without getting dirty?" Sediba replied: "My mother made sure of it."

We laughed at that. Everyone knew Sediba's mother was as clean as they come, so this led to us talking about our mothers and their cleanliness. We stuck to the polite details.

They stayed longer, finishing their beers and looking more and more sloshed by the minute. Then of course it was Lelo's turn— because Lelo always needed a turn, to have us engrossed in one of his stories.

"Eintlik, I'm happy the two of you are leaving," he started, pointing from me to Sediba. "I'm going for one of your Gradus."

The guys called the girls from the multiracial Model C schools "Gradus," for "Graduates." I didn't really know why. Lelo had long been pulled towards the kind of girls Sediba and I went to school with, finding them annoying, fascinating, and amusing all at once. Mainly, I think, he treated them like a challenge he had to take on. Something to do with not being able to go to those same private schools himself.

"You have the ones who want a movie date before taking their panties off, *Jo*," he liked to tell us and that night he repeated himself. Adding: "But not with me. With guys like me they want to go home first. Girls like that, they live for that moment when their mother wakes up to find you running out of her bedroom, pulling your shirt on. And me," his laughter came up like a roar from his belly, "me, I love to hear that ou' lady screaming, 'What school does he even go to?' " We were always thoroughly entertained by Lelo, even though I never missed the hint of scorn in his jokes about the Gradus.

"So now I have this sweet one, neh? Her name is Masechaba. She's the head girl at St Mary's. So, I'm running out of her room the other day and her mother says: 'Sies! What school does this one go to?' She has her fists on her hips and my girl is in nothing but a t-shirt behind me. Die ou' lady looks at me like she's never smelled anything so foul. She says: 'What does he want?' and my girl says—hahaaaaa!—she says: 'Mama, he wants *me*!' Yoh! I'll never forget it Gents."

He rolled onto his back. "Fuck your schools Mama. Your daughter

wants a real man," he quickly glanced at me and then took a swig of
his beer.

I wiped my brow because I imagined I was sweating, but I wasn't. I
could have let it go on but instead I turned to Base.

"You know I was just saying to someone the other day," I said,
without looking at Sediba, "That you could be like that guy Mike
from Boyz II Men!"

Base smiled, chuffed. He asked, "Who were you saying it to?"

I shrugged and bit my lip. "*Haai*, just one of my friends from
school."

"Not a *cherrie*? Come on *Jo*, tell those things to a *cherrie* around here
and I can"—he held out two fists as if grabbing hold of someone and
moved his hips back and forth.

We all laughed. Then he was fishing through his pockets and came
out with a purple box in his hand, which he threw at me and said, "For
you, Mfana. Use it before the end of the first week. All those cherries,
far from home and looking for a man to hold onto." He wrapped his
arms around his chest, demonstrating. Lelo nearly spat out his beer
from laughing. He walked over and opened the box, pulling out the
condoms in a black wrapper and letting them fall down in one long
line as if he'd just performed a magic trick. I shifted in my seat and put
down my beer, laughing, careful to keep my eyes away from Sediba.

Lelo cut one off. "I'll take one just for tonight." His eyes stayed
on me like he was examining suspicious fruit. "Will you use these?"
He made as if to hide them behind his back. I laughed, coughed.
"Seriously. Because if you won't, I will, *Jo*."

I snatched them from him. "That's my present, neh? Give it back."

Base said, "Of course he'll use it, Lelo. He's a free man now. No
parents watching."

Admittedly I did have what I called a girl-of-the-moment situation.
I was always seeing someone, playing coy when anyone asked for
details and then getting to know the girl just enough to be able to talk
about her. I had chosen to stay at home and not be at boarding school
like most of my friends because then I could avoid the weekend jaunts

into town and into our sister school. I could tell my school friends about a girl without them having a chance to get a good idea of our relationship.

So, just before I left home and right after I started spending time with Sediba, I had stopped speaking to a girl from our sister school. We'd been dating, meaning that I took her to the movies and paid for everything, kissing her afterward even though she was not who I thought of when I did. She phoned every now and then, making my mother giddy with approval. Mamello was her name. A big-eyed, petite girl with lips that looked as though she wore dark lipstick when she didn't. I wished—as I had with other girls before her—that I could tell her I liked her and mean it. Whenever she phoned my mother would pick up and call my name in a sweet melodic voice: "Kabi! Ke Mamello." It didn't matter what I was doing, my mother would insist I stop and come to the phone right away.

"She has a nice voice," she'd whispered to me once. "We'd love to meet her."

Now, as if knowing exactly where my mind was Lelo said, "Mamello's not coming with you, *Jo*. So have the time of your life."

My eyes flew to Sediba. "That's over," I said.

I had never mentioned her to Sediba, only to Lelo a few times, because I needed to keep him up to date with my attempts at becoming the type of man he and my parents wished I could be. I winced when he said her name, clutching the condom box my eyes shifty. It felt like a betrayal.

Trunka asked, "Who is Mamello?"

"A girl who wants him. Or does she have you, *Jo*?"

Lelo rarely spoke English and I couldn't help but think there was always a hint of mockery when he did. I sat up and smiled, shaking my head.

"It's old news, gents. I'm going to Cape Town a single man."

"Sure. Sure *Jo*. It's your time." They spoke in such sincere, encouraging tones that I very nearly cried. Then I did look at Sediba and found him less bothered than I had expected. I thought his smile was some mixture of pity and understanding and I wished I hadn't seen it.

Pocketing the box of condoms, I gathered the empty beer bottles and took them inside the house. Through the kitchen window I could see them all in the backyard, teasing and playfully hitting each other and laughing.

I was grateful to have this loving group of people who had known and played with me for as long as I could remember; almost all of us had been growing up in the houses our parents had bought before we were born. I panicked at the thought of them not being there with me in this next phase of my life, wishing I could take them with me because even though I was going with my friends from school I thought about how large and scary UCT was going to be and I wanted to have people who spoke the same language as I did in more ways than one.

Then I looked at Sediba lying on his side, his eyes closed as he took in everything being said, and realized I wanted, maybe a little more desperately, to take him too, but if I wanted him the way I did then I couldn't have the others. And if I did take them, then I would live separate lives at varsity, with my school friends up in the quiet residence at the top of the mountain and my home friends down in the more crowded, less polished residences that were typically reserved for Black students from Kasi schools. It wasn't the first time that I was aware of the many lines that separated my many lives. It just seemed a little less bearable at that moment.

When they finally got up and sauntered towards the gate, Sediba slowed down, staying behind and patting his pockets. "I think I left my wallet where I was sitting," he said, and I realized then how little he'd spoken that evening. We stood side by side and watched our friends go, moving in drunken zigzags down the hill.

"I'll catch up!" Sediba called out to them. "Don't wait, I have to look." They were too drunk to hear or care.

Then it was just the two of us.

My parents had left earlier to take the party to one of their friends' houses. Sometime in the middle of our drinking, joking, and singing the sun had disappeared, leaving only the nightlights, which lit the path leading from our backyard to the river rock. I bit my lip and followed Sediba to the backyard.

He walked past the house and the backrooms towards the pool and I walked behind, as slowly and as steadily as I could. Our shoes crunched the river rocks along the path, the only sound you could hear apart form the crickets. Here and there a lizard slithered up a wall. I was surprised at how fearless I suddenly felt, how much I wanted to leap forward and put my arms around his waist.

I had led a girl away from a crowd and into one of those spaces people disappear to when they want privacy, when they want to feel things that their friends talk about on Monday at break or in the change room after a game. I had been here before, but it had been as an actor in a play—only doing what everyone else did, without my heart in it. Now it was like going towards something both exciting and dangerous, like I had spent my teens waiting for this door to open and couldn't wait to find out where it led. It was hard work trying not to run over, not to rush.

When we got to the back, behind the house and in front of my mother's pissing-boy fountain, Sediba suddenly turned around and pushed a small, gift-wrapped box towards me. I saw the corners of his mouth tremble, his eyes darting from me to the box and back like he was worried this might not end well.

It was not quite as bright in the back as on the path, even with the lights around the garden. I swallowed and tried to smile but I couldn't. All I did was shiver slightly. I said, because I couldn't think of anything else, "What? You got me a gift?" It sounded like something I'd heard in a movie.

"Open it. Now or tomorrow. It's up to you." His shrug was forced, his eyes on the box now in my hands.

My fingers fumbled with the wrapping. Then I tore it off, sorry because it had been wrapped so perfectly. Inside was a camera. He had remembered that I had wished for one and had one day mentioned it when I had read in a magazine about exactly this kind.

I was overwhelmed with gratitude, sadness and excitement. I felt that part of me that was always hiding, that was always alone, come out even more than it had in the times we had spent together. My heart raced, the weight of secrecy lifting. I wanted that very moment to go on and on, for my parents to never come back home, for Sediba never to leave. I looked at him without saying anything, my eyes on his, my right hand going to take his left.

It was he who came forward first, hesitantly, as if confirming I was alright with it. There was a lilac and mint soap that he often used— that he had shown me once when I had boldly asked him what he used because I liked the smell. Now I could smell the green and white bar on his clothes. It made parts of my body shift in understanding—it made me close my eyes and put my hand on the back of his neck and pull him into me. His lips landed softly on mine and then I opened my mouth, the tip of my tongue brushing against his.

It only lasted a few seconds before we heard footsteps and a soft voice say, "Kabi?"

In a moment of fear and panic, I pushed Sediba into a nearby rose-bush and watched his body land helplessly against the thorns. I could tell by the sound he let out that he was more hurt than surprised.

Aus' Tselane had returned. I wasn't sure how much she had seen in the dark but I was sure she hadn't missed the push. Sediba came back up with great effort, then bent double as if he'd been punched in the stomach, letting out a small whimper. I turned around and ran into the house and left him and Aus' Tselane there, staring at each other.

In my room I cried more than I ever had in my life, sobbing until I fell sleep. I dreamed of him falling, then getting up, coming away with me, running his hand down my bare back. All night his scent stayed in my nose and I held his hand, and when I woke up there was only the camera in my hand, my eyes puffy and my body refusing to get out of bed.

I hated him—or wanted to.

Later, after rearranging the clothes in my bags, double-checking the list my mother had made for me, I went out and walked around the backyard—saying goodbye to the place—and found the weight of my sadness too much to bear. My mother's roses were in bloom: the green garden dotted with yellow, white, and red flowers, all wrapped and cheerful along the high wall that was our fence. The pool was empty and the backyard clean—there were hardly any traces of the party left, except where Sediba and I had stood there was a piece of paper that must have fallen out when he gave me his present. I picked it up and put it in my pocket without reading it.

I decided then that I would go away from here, become someone else, find other people to be gay with, far away from anyone I knew. And I worked and worked at my heart, telling it not to stay here, in this place that didn't know me. I tried to remember how desperately I had always wanted to leave, but I couldn't quite capture the excitement I had felt when my father had brought home that acceptance letter from UCT—because he had given the university the surgery's address, wanting to be the first to get the news.

Sediba was merely a crush—a first boy kiss—I told myself. I would leave Kasi and so would he and we would forget each other. Maybe someday we would see each other across the street and then stop to talk about how we were. Anyway, we were eighteen and going off to different parts of the country—seventeen hours apart.

I went inside and rearranged my packing once again and then stepped out again. My mother made me food and my father was in and out of the house. Finally I sat outside and waited for them.

By the time they both emerged from the house with my bags, my mother's eyes red and my father anxiously throwing his keys from one hand to the other, I was more than ready to go. In one hour I would be at the train station. In just over twenty hours I would be in Cape Town. When my mother took a step away from my father's touch I pretended not to see.

"Kabi? O right?" she was saying as she brushed off nothing from her dress like she was brushing away his touch. "Let's go, it's time."

My father's eyes were all sadness but he managed a smile. He put his hand on my shoulder and said, "This is it, monna." I nodded and walked to the car. This was it. I wouldn't take any of this with me, I would become a free man, I insisted to myself. Yet even as our car drove down the hill and my mother hooted at my friends sitting around Trunka's family tuck shop, I was bitterly disappointed not to get one last glimpse of Sediba.

Cape Town

WHEN I CUT THROUGH THE CROWDS inside Park Station that February morning, sweating from the end-of-summer heat, I didn't even look back at my parents or wait for them to catch up. I ran ahead with my large suitcase and equally large shoulder bag, the box of condoms in my right pocket and my grin too wide for me to pass for sane or sober. For that moment I'd put the previous night behind me: I was eighteen and couldn't bear it anymore: perfect school marks, impeccable behaviour, the son the neighbours wished they had. Fuelled by curiosity about a world in which I didn't have to be anything to anyone, for me varsity couldn't have come soon enough.

My parents were dressed up as if they were seeing off a dignitary: my father in a navy blazer and my mother with makeup a touch lighter than her summer skin, too much lipstick, and heels too high for just a quick 'bye at a dusty train station. She was fussing: "Do you have enough toothpaste? We bought everything we could think of, but there's always something . . . " When she asked if I wanted to open my bag again and count the number of shirts I had, it was too much. I exchanged a solemn handshake with my father and kissed my mother goodbye and then I just ran forward and hopped onto the train.

I couldn't believe this trip across the country, all the way to the tip of Africa, was mine and mine alone. The friends I was traveling with from school would be the only people I knew and they were already putting on their earphones, getting ready to settle in and relax all the way down. Seventeen hours was how long the journey would be. My body may have still been in the north of the country but my mind had leapt forward and was far away already.

In my pocket of course I still had that note—and when my fingers went to touch it my heart swelled, a bubble caught in my throat. I had memorized it on the way to the station, sitting in the back seat as my parents turned up the music to disguise the silence between them. I read it over and over until I couldn't anymore, until all I could do was watch the landscape change from the flat and dusty streets of Kasi to the vast expansion that separated Black people's cluster of homes from White people's paved residential streets. I watched the buildings rise and rise until I couldn't deny that while I was anxious to leave, I felt wretched about the night before, the note, the kiss, everything.

The handwriting was so neat. It said:

Kabχa,

Take this and don't be afraid to use it. Use it every chance you get.

Forget about everything. You are destined for great things. Show them what you're made of!

Have a safe trip *Jo,*

S

I kept it in my left pocket, pressed against the condoms. Then I chewed mindlessly on some peanuts from the bag my mother had packed me that morning. The beer swirling in my brain, I recalled her hands trembling as she sliced my cheese-and-tomato sandwich into eight perfect triangles—the way I had liked since my first day in grade one. My father had supervised the cleaning of his car as a way of staying out of the house and I had busied myself with the packing, pretending I didn't know each was terrified of being left alone with the other.

When remembering home became too much, I reached into the other bag and caressed the camera that had come with the note. It was a small Kodak Eastman, 35mm. Exactly the one I had talked to Sediba about for weeks as we sat alone in my parents' backyard trying not to look each other in the eye. But that memory proved to be too heavy as well, and I quickly pulled my hand away from my bag, as if I had just teased a caged animal and had to suddenly escape its bite.

———◦———

So it was a great relief when Cape Town first came into view.

I arrived wide-eyed and hopeful, trying to ignore my sadness, pulling at some of the reasons I had wanted to leave home and yes, the thought of medical school helped. I couldn't wait for that part to begin.

As the taxi made its way up the hill towards the university I watched the animals grazing at the foot of the mountain, the university's stately buildings behind them. Cape Town is first-world-city-meets-jungle, an old colonialist city world both lovely and unsettling. I watched the wildebeest, so comical and ungraceful compared to other animals. The Khoi said that it was formed from all the leftovers after the creator had finished making the other animals. But just then they looked quite peaceful, going about their business, and behind the noise of the cars on the road below, they were so quiet as to seem mysterious, eerie.

Further up and closer to the mountain, a mist rose up steadily like a curtain, unveiling Devil's Peak, the rocky mountain on which the university stood. The harmonious union of the wild and the city drew me in, if only because of its strangeness and vast difference from the flat and dry urban landscape that I had just left behind. When I caught my first glimpse of the ivy-covered buildings, a chill ran down my back. I was finally here.

I saw endless possibilities. Maybe this was where my life would finally feel complete. Maybe this was where I would stop feeling that pieces of it were always falling off as I walked through different doors.

And at first the city seemed to welcome us all with open arms. Smuts Hall was where we would stay, one of the two residences on upper campus. The university had been divided into three: upper, middle, and lower campus, and its buildings seemed to conform in elegance and stateliness to those distinctions, so that "upper" actually seemed to refer to upper class. Not unlike the township then, where the wealthiest were at the top of the hill.

I suppose as we were boys from St Joseph's, the brother school of some upper-class British boarding schools, it seemed like the natural choice for the university to house me and some of my schoolmates at Smuts. Upper class schools led to upper class housing. Fuller, situated across a stone path, was for the girls. Smuts didn't have a dining hall, so all our meals would be taken at Fuller. In that first week I would hear guys call it "our point of entry."

I threw my bags on the floor and jumped on top of my bed as soon as I shut the door to my new room. Light flooded through the sparsely furnished space, a small one that would belong to me only for the first year—at least—and what I wanted to do here, who I wanted to do it with, could remain my secret if I wanted. As I saw it, what UCT had to offer was mine for the taking. It was so large and sprawling, I thought it the perfect place to hide and to seek the kind of company I desired. In fact, looking back now, I'd say I've never before or since approached anything with such stealth, caution and unparalleled determination.

It was sheer good fortune then that I met Rodney Myburg during Freshers' Week. The Black student body being so small and close-knit, I guess it makes sense now that it would be a White guy with whom I escaped. Short and skinny, all his pants just a little too big for him, Rodney seemed to be waiting for me the day we met. He had a grubby look suggesting he was so easy-going that he might pull out a guitar in an instant and start strumming. He wore his sun-burnt blonde hair a bit longer than most guys, letting it cover his ears and grow down to his chin, and he was never without his leather bracelets. I found his look to be a refreshing change from the people I normally hung around with, and from the other medical-school students, who looked so serious they drew no interest from me and I wondered if I would ever get to know any of them.

It was Tuesday when I met him, our third full day at UCT, and

I was late meeting my friends. We had spent the previous night in a restaurant in Muizenberg as part of the Freshers' Week festivities. In the middle of doing tequila shots I had watched my friends watching girls, while I stole glances at good-looking guys. Everyone had generally had a very good time. But it had been my first time drinking tequila and that Tuesday morning I had a terrible hangover. So I had woken up later than I was supposed to, missing breakfast and a bus to somewhere I couldn't remember. Then I had gone in search of one of the university's cafeterias and bought myself an egg and mayo sandwich. I walked with it in one hand, my feet moving with caution, my eyes on the steps of Jammie, the hub of student life. It took no time to understand that this was the sun-tanning, people-watching centre of the university, where people lounged around chatting, reading, or scouting out their next date. Drama students, in capes and black boots despite the heat, business students in jeans too high and shirts tucked in, and political science people arguing about the state of the country.

All I wished for was a pair of sunglasses and a quiet corner. When I found a spot near a young woman reading, I opened my sandwich and took in the rest of the campus. The world looked startlingly beautiful from up on the mountain. It was calm, refreshing. And even as the memory of Sediba and the previous few weeks stabbed at me, I insisted to myself that I had escaped a place I had never really fitted in.

Rodney sat two steps ahead smoking a cigarette and looking slightly dazed, not entirely sober. He had an easy smile, his long hair swept in that careful side sweep meant to look effortless but that actually takes some hair gel and a bit of skill to achieve. His fingers were long in spite of his height and his jeans grazed the floor of the steps even as he was sitting.

He was looking up at me and I smiled at him and started to unwrap my sandwich. It didn't look fresh.

"You're not going to eat that!" I heard him say with a chuckle. I looked back up, squinting against the sun.

"I don't have a choice. I just bought it."

He shook his head and took a drag from his cigarette and then offered me one from a pack lying next to him. He stood up to come sit next to me.

"Have a drag and I'll show you proper food."

I smiled at hearing the skinniest boy I had come across so far telling me about proper food. I waved away the cigarette. "No thanks, I need to eat first." I took a bite of the sandwich and made a face. The guy, with his hand on his mouth and his cigarette burning away between his fingers, started laughing so hard I thought it might hurt his stomach.

"Spit it out. There's the rubbish. Spit it, spit it!" He was pointing at a rubbish bin just below the steps to our right. I stood up and ran to spit into it, hurling the sandwich in as well.

When I turned around he was standing behind me, his old leather postman bag swung across his chest and his thumbs in the belt loops of his jeans.

"Come with me." He didn't wait for me to answer, just turned around and started walking and I followed him down the steps.

"Rule number one: don't eat on campus except for the doughnuts. Now those are worth every cent." Again, he gave me his charming broad grin and, extending his hand to me he said, "I'm Rodney, by the way. You can call me Rod. My mother calls me Roddie, which I don't appreciate."

I laughed and shook his hand. "Did anyone call you Rodz in high school? I'm Kabelo."

"Yes! Black guys! You're always adding a Z or an S to people's names. Then you Anglicize your own names. Zukiswa is Zuks, Tebogo is Tebz. Mpumi is Pomz. Why?!"

I said, "I have no idea."

"Then you must be Kabz . . . and you don't know about the food here, I see."

"Have you been here a long time?"

He shook his head. "Not a long time. Just long enough to have spat out a few things myself. I once had something marked 'turkey sand-wich' but I swear it was a cow's arse or something." I had thought that we were going all the way down to Rondebosch on the main road for food, but at the bottom of the steps just above Fuller and Smuts, he turned left and took out a set of keys from his pocket.

"Oh, you have a car!" I said, staring at the red Golf VW whose lights had just beeped when he clicked his keys.

"Yup. Because, one: I got accepted into medical school. Two: I promised to never do drugs again."

We both started laughing. Rodney had a loud, easy, from-the-belly laugh that was infectious. He threw down his cigarette butt and gestured for me to get into the car.

"You didn't stop the drugs, I gather?"

"Nope. But the promise got me this car. Do you like it?"

I nodded.

"It's a car, what's not to like?"

"I feel the same way."

We drove down the one-way street out of campus, turned right and entered Rhodes Drive. Rodney turned up techno music.

"Hey," I said in an attempt to block out the awful music, "I'm also here for medical school. You're the first person I've met so far who is doing the same thing."

Rodney shook his head. "Not my first choice. But it is the family business." There was something hopeless in his tone and there was the slight yet unmistakable droop of his shoulder.

"Yes, my father's a doctor too."

"Really? Your father is?" His surprise irked me but I tried to ignore it, since I wanted to have a nice time and I was eager to eat something better than what I had just had.

"Where are we going?" I asked, my voice rising.

"To eat! I know a place."

"Are you from Cape Town?"

"Yes, all over Cape Town really. My parents have a few houses. That's why I'm not in res."

The little car went roaring up the mountain as Rodney tried to change gears but his movements were so uncertain that it made for a bumpy ride. Below us the many levels of Cape Town spread out.

We were above the campus, which was above Rondebosch, Mowbray, and Observatory, and then we were turning away from the city and towards the water.

The sound of the gears changing was like a rough shove of furniture against stone floors.

"How many times have you driven this car?" I asked him, amused.

He gave me a sly smile and shook his head. "Without my brother? Um . . . twice. The first time was when I drove to campus this morning!"

Then we were going up hills, the ocean below, passing a much posher part of town, which I vaguely recognized from my family's visits to the city.

"This is Clifton, right?" I asked. Rodney nodded with a grin.

"The parents' humble abode—one of many—is about to present itself."

Soon the hill was getting steeper and steeper and the road more winding. I was worried the car would roll back down with Rodney's insecure gear changes, but suddenly we were in front of a large garage on a very quiet road. When he pressed a button above him, the garage doors slowly went up like a theatre curtain and we drove in. There was another car in there but it was covered with a white, polyester cover. When he saw my curiosity he said, "That's my father's Porsche. Or my mother's. Depends who has the keys."

"Nice."

We went down the stairs from the garage and into the house, which seemed to descend further and further down and forward, towards the ocean. There were windows for walls. Light was all around.

"This is a nice spot," I said, looking at the magnificent view of the ocean from the sitting room.

Rodney had gone to the kitchen, taking out several types of cheeses, cold meats, and what looked like leftover salads—then he took some sliced bread from the bread bin and put it all in a pile on the kitchen island, which was itself large, like the sofas and the tables and the TVs. He now took out a small plastic packet of grass and started rolling it into a piece of paper, moving with the focus and precision of a seamstress, barely registering my question. I was hungry but didn't want to be rude, so I stood across from him, separated by the delicious spread of food, my mouth watering. I hadn't eaten since the previous day.

"Eat as much as you can," Rodney said, eyes still on the rolling paper.

I put together a sandwich with cheese and slices of turkey, worried he might have noticed how quickly I had done it and that he might think I had never seen food like this before. When I was finished eating I took puffs of the weed and lay back on the sofa. Rodney stood up and went to the kitchen, and to my surprise, rolled another one.

"Still going?" I asked in a daze. With me it only took two puffs and I was out, mind swirling with funny images: trees all around me, everything wrong side up, talking animals. I loved being here: Everything I needed to forget was even farther away: Kasi, my parents, Sediba. I could stay.

"Do you come here a lot?" I asked him.

"Whenever I need food," Rodney laughed and offered me a few more puffs. I'd reached my limit, but what the hell. I accepted.

"Do you cook?"

"No, we pay someone. She lives in Juju Le Toi."

"Where?"

"You know. Gugulethu. I heard someone call it that the other day. Thought it was funny."

"Juju Le Toi," I sounded it out in a drugged haze. "Juju Le Toi," I kept saying. It made Rodney laugh and he fell off the sofa, shoulder hitting the coffee table. I could see it wasn't the first time.

"Oh, Monsieur! Say it again. It turns me on," he was saying as he rolled around on the floor. Soon I was laughing so much that I was also on the floor, and our day turned into an evening and the evening turned into the night. We would smoke then eat and repeat. He seemed to have an endless supply of zol. At one point we were feasting on gherkins from a large jar that we found at the back of the fridge. The swoosh of the waves outside sounded so soothing that I put my finger on my lips and said to Rodney, "Sshhh . . . the sea is putting us to sleep. Sssshhh." He also put his finger on his lips and said in a whisper, "Ssshhh, I hear it. I hear it."

We didn't leave the house until the early hours of the morning, to search for more food.

This was the first place I had been to in a very long time where I felt at ease. Rodney dropped me off at the res sometime after lunch and I slept through the afternoon, in my dream swimming in the ocean outside Rodney's house. Sometimes his house was my parents' home in Kasi before turning back into Rodney's, and then back again. I felt sad when just as I was about to step into the shower, Mohale, an old school mate and one of the guys in my Res flat, poked his head round the door. "Hey Kabz? Your parents have phoned about ten times. I spoke to your mom, she says you haven't phoned home much since you arrived."

He sounded disapproving , and I was embarrassed. He stopped to think a minute and then, "Actually, where have you been? You're not the sort of bloke to just disappear and I haven't seen you since Monday night." He stepped into the next shower, turned it on and spoke above the water's noise. "Have you not been feeling well?"

"I think it was those tequilas that first night. I'm still recovering."

Mohale laughed out aloud. The thought that he believed me brought on a familiar feeling of satisfaction followed by disgust with myself. Yoh! I could lie. I could lie so well that sometimes I even convinced myself that, in a way, when I really thought about it, it wasn't really a lie.

I pushed aside the guilt, saying I would phone my parents, but I couldn't stop hoping that Rodney would come and find me, because now the house on the hill overlooking the beach was the only place I wanted to be.

The sun had already gone down by the time I finally steeled myself and made my way down to the phones in the poorly lit basement below our rooms. I knew my mother would still be at the shop and my father would be at the surgery, so I had to make two phone calls. I

played with the coins in my hand and bit my lip, knowing that what I
was about to do was the easiest and most cowardly thing. I phoned our
home line and let it ring, left a message and put down the phone.

Walking back upstairs I kept thinking: *You can have a whole life that
people close to you know nothing about.*

Longing for some fresh air, I went to sit outside on a small bench
near the main entrance to Smuts. Students were out, standing in
groups or sitting alone, some gathered around the Cecil John Rhodes
statue, talking with old friends and getting to know some new ones.
The evening was thick with summer heat as is typical for February. I
leaned back against the old stone of the residence wall, feeling it cool
my back through my thin cotton shirt. I didn't smoke cigarettes very
often, but at that moment I wanted to be holding one between my fingers, just to have something to do. It worried me that to passersby I
might look lost and in need of company; people don't like the burden
of being needed, feeling they have to make an effort towards some
lonely fresher. So I struck a pose that I hoped made me look aloof and
was glad I had my sunglasses this time to cement the effect, even as
there was no sun. I listened to the chatter around me, piecing bits and
pieces of conversations, working out where I belonged—if anywhere.
But I was too jittery, the guilt getting the better of me as I remembered
Mohale saying my mother was worried. So then I did have to get up
again and phone home and this time I made an honest effort.

As I dialled with trembling fingers I willed my voice to be cheerful.
You're never far enough, I thought.

My mother's voice was hoarse as it tended to be when she was upset.
She couldn't say she was angry, you had to think she was sick and feel
worried and then guilty for not checking on her, that was the point.

"I'm just thinking now we should just come."

Someone had left a piece of paper above the phone: "Lilian, E Flat,
room 6."

I felt it between my fingers. It was about that time. Not even a week
had passed and they needed to get away from each other, come find me
and work on . . . what? My schooling? How clean my room was? Who

I was dating? My mother was nothing if not relentless, so saying she couldn't come would have been useless.

So I said: "When?" and started preparing myself.

The day they arrived I felt twitchy, trying to remember if Rodney and I had made firm plans as I saw him walking up the steps on his way to Smuts.

Smuts was quiet, as it always was on a Sunday, and I was hungover, as I always was on the weekend. I was sitting up on the lower end of the campus steps closer to Smuts and Fuller, people-watching and telling myself: it would only be for two days, no they were not coming to stay and yes, they would leave and go back to Kasi. I could see Rodney in his oversized torn jeans and shaggy hair shuffling his feet up to Smuts, looking forlorn even from a distance. From where I sat I couldn't see his shoes but I guessed from the way he walked that he was in the flips-flops he had been wearing the day before.

My parents would arrive in a few minutes and I couldn't be with Rodney. I couldn't go back to his house and smoke zol or drink too much. I had to stay close to res., introduce my parents to the friends they would approve of, take them around the medical school and then the rest of campus, pretend I had a girl I liked in Fuller and then watch with both guilt and relief as they went back into their world without me as the buffer they needed.

Almost as soon as Rodney walked away, my parents arrived, my mother a little overdressed for a simple visit, both trying to look cheerful. My mother wrapped her arms around me as if I'd been gone a year and my father put his hand on my shoulder with a firm grip, holding on. He still couldn't believe his son was here—almost as if he'd come to see for himself, to make sure.

As I had anticipated, two days felt like ten. I took them around, they bought me things my mother thought I needed: more pants, another pillow, stationary. She had made a list, walking around my room taking notes and saying things like: "Had I known, I would've brought more soap. I was just at Makro last week."

When they asked about a girl I said, "We're right across from Fuller,

Ma. I'm not worried," she smiled adoringly at me. My father looked down at his plate and said: "Of course. Of course. Every doctor needs a good wife." To which my mother pursed her lips.

I suppose the three of us tried not to think of what that meant about the two of them. I cupped my glass instead of holding its stem between my fingers and it was enough to get my mother fussing again about proper table etiquette. My father gave me a knowing smile; always the son who could take attention in the right direction.

I smoked too much zol anyway but I smoked even more the night after they left, sitting on the floor in Rodney's house listening to music that was too bad and too loud.

That was probably Cape Town in a nutshell: booze, zol, loud music at Rodney's house, and then being hungover and catching up on work in the library on weeknights right up until closing time. I loved it at the time, the freedom and carelessness of it. Sometimes the memory of that time is hazy but that's just fine. It didn't end well, so I like to remember the fun. The way it was easy to be with men, the way I never saw my friends from high school anymore because I was on a different campus and at night I was in a different part of town. The way my parents stopped visiting for some time because, I think, it was too long a trip for them to take together. They left me alone (except for the four phone calls a week) and for a long time Cape Town let me be me. Until it couldn't work anymore.

It was not until well into the first semester, after I had settled into school and a routine that I finally had my first sexual encounter at Rodney's house.

The guy was a newcomer. He was visiting from England, he said, and was "unimpressed with the gay scene in Cape Town." His name was Danny and he had a refined, upper class English accent, which to the trained ear sounded thoroughly put on, but with a soft voice and an easy smile. He was about a few centimeters shorter than I, with long delicate hands, a pretty nose, green eyes and eyelashes so long they touched the tips of his blonde strands: very attractive and quite sure of himself.

Danny's manner was a pleasant surprise since most guys who came to drink and party at Rodney's house were generally either aloof or just too high to engage. He opened the door for me and smiled in such a welcoming way that I instantly warmed to him. He didn't appear to be on drugs, though he later said something about going only "where the good drugs are." He put his hands on his hips and moved his eyes up and down, taking me in slowly. "Well, *you're* different," he concluded with a grin.

I thought: "Ugh, not this again." But I could see by the look on his face that he meant different as in exotic and not as in too strange, like other people. I followed him willingly.

When Rodney saw us walking through the house he flashed me a knowing smile and said, "I've told Danny about you," but as usual he was already so high that I couldn't get an answer from him about what he had in fact told Danny. All I got was: "Danny is a family friend."

Danny tossed his locks and added with a sly smile, "He was *not* lying."

I felt rather shy around him at first because he seemed so sure of himself and said the word 'gay' as easily as if he were pronouncing his own name. He motioned with his head for me to come outside and I happily obliged, intrigued by this stranger who unlike the rest of the party, didn't seem turned off by me. On the balcony he offered me a cigarette but I declined. I was already eyeing the zol he had rolled up and placed on the table for me.

Between puffs Danny and I made attempts at a conversation. Elbow on the railing, he examined me carefully, as if he were trying to decide which one of the books he had read would explain me to him.

I didn't need to do a lot of thinking: Danny being the first guy around here to show any interest in me, I was going to go along with his looks and his lines until something happened between us. In the end he must have seen the conversation for the loss that it was, because now he put his hand on my arm, stroked it suggestively and said impatiently, "Finish that thing and let's go find a room!"

I rushed through my spliff. Yes, you could say I was overeager.

Unlike my friends from high school and just about everyone around me, my sexual frustration seemed only to rise with each week. By then my friends seemed to have abandoned their plan to have us all rooming in one flat, their attentions now having turned to a few very pretty Fuller girls they had met in the dining hall. All of them had found lovers as easily as picking apples from a tree—it was uncomplicated and they could do it in broad daylight for everyone to see.

Even though my eagerness had done nothing but intensify, I was the only one still carrying the same pack of condoms from the first week of varsity. Now here was a guy my age, quite attractive, practically demanding that I have sex with him. I couldn't believe my luck. I followed him to the nearest bedroom, where we groped our way through the dark and didn't bother to turn the light on.

I felt clumsy because I had no idea what I was doing. I mean, I had kissed a boy but that hadn't gone very far nor had it ended well. In the darkness of that room alone with a strange boy who was quite attractive, I was terrified of disappointing.

Danny, on the other hand, was neither clumsy nor lacking in confidence or experience, clearly. He pushed himself against me and started unbuckling my belt with fascinating skill and speed. When I felt his mouth around the tip of my penis I shut my eyes and inhaled sharply, grabbing his limp straight hair with both hands. I stepped back and found myself flopping onto the bed, but skilled Danny's lips never left my cock.

When he did speak he said, "Put your finger in here!" and I was so aroused that I instantly obliged. But the whole thing was quick, and once we were done, Danny and I had nothing to say to each other and left the room in awkward silence to join the group outside.

I felt like a new man. I smoked two or three spliffs that night, skipping the drinks, watching as people went into the rooms in pairs, or groups of three, and sometimes four. It finally felt like I had joined the party.

Still, when I was alone I was filled with intolerable amounts of shame. I would look back one minute and think of how aroused I had

been and then the next minute I'd remember how Danny had looked
at me like I was stepping out of an old painting in a museum: I was
something to grab and taste, not someone he was really curious about.
Had he been straight and in one of my classes, speaking to me about
"your people" and "your dialect," I would never have given him the
time of day. Loneliness and boyish sexual frustration meant that I
overlooked a few things. But after that experience there was confirma-
tion of my feeling that I could get pleasure from sex with men. I had
enjoyed myself far more than I had thought I would. I had loved it. I
had been very open to every bit of it, however brief the encounter had
been, and I looked forward to doing more.

I hardly ever went home. Even for the longer winter break, I was in
and out of my parents' home in a few days, unable to stand the feeling
of being alone around other, familiar people. Cape Town had been
such an intoxicating escape that back in Kasi I felt like a caged animal.
I might have stayed longer if I hadn't seen Sediba briefly one Sunday
afternoon at Trunka's house.

I think he must have already been there when I walked in, but I
hadn't noticed. The place was always full of people chatting, laughing,
dancing, having drinks. Trunka, Lelo, and Base were sitting on turned-
over bottle crates drinking when I joined them. It was easy, getting
back into our old ways, talking about the same things, and I, as always,
avoiding the stuff I needed to avoid. So while I was a little bit taken
aback when they introduced me to a girl whose name I can't even
remember now, I went with the flow. I must already have been drunk,
and I was standing with my back against the wall with her hand on my
arm, the two of us laughing about I-don't-know-what. Suddenly up
walked Sediba in his usual easy style, wearing white t-shirt and dark
jeans. His face expressed no surprise, it was as though he were seeing
me for the first time. I, on the other hand, was startled.

He said, "*Heita*," voice breezy, the smile on his lips not quite
reaching his eyes. With such a casual Kasi greeting, he was putting distance between us. "*Ey . . . ,*" I managed, rubbing my eyes as if to help
my mind focus. The girl didn't go away even as I willed her to. She

seemed instead to squeeze herself even closer. Sediba kept walking, going towards the gate. I excused myself and followed, catching up with him just as he was lifting the latch.

"*Ey* . . . I haven't seen you in a long time. Stay and chat." I knew even in that moment that I sounded like an arse, trying not to slur my words.

"How long have you been back?" he asked, no smile this time.

"I don't know, a few days."

He looked me in the eye for a moment. It was hurt I could see in his face, not judgement for the girl, which I might have preferred. He said, "I have to go," but didn't move or take his eyes off me. I couldn't think of anything more to say but I felt sober now, my eyes now starting to focus. I cleared the lump in my throat. I could barely stand to see him, to be standing right in front of him and feeling so far.

"Come over later . . . we could . . . " I hesitated.

"You're busy, Kabelo." He was looking at the girl, who was watching us curiously from where I'd left her. "Don't be rude."

He marched off and left me holding on to the fence. Behind me I could feel the girl still waiting; I could feel everything still waiting. My parents, my home, my friends, my school work, the expectation of coming back to work at my father's surgery. Everything waited for me to face it and all I wanted was to go wherever Sediba was going.

The girl delicately brushed something off her pants and then waved. I felt her eyes wide with expectation when she looked at me, her smile eager, inviting, sweet.

I have rarely felt as lonely and ashamed as I did at that moment.

I was drinking and smoking too much, I knew that. But in Cape Town there was no one and nothing to tell me this, or that my excesses wouldn't change my parents' expectations or drive away my guilt about their expectations. They wouldn't fix me. Couldn't make me love a girl or be the kind of man Lelo was. In Cape Town I could pretend they would but in Kasi there was a lot that would admonish me: like when I stumbled after too many beers and Trunka said, "Yoh, did you pump up that whole crate?" Or Lelo saying, "I don't remember you liking zol, this must be Cape Town stuff."

Cape Town stuff. He had no idea.

And Sediba. Sediba's eyes going from me to the bottle in my hand and back up to my bloodshot eyes. Sediba talking to me but looking at the girl whose name I was not respectful enough to remember. Sediba, walking away instead of wanting to be alone with me.

I couldn't stay there. I was back in Cape Town forty-eight hours earlier than I was meant to be. But soon Cape Town also had to come to an end, because when things are out of control, something has to give.

The evening that was the last I saw of Rodney, we were alone at his house sitting in the sun on the pool deck, smoking zol. I had spent part of the day alone with my books, catching up, trying to make a dent in my studying before I made my way to Rodney's. I'd been on thin ice at that point, a little bit afraid that I might not pass my exams, having been too much into parties and let a few crucial things go.

I found Rodney already high, jittery, eyes red and puffy. He was talking about a guy called Akhu who was from a political family in a neighbouring country who was sort of hiding out at UCT, coming to our gay parties at night and pretending to have a girlfriend in the daytime.

"Akhu could never hide that he's such a fag. Imagine him going back there and dealing with his father."

"Why do you use that word?"

I turned to lie on my back.

"What? Fag?"

"I always found it . . . unsettling. Jarring. I mean, doesn't it scare you when people use it?"

Rodney shrugged. "I've been called that, punched by some fuckers on Front Street. I use it to defend myself, if that makes sense. I use it the way black Americans use n____. I take it back. Reclaim it."

"I think that's a load of shit."

He chuckled. "You're probably right. But I like the sound of it. I can't help it. I mean if not that, then what are we? Homos? Do you like that better?"

"How about gay?"

"All right then," he said like he couldn't care less. "We'll use that."

We went quiet, listening to the happy sounds of sunbathers and swimmers frolicking on the beach, somewhere on the other side of the high white wall.

"He's going back, you know."

"What?" The ganja hit. I'd half forgotten what we were going on about.

"Akhu. He's going back. To enjoy the path his father has laid out for him. Nepotism. That's how it goes. He's going to be groomed to be a minister or something. I think eventually they're hoping he'll take over."

"Are you joking? He's . . . isn't he our age?"

"That's the plan, from what I hear. Hey, why don't you and he ever, you know? I mean, you're both so attractive."

I vehemently shook my head.

Without asking for an explanation, he said, "And you know what else? Akhu isn't his name. Not the name everyone knows him by anyway. See? You go away to South Africa and its all debauchery, you get it out of your system, and then you go back home and be a nice, respectable, *straight* African boy."

I winced at the thought. My father and all of my community expected the same from me. I liked the fact that medicine took seven long years—I didn't have to think too much about what I would do next, but I knew what was required of me: to get a degree and then come home and follow in my father's footsteps.

Township doctor. White coat and old neighbours as patients. My mother and everyone finding me a wife. The thought made me ill every time it came up.

"Ha! Someday we'll watch him on TV," Rodney was carrying on. "He'll denounce homos as filthy and unnatural and then he'll come down to South Africa on an unofficial visit and spend some gay old time with a nice South African boy."

He was now standing up, closely observing the sunrays landing on the turquoise pool. I got up and pulled him back, because he was too high and standing too close. He came back to sit down and continued talking.

Through my haze I noticed him blink as if fighting back tears.

"Yesterday I told my mother. I just came right out with it."

"With what?"

"I said, 'Mum, I'm gay.' "

"No! Why? What . . . what did she say? That does not sound like a good idea man." I was standing up now, towering over him, my heart racing like he'd just told me he tried to kill himself. Which I thought was the same thing.

"Wow. If you had been here you could have stopped me from doing it. Too bad, then." A lone tear ran down his cheek.

I knelt beside him and put my hand on his arm, more to settle myself than to calm him.

"Rod, what happened?"

"She stood up and stepped away from me. It was . . . so . . . I thought I had imagined saying it. It was like I hadn't said anything. She just stood there and said: 'Rodney dear, we really should start supper.'"

I had never met his mother, but Rodney was now speaking with a haughty British accent that I knew he used all the time for his mother.

"I said, 'Mum! I'm fucking gay! Did you hear me? I said I'm gay! A homosexual, if you like. I like sleeping with men!'"

"You didn't!"

"I did! I screamed it in her face: 'I like sleeping with men!'"

I laughed at the absurdity of saying something like that to one's parent. Was Rodney going mad? Were the drugs taking over his brain? If you had asked me at the time I would probably have told you I planned to die before ever telling my parents I was gay.

"What happened then?"

"She picked up her handbag and said, 'I'm going to the shop, Rodney dear, we need olive oil.'" He stood up and demonstrated, then let out a strange, bitter laugh. So unlike the carefree, delightful sound I often enjoyed hearing from him.

"Do you know what the thing is, Kabelo dear? I neglected to see that it was time for *olive oil!* Do you see my mistake? I *fucking, stupidly,* thought we could talk about me. But no, it was time for olive *fucking* oil."

"Shit man, I'm so sorry."

He picked up a cigarette, fingers trembling, and lit.

"Do your parents know?"

A picture of both my parents came to mind and now I laughed bitterly. "It's not the sort of thing . . . well, where I come from, it's not the sort of thing you say."

"Apparently not where I come from either." His eyes closed and he curled up in the chair with his arms around his knees. Not unlike an infant.

I'm not sure what happened next exactly. Two of Rodney's friends arrived, and shortly afterwards I decided I would leave. They were friends I didn't particularly like, their noses were always turned up, they never looked you in the eye and were never sober.

It wasn't long before they were supplying him with a bag of coke and another bag of pills. I got worried and said, "Don't you guys think that's too much?" They snorted the coke and sneered at me and my question. I hesitated, trying to catch Rodney's attention. His feet were in the water, his hand rubbing off a stream of blood from his nose. I needed to get out of there.

I started walking towards the house and out through the garage. I don't think Rodney heard me when I said, "Bye," and I hurried out as if I were in danger. I thought I'd come back, see how he was doing. But there were ugly scowls on those guys' faces. I ran, I suppose. It was cowardly, but that's what I did. I kept going past the large houses and down the winding roads until I was down on the main strip and across the beach, hoping to find a cab back to campus.

Things were going dangerously off track, I thought. I was doing too much of this and not enough of school. I was falling behind. The last thing I wanted was to be on the front page of the papers, lone

Black guy in a house full of drugs.

I could see what I was turning into; and even if the thought of going back to work with my father was painful, I still wanted to finish my degree. I still wanted to have good options, be able to go and stay where I chose and live the way I wanted, as much as that was possible. I could do that with a degree. Then of course there was the thought of both my parents being disappointed if I failed and got excluded from varsity. That, I couldn't bear. It was a lot. I had to leave Cape Town, it wasn't working anymore.

In the following weeks and months, I immersed myself in my work while I thought of what I would do next. I stopped seeing Rodney— which would come back to haunt me but wasn't completely out of character when I think about it now. News of him being in the hospital didn't surprise me. Talk amongst medical students about how he had nearly overdosed came to me days later and I looked the other way, glad he was alive but also refusing to bear the guilt and shame of my part in that last day. I had now separated myself from him. In being so practiced at putting my many different selves in different compartments, I'm embarrassed to say it wasn't difficult. Even though he was such a good friend. By then I had learned to let go of bigger things.

I started running, as always. Every day I thought of ways to convince my parents to let me switch to Durban and in the end they didn't need much convincing. I spoke to my father first, while I was at home one year after a particularly lonely stretch. We were sitting in his office and he told me about his latest concerns: breastfeeding mothers who preferred formula, an aging population, younger patients not coming to him. I twirled a set of keys on my finger and said, "I've noticed that the teaching at UCT is not as good as it used to be. I have friends in Durban," I lied, "who are raving about the work there. And some of our best teachers have moved to Durban." This was half-true.

My father looked up: "But UCT's the best."

"Sure, but I'd be six hours instead of seventeen away by car. I could come home . . . "

I was skilled. He didn't need to hear more than that. A year later I left Cape Town the same way that I had left home: promising myself I wouldn't look back, that I would reinvent myself, that I had nothing to stay for and that city, like home, had spit me out anyway. I'd had no choice. I missed Rodney, the parties, the freedom and the hiding place that was his home but once again I relished the opportunity to be where no one knew me.

Durban

I ARRIVED IN DURBAN with my parents, who helped me move into a flat—it was mid-semester and too late to find a room in residence. The flat was bright but it felt bleak—at first, empty inside the way I was always feeling those days. I hadn't counted on the fact that arriving somewhere without a single friend might take some getting used to. I had to work hard not to hate it.

On the plane, as I sat with my mother to my left and my father to my right, the three of us exchanged very few words. Familiar silence. We read the paper and occasionally smiled up at each other. If we pretended we were fine then we were fine. I suspect they were just grateful that I was continuing with medicine. When I told her I was switching universities, my mother had thrown in some gossip about someone's child who was dropping out or changing courses because he couldn't cope. At least she didn't have to say the same about me. "It's a good change," she said more to herself than to me. "You'll be less distracted in Durban. All your rowdy friends are in Cape Town." It was the story she was telling everyone at the shop and in all of Kasi. I went along.

They took what they could from my reasons and ignored the details. Of course they had noticed my marks plummeting but I made excuses about not being in the right place and they were fine. Durban was still far enough from home for it to look exotic: it was still going away to varsity, by the ocean. It worked with the image of me we were all selling.

"You know you'll meet a nice girl and get used to the place," my father mumbled, keys to my flat in one hand, eyes on the door.

"If you can pick just one!" My mother said, giggling. It was the only time they agreed on something. "I'm sure there'll be a lot to choose from."

"Mum . . . " I started, but stopped as I always did when they mentioned me finding a woman.

My mother put her arm around me and squeezed. "Ah. Don't always be so shy, Kabi. I think everyone knows you'll bring home the best kind of Makoti. Who knows? Maybe another doctor. You know you can't marry just anyone. You have to choose right."

My father chuckled. I eyed the dust on the kitchen counter.

I felt more alone than ever when they left, waving to me through the car windows as they sped off to the airport.

Every day before opening it, I hovered around the door to my flat, afraid of being harassed by the silence of the new place. The walls were bare, the floors were tiled and unlike the hardwood flooring of res., they were sure be cold in the winter. I seriously wondered if I could make it my own and from time to time weighed the benefits of dating a girl for company against the trouble of being gay.

Over time I learned to open the windows and discovered a beautiful view of the beach and lovely aromas coming from somewhere in the neighbourhood: lilacs, lemons, and frangipanis. The houses were so pretty and the lawns so manicured that I couldn't help but insert the most charmed lives into them. I discovered that I could hear music from my neighbour's flat through the kitchen walls and I liked it because while it was only a faint sound and it always took me a minute to work out which song was playing. It felt cheerful and like I had a friend next door.

The hospital was much smaller and much busier than the one at UCT, and Durban seemed a lot quieter in the evenings, with the streets empty by nine o'clock at night when the shops closed. In the daytime if you wished to venture out, there was the beach and the lush countryside. The beauty was expansive and breathtaking, although it paled compared to what Cape Town offered. Daytime Durban felt chaotic, parts of it dirtier than I could stand. As someone who was always easily overwhelmed, I rarely ventured out into the streets during the day, even when I was not working. I didn't miss Cape Town as much as I missed home, memories of it arriving in vivid dreams or brought back by a song in the middle of the day. Was it because I was now only a few hours away, or was it because I had absolutely no one I had known here since before adulthood?

It would be three more years before things would start looking up, but at first I retreated. School was demanding. This wasn't just pre-med anymore, we were fully in medical school, seeing patients, and our housemanships would soon start.

Then there were times when it was painful how much I missed Rodney. I missed his laugh, our car rides to his house, the parties, and the way he'd always open his door like he'd been expecting me. I had managed to push away the guilt for a time but now it came gnawing at me. The distractions here in Durban were not enough. I had essentially left a friend to die and I felt sick about it. I don't know if it was youth or a well-established understanding of the importance of secrecy, but I had listened and carried on like Rodney was just another secret to bury.

Finding people to spend time with was as complicated as it had been at UCT. I met a few guys on campus and went to some parties with them. They were nothing like the ones at Rodney's house: the houses were dark and seedy, the music was too loud and it was sometimes hard to know if people actually lived there or if someone had simply rented the place for the purpose of the party. I didn't feel as close to anyone as I had felt to Rodney, maybe because I was so preoccupied and distant that I could barely manage simple conversation. So I continued sleeping with other students or guys who had come from the townships into the parties in town because here they could be gay without judgment. We'd look past each other before, during, and after sex. Acknowledging each other was too frightening and too painful; if we crossed paths outside the party in broad daylight we were complete strangers.

There was a guy, Dumisani, with whom I met from time to time at these parties and had sex. He was a lot of fun, telling jokes to the group when he was high but never really speaking directly to me when we went into a room or a corner alone. He had a long athletic body, always looking like he'd put extra effort into his clothes. I think that had either one of us been less afraid, we might have found out what else we had in common. At the time we just enjoyed sleeping with each other. Apart from his name I didn't know who he was or what he did. I pictured him as a commerce student or an engineer—he was so very clean-cut that it wasn't hard to imagine him passing for straight on the street. Once or twice after sex we shared a cigarette but that was the extent of our intimacy.

Otherwise I heeded my father's advice and kept my nose in my books. In Durban I grew up and grew quieter. More afraid and less joyful. I understood what had happened to Rodney: he had needed to free himself from his own demons. He wanted to stop the parties and the drugs and wanted his mother to lift him up, to promise him her love. He had opened up and invited his parents into the most frightening part of his life and they had refused to look. Sometimes I admired him for it and other times I cursed his stupidity—his sense of entitlement. Rodney's problem was that he hadn't had enough sense to know that it shattered people's sense of safety—muddled with their need for equilibrium—to think that we were not just characters in books they chose not to read; that we in fact lived and grew up right next door or even worse, in their homes.

How terribly, terribly moronic was Rodney not to know that people would go to great lengths to feel safe again, to live with at least the illusion of equilibrium? He'd been foolish, I decided. It helped assuage my own guilt.

I would sit in my flat seething with rage when I thought of him telling his mother that he "liked to sleep with men." What did he expect? I went with that anger for a long time, until I couldn't any- more and I missed him reminded that we were all seized with the need to tell someone sometimes. I could see that he had in fact been brave because unlike him I couldn't think of a single person I could tell.

And my parents? The only feelings my parents let into conversation were pride and excitement. We were not a family that spoke about what was difficult—we cried in private, alone. My only job was to keep making them proud.

I had developed a routine in Durban: within the first year I had taken up jogging in the mornings, running along the sandy beach at low tide. It was one of the things I had written down and promised myself to do as part of an effort to at least like living where I was. I enjoyed jogging on the beach rather than along the pavement, even though my tekkies got wet and sandy; it felt romantic and of course it was an experience I wouldn't have had if I'd lived in Jo'burg or Pretoria. I ran at sunrise, since my rounds at the hospital started very early. Hardly anyone was on the beach at that hour except for those who lived on the beach or on the streets and after a while I recognized everyone, waved and kept going. It was the only place outside the hospital where I felt someone was expecting me. Something I liked about running—apart from gradually seeing my body get fitter—was watching the sun rise as if coming out from the deepest sea. It was one of my few pleasures, watching the morning come to life. It was also a time to be alone with my thoughts and my longings before throwing myself into the chaos of the hospital.

I was getting used to being in Durban finally, this place in between my divided past. School was fine, the flat was home. Even speaking to my parents was half bearable.

On the phone my mother asked how I was doing, without really wanting to know, and I didn't expect more.

One morning at the end of November and close to the beginning of my year of community service I went for my jog as usual. At some point I decided to stop and walk along the boardwalk. I had started earlier than usual that day so the sun had only half risen and no one else was around, not even the woman who showered with her male companion at the beach showers. I walked all the way to the end of the boardwalk and stood at the centre of the square lookout area, watching the waves crash against the poles holding up the cement walkway. I was about to enter my fourth year in Durban and was surprised to realize that this was the first time I had come down here. When I was growing up my mother and I would take walks to the end of the boardwalk on family holidays and one of my favourite things to do at those times was to watch the ships in the distance, looking as if suspended in midair. I would look out until my eyes and back hurt, and when I turned to look up at my mother she'd be in the same position, standing upright, forearms on the railing, eyes squinting against the sun. She always looked distant and forlorn on these occasions, but I didn't mind, feeling that the longing in her face somehow suited the mood of the ocean. I had come to associate ships and the ocean with sadness and I don't know if it was because of my mother's mood or mine on our holidays, but it was a comforting sort of sadness. She and my father didn't spend time together even when we were on a family holiday. They took turns taking me to different places—which meant time alone for me with each of them.

I was lost in thought and longing again for my home, for things I refused to name, when it occurred to me that I was running out of time to reach the hospital for my shift. Turning around, I swiftly gathered my spirits and started jogging back home. The sun was higher up in the horizon and the vendors were up and running now, putting their stock on the ground, standing wooden artifacts—West African masks and wall hangings—on their tables and hanging hand-made leather sandals against the poles. On the way I was distracted by a woman calmly shifting a screaming infant from her back to her front, cradling it against her chest and taking out her breast to soothe him. There was something so beautiful about the ease with which she did this that I was overcome with a devastating sadness. In the meantime I was running across a busy street without looking and the light had begun to change. A small, white VW hooted and came to a screeching halt to my left. Holding both hands up in apology, I sprinted across but when I stepped onto the pavement I realized that the car had come around the corner and stopped in front of me. I was late and not in the mood for an altercation. Worrying that the driver might want to have a fight, I walked away, picking up my pace. Then I heard a shout: "Kabza!" The door of the car opened and when I saw the driver I stumbled from the shock.

There in front of me was Sediba giving a big grin, arms stretched out and offering a hug.

"*Heita!*" he said, shaking his head. "Ao, I see you want to die in Durban."

I was speechless. He walked over and wrapped his arms around me with the warmth of a good old friend. His touch and smell felt like home. He looked even better than I remembered and had changed his look: his head was shaved and he had a tapered beard that was so finely cut you could tell it was done by a skilled barber. I wondered if he had done it himself.

"You're sweating," he said, pulling back and looking me in the eye.

"I . . . I was out jogging. What are you doing here *Jo*?" I had my hands in the pockets of my shorts, feeling terribly self-conscious.

Sediba shook his head. His eyes locked into mine, his grin widening. "Long time *Jo*."

I laughed nervously, looked at the ground because I couldn't think what else to do. There were cars coming around the corner and hooting at us to get out of the way, so Sediba gestured towards his car. "Are you going somewhere? Do you want a lift?" He was still holding my gaze, eyes dancing like he couldn't believe the delightful coincidence.

I gathered my thoughts and quickly said: "Yah! Yah. I have a morning shift and I have to shower—"

"I'll take you home," he started walking towards his car before I could respond. My eyes darted from the car to his crisp white shirt and blue jeans to the muscle definition on his arms. I swallowed hard and walked around to the passenger seat and, once seated, opened the window for air. A lovely whiff of Lilac and peppermint filled his car, so strong that I had to close my eyes and keep my nose to the breeze. I felt my mind drifting, returning to a time I had long left behind.

When the car started, Mdu came on the CD player but he turned it off.

"Still a fan of Mdu?"

"*Eish* man, you know, you know me!" We laughed as the car gathered speed, roaring up the hill. I think we were both making an effort not to look at each other and me pointing out directions to my place seemed the easiest thing to do.

When we reached my flat I quickly led the way, thankful that it was in a good state. As I was walking up the stairs, I turned around to say something and caught his eyes on my legs. A felt a fizz of pleasure.

"So what are you doing here?" I asked.

"Ah . . . you remember I had an aunt here, my mother's sister?"

"Yah . . . Yah."

"Mama wanted to see her so we drove down yesterday. She stays in Umlazi, so we're there for three days."

I opened the door and looked for a place to put my keys, feeling somewhat disoriented in my own home. Sediba looked around with curiosity and I was not quite sure what to say just then.

He met my eye briefly and then turned away, walking towards the sitting room window.

I said, "Have a seat, I'll take a shower and then . . . "

"I'll drive you to work," he said, not looking at me but at the collection of CDs on my shelf next to the window.

My shower was brief. I exhaled dramatically as soon as I stepped into it, feeling as if I had been holding my breath for the past half hour. A rush of great pleasure and anticipation ran through me. How long had it been? I hadn't seen Sediba since that fateful afternoon when I had been too drunk to make sense. Since then, whenever I went home to visit I very rarely saw him, and I never stuck around for more than a day or two anyway. We had gone back to the way things were before he injured his hand, eyeing each other from across the street like strangers. I was excited to see him now and found myself wondering if he may be seeing someone. His presence along awakened something old and familiar in me, something I wanted to hold on to. He looked happy to see me—but what if he was not past what had happened between us?

When I walked out of the bathroom wrapped in a towel, crossing the small space between the bathroom and the bedroom, I saw him making an effort to keep his eyes on my CD collection, his back to me. I darted quickly into the bedroom and got dressed in a hurry, conscious of the time.

When I came out in my work clothes, tugging nervously at jacket, Sediba whistled and we both laughed. He looked me up and down and said: "*Ao, ao*, Doctor Mosala!"

I ran my hand from the front to the back of my head and then looked at my watch without seeing the time.

"They must be lining up to see you at the hospital," he said, reclining against the sofa, still watching me closely.

"Do you want something to eat?"

"No," he said, standing up. "No, I ate very early."

I nodded, picked up my bag and tucked in my shirt. Sediba walked towards me and straightened my tie. At the sight of his hands on my tie, his body's proximity to mine, I felt my breath quicken and cleared my throat to make it go away. His voice was serious and he looked me right in the eye when he said: "So, are they lining up?"

I shook my head. "I . . . I'm not seeing . . . I mean, yes. Yes, there are many very flirtatious . . . *women*. But . . . "

"Only women?"

"Yes." It took all my courage to look him in the eye. Although I was waiting for him to, he didn't make to move closer but still kept his eyes on mine. We both laughed nervously.

"I have to go to work," I said, fiddling with my keys.

He opened the door and we went out.

We made our way through Durban's early-morning rush in silence with the radio off. When we reached the hospital I found myself looking around for familiar faces that would see me. The unreasonable, fearful voice in my head said that anyone who saw me next to him would know. Sediba put his elbow on his open window with the other hand on his gearshift. He looked around outside at the people and I felt he was making an effort to keep his eyes away from me.

"So this is where I work," I said.

"OK," he cleared his throat and nodded slowly.

"When do you go back?" I asked.

Sediba smiled and looked at me. "What time does your shift end?"

I paused to think, running my finger along the edge of the dashboard. I was afraid of what was starting but also very tired of being afraid. I didn't want him to go back home, to be so far away again; in Durban, where no one knew us, I felt more courage to let something happen.

Finally I said, "Come to my house around seven tonight . . . if, if you want. We could go out for supper."

His eyes widened and he cracked a smile. I think he was surprised.

"Sure, *Jo*," he said.

As I stepped out of the car, one foot in and the other on the ground, I turned back and looked at him. "It's really nice to see you."

"Sure, *Jo*. Sure, sure," he was nodding, eyes understanding.

I really wanted this time to be different. We were not teenagers out of high school anymore and I was nowhere near my parents or my childhood friends. I was exhausted by my own loneliness—even ashamed of it, especially when I could feel my old school friends' awkwardness through the phone or see it in their faces as their eyes darted around, attempting not to look at me. When the topic inevitably veered towards women and marriage I would let them do the talking, nodding in agreement, dreading the moment the conversation would turn to me. When they'd inevitably ask, "So . . . what about you? Are you seeing anyone?" I forced a smile and said, "You know me, I'm never seeing anyone in particular." I think most of the time they were grateful I was evasive and were happy to let it go.

Seeing Sediba had awakened my senses. Things felt a lot brighter that morning. Even the chaos of the hospital was exciting instead of overwhelming. I couldn't remember the last time I had had something to look forward to.

And the day was not moving fast enough. I had to tell a patient's family that he would need to go to intensive care, and instead of my usual calm, composed, and compassionate approach, I worried that I had rushed through the consultation and not given them the empathy they deserved. Luckily the attending physician didn't seem to have noticed. The patient's wife had held a tissue to her nose and cried for the duration of the meeting, and I was ashamed of feeling impatient with her, wanting her to sort herself out so I could get back to my work. My father would have been appalled. I was acting so unlike the physician he had groomed.

By six in the evening my shift was finished and my colleague Andrew gave me a lift back to my flat.

Andrew and I had started at the hospital at the same time. He had been brought up in America by South African parents and had returned after the first democratic elections in the country. He always spoke about the disparities between people of different classes and different colours. I saw him as a man sorting out his roots, yearning for South Africa to finally feel like the place his parents had spoken to him about as they raised him in a foreign land. He wanted to be friends with me, and I liked him well enough, sometimes had drinks with him after work but I'd never made a solid effort to befriend him.

I wanted him to be quiet so I could sort out my thoughts but he was chatty that day.

He turned on the radio and said, "So when are you getting a car? Not that I don't want you to keep riding with me, but you've been eyeing that BMW for so long dude!" He laughed his light, easy laugh that always surprised me because it seemed so incompatible with his very low voice, and looked from me to the road. I stuck my face out the window and felt the fresh, warm breeze against my face, and it was calming. Every day I took time to feel the fresh air to wash off the smell of cleaning products and human fluids from the hospital.

"I don't know. Still saving up," I grinned at Andrew.

"I'm thinking of selling this thing and buying a new car. But not a BMW. That's a German car. My dad would freak if I bought a German car."

I turned to him and tried to engage. "Why?"

Thankfully we had turned a corner and were approaching my home.

"Because he's Jewish, his parents survived the Holocaust. I think he has to be more Jewish than the average guy because he married a Christian girl."

I shook my head and smiled. Andrew mentioned his parents' marriage a lot. The difference between his parents' backgrounds seemed to consume him.

I said: "Yes, you said. That sounds like it was not easy to accept for your grandparents."

He shifted in his seat and wrinkled his forehead. I could see he was getting ready to have a long, involved discussion and now I regretted saying anything.

"You're never with the person your parents want you to be with," he said, then ran his hands up and down the steering wheel and focused intently on the road. I often had the feeling he was trying to say something to me but didn't know how.

"Do you know what I mean?" he asked, but the question came too late and it was time for me to get out.

I shrugged and gave him a friendly pat on the shoulder. "Yup! Thanks man. Thanks for the lift!" I hopped out in a hurry.

"Hey Kabelo, if you ever want to just hang out and chat this weekend, let me know . . . "

I nodded and waved as I walked away.

Making my way up the stairs of the complex—skipping two stairs at a time like a little boy—I suddenly found myself missing my old friends from school and the comfort of our rowdy schoolboy relationships. I missed friends who were willing to just let me be. There was something very anxious about Andrew. He seemed to want to have everything out in the open in a way that was unfamiliar to me. He once told me about a brother who was mentally ill. "Schizophrenia man." I had known him only a few weeks then. Whenever people disclose difficult personal information, they tend to expect the same from you. It was an exchange I preferred not to be a part of. The point of me moving to different places was usually to get away from intimacy.

Feelings. They were like tools I didn't know how to use. Give me a wound any time, I thought, and I know what to do. I could never work with people's sadness. When I reached my flat I raced around getting ready. I cursed myself for not taking a cab that would have taken a straight route and dropped me off twenty minutes earlier. Andrew had been slow and chatty, obviously hoping to be invited up or out. I should have known better.

My flat looked fine but my clothes reeked of hospital scent. A quick shower, two pairs of boxer shorts and three pairs of jeans later I was ready, sort of. A clean white t-shirt was in my wardrobe next to a soft, light grey one that I hardly ever wore but I knew Sediba would be in a white t-shirt, so to avoid looking like twins I put on the grey one. I wanted to shave, but was afraid I would cut myself if I did, my hands could not be steadied. Still, I splashed a dash of aftershave onto my palms and dabbed it onto my cheeks, washing my hands vigorously afterwards and then rushing out of the room to reevaluate my outfit. There was a photo of us from years ago, at a party at my house before varsity, me sneaking a glance at him from the edge of the pool and Sediba glancing at me with a secret grin. It was framed and on my windowsill. It was not a picture of us so much as it was of the day. It had half our friends in it, people scattered around the pool laughing and drinking. There was a braai stand in the background and my father with a piece of meat on a long fork, his eyes looking in the distance where my mother was talking to Aus' Tselane. Lelo was caught midair, diving feet-first into the pool. It was a picture of my childhood, of lazy Saturday or Sunday early evenings in my parents' backyard, with half the neighbourhood enjoying themselves. Sediba and I were at the far ends of the picture and Lelo was in the middle with my father behind him, but I had always seen it as a picture of me and Sediba because it had been taken in the last few days before I left home, in the days when our times together were a delicious secret.

Now in my bedroom, with the billowing white curtains before me and a gentle breeze floating in through the large open windows, I suddenly worried that he would see it and it would expose my longings, my never having fully let go. So I rushed to find a place to hide it.

Once I had thrown it into the drawer, the buzzer rang. I froze, then, taking another look in the mirror, sniffed at my armpits. I stood looking at the white intercom receiver, unsure whether to let him come up or tell him I was coming down. Much to my dismay, when I finally picked it up to answer there was no one there. I panicked.

There was a knock at the door and, taking a moment to compose myself, I turned the doorknob and opened. Sediba stood a few feet away, leaning against the white wall of the corridor, in loose-fitting blue jeans and blue and white lace-up canvas shoes. There was the whole width of the shiny red floor between us and I immediately felt he was too far.

"Someone let me in," he said. His white shirt hung nicely over his jeans, barely covering his black belt. I wanted him to step closer and come in but was still too nervous to ask.

"You OK?" he asked with a shy grin.

I nodded. "I was just getting ready."

"So come. Let's go," he held out his hand but dropped it before I reached him. As I followed him down the stairs he asked about my day and I asked about his. By the time we reached the car we had fallen into talk about our old childhood friends and he was bringing me up to speed on township news; it seemed suddenly like we were sitting in my parents' backyard talking the way we used to.

In the car on our way up the road, however, I started to feel a wave of regret, thinking how we had left things the last time I saw him—and then I was gripped by the urge to tell him how sorry I was, properly, the way I had practiced in my mind many times but had never had the courage. Over the years I had thought of calling him many times—especially in those first few months in Cape Town—but between regret and a pull away from everything back home, I couldn't quite bring myself to do it. Now I started, "The last time I saw you was so long ago," my eyes were on the street life as we drove up past some roadwork and Durban's newer buildings towards Florida Road with its many restaurants and bars.

Sediba looked over and smiled, playfully hitting my shoulder. "You were just getting settled at varsity *Jo*," he said.

"I was . . . " I rubbed my neck, looking for the right words to say.

He didn't let me wallow. "It was your parents' house . . . and it was a long time ago." Then he opened the window. "I think I like Durban," he said. "You know, I've been driving around looking for products for the salon. I ended up eating around here this afternoon. My mother's busy with my aunt and it's so hard to watch my aunt in her sickness, my mother cries to me when my aunt is asleep. When daytime comes, I just want to come out here and be alone. Think about my own things . . . "

I understood that for him the past was behind us. We drove slowly up the busy road, passing diners sitting on terraces and groups of young people loitering around, loud music coming from the bars. The scene took me back to Cape Town, but I didn't want to bring up Cape Town.

"How long ago was the last time you were here?" I asked him.

"Last year."

"Yah . . . " I picked up his CD collection that lay between us and looked through it. He hadn't tried to find me even when he knew I now lived here. I hadn't been in touch with him, but my mother talked to everyone and I knew people in the location were aware of my move from Cape Town to Durban. I felt somewhat hurt but didn't want to spoil the evening by showing it. Then, as if he had read my mind, Sediba said: "It was only for a night or two that time and I hardly left my aunt's side."

It sounded like a lousy excuse but enough for me to let it go.

On Florida Road we walked up and down trying to decide where to go, bumping into people, avoiding the long lines outside restaurants. Everyone seemed young and ready for a night out, people were dressed for a good time.

Increasingly I felt frustrated and knew it was not because of trying to find a place to sit but because my longing to be alone with Sediba was rising with every filled restaurant, every long line we had to walk past. Sitting at a restaurant and chatting for any length of time didn't interest me at all. I didn't know if I were imagining it, but I sensed he was frustrated too, as our conversation began to feel more and more forced.

Finally, we were about to enter a place that looked quieter and not nearly full when he tugged lightly at my shirt from behind. "We could get take away," he said and with a slight shrug, "or we could sit."

My heart racing with excitement, I nodded. "Take away," I said.

We bought steak and chips and got back into the car without looking at each other. He turned up the music, Mdu singing "Jola," and we sped back down the hills under rows of large Jacarandas towards my flat. The windows were open; with the breeze and the music and Sediba sitting only a few inches from me I felt, at that moment, freer than I had felt since I was a child. Even at UCT, even when I had lain naked in Rodney's pool or was smoking zol on his balcony, I was still aware of hiding parts of myself. Now I felt at once nervous and open, unafraid.

Then unexpectedly the image of Rodney on that day when we met flashed through me. I saw him fumbling with the gearshift and then throwing his head back, laughing from the pit of his stomach. The memory was so sudden—so quick and jarring that I felt dizzy and held on to the door handle for support. Images spun around in my head. I knew they would only grow bolder if I tried to swat them off, so I sat still and let the mind remember, the body shiver and then stiffen, so that when it was all finished I could carry on. Thankfully Sediba didn't seem to notice.

Once we were in my flat, I took the food into the kitchen, and Sediba again walked to the window, as he had done that morning. My place looked out over the city and the beach so that in the mornings you could see the sun rising above the ocean, but at that hour of the night only the city lights were visible and the view was spectacular.

Sediba said, "I guess this is what foreigners mean when they say it's not the Africa they imagined."

Then, looking restless, he walked over to the music player and looked through the CDs. I stood watching, meaning to move but unable. He pressed the glass door of the music stand and then the button to see what was in the player. When he was done Boyz II Men came on, singing "Yesterday."

He started to laugh quietly, shaking his head. I had been fiddling with my keys and staring at the package with food as if it required a key to be opened, but now I stopped and watched him sitting on my coffee table, shoulders broad and his shirtsleeves revealing his toned arms. In my mind I could see the scar above his navel, the burn mark I had noticed years ago.

I put down the keys and the bottle opener I had been holding in my right hand, and started making my way towards him. He didn't turn around even as he heard my footsteps, which were slow as my body was now oddly relaxed and everything seemed to come to a complete standstill around us. I could smell lilacs as I got closer—either from his scent or from outside. Then I sat at his side and asked, "What's so funny?"

His eyes on the CD player, he said, "I can't believe you still listen to this!"

I laughed too, recalling high school days, December at Trunka's house with the guys, lounging on the trimmed lawn or sitting on turned-over beer crates. I remembered how we'd play those early R&B songs until the tapes were scratched and sticky.

Sediba said: "These guys! Remember that video? Shorts and ties? *Eish*, no man."

The sound of our laughter rose and then faded into the quiet of the room at the end of the song.

I reached over and turned him towards me. He was serious when he looked at me, no longer thinking about the shorts and the ties. And I was the one who went forward first, thinking I'd kiss him gently but was surprised by the rush through my body, how much it felt like that first time, all-consuming and dizzying. His hand went to my waist and he pulled me in. When I drew my head back it wasn't because I wanted to stop, but because it was all so powerful I had to take a breath, calm my racing heartbeat. And he seemed to understand because he said nothing, only resting his hands behind him on the coffee table, waiting. My palms were on my knees as I breathed in, my eyes closed.

When I looked back, his eyes met mine and there was a gentle calmness about him that took me back to the younger man I used to spend evenings with, lying on my parents' lawn drinking Coca-Cola from tall glasses and eating tea biscuits. I said: "Stay" and he kept his eyes on me, his expression not changing. So I took his hand and led him to my bedroom, where the windows were wide open and you could smell the sea breeze like we were two steps from the beach.

When I put my palm on it, the skin under his t-shirt was smooth and warm. He was brushing his lips against my bare shoulder when I pulled his shirt up, and I stopped before it was all off, letting him kiss me some more, my body moving to the rhythm of the mood. I had never seen his whole body so bare and so close, yet whatever part I touched, held or moved my lips against felt familiar.

Still, what we were doing—my teeth on his skin, his palm around my erection—was different from what I'd imagined in the many moments alone in my room at UCT or here in my bed when I could think of him without the guilt and old shame. Every time I had imagined something hurried and clumsy but this was nothing like that. Our lovemaking was slow and rhythmic, steady but uncontrolled. Sediba's movements on top of me, while charged, were graceful. He had always had a powerful body and moved in it with confidence and deliberate, incredible skill. By then I thought of myself as a good lover or at least impressive enough. For me it was all about demonstrating your competence, showing off, and letting your lover see what you were good at. Sediba had a different idea of it. With him lovemaking mimicked the back and forth of a good conversation. He was interested in how I felt, what I wanted; the kind of lover who appreciated a response. And I found out that that was an intoxicating and wildly erotic thing: making love with someone who wants to look at you.

I slipped away from everything I had known until then, my world suddenly making sense. Inside I was falling into a more peaceful place, a place I had spent many years looking to find. That night we were in bed for hours, kissing, caressing different parts of each other, slowly discovering, learning what the other wanted and then resuming our lovemaking. By the time the sun came up I was both achy and relaxed, wanting more and already regretting that he had to leave.

It was dawn and my day off when Sediba started getting ready to go. The sun had not yet begun to warm the rooms and there was only a little bit of light coming in when I pulled back the curtains. He kissed me at the door holding my head in his hands, reluctant to let me go.

"One more hour," I begged between kisses.

He stepped back inside and leaned against the wall near the door, head just beneath a photograph of Winnie and Madiba that I had bought in Cape Town from a dodgy-looking man reeking of weed.

"Don't say that, I'll never leave."

"There's a thought."

He threw his head back so that his laughter was so delightful I almost wanted to him to do it again. Then he patted in his pockets looking for his keys before he took my hand, saying: "Walk me to my car."

Durban was hot and humid, the air heavy with both sweet scents and stale odours. He had let go of my hand by the time we closed the door behind us. Distracted, I tried to get us back to easy conversation. "How's the salon?" I asked.

"Actually, it's great. We're doing really well, but I'm busy with something else."

"What's new?" I asked him once we were inside the car. It felt more awkward here than it did inside the house. Maybe it was the anticipation of parting, knowing he would now be six hours away, and not knowing what would follow next.

Sediba clasped both hands in his lap and said, "I see this guy sometimes, about starting my own product. You know how I was thinking about that before?"

Of course, I remembered. "Ao! That's grand, *Jo*!" I said, truly excited. "Wow, so it's happening?"

"Yes. I'm going to start coming here in about two weeks to start working on it."

"Sure, *Jo*. Wow. So . . . "

"So . . . "

He was now nervously running his finger along the outer edge of the steering wheel. "Ummm . . . look, I don't know what you're thinking, but last night was . . . well, I had a really great time."

I nodded and said, "Yah. It was. It was really great."

"So when will I see you?" he said, now bringing his face closer to me.

Nervous, I took a breath. "OK." he said "I don't know. I mean, I remember you were never the kind of guy to be tied down . . . "

He was being playful, but I was embarrassed. This took us back to a time when I had my arm draped around a different girl every month, thinking only of myself, as if it didn't matter—as if the girls didn't have feelings. I looked away from him and through the tinted windows.

His voice dipped slightly like he was not allowing himself to hope. "I don't know, this may be a one-time thing for you . . . but, but I want to call you."

I turned to face him, wanting to say something to make him see that I was not like that anymore, that I wanted the same thing, but all I could say was: "No. Not a one-time thing."

He smiled delightfully and gave me a quick peck on the lips but I held his cheek and leaned in for a long kiss goodbye. "Call me," I said.

He nodded, and bit his lip.

Afterwards, as I stood outside his car I thought of how, if you were seeing us for the first time and your mind didn't tend to think of two men or two women sleeping together, you would only guess that we were two friends or colleagues, nothing else. And as I watched him drive off and images of the night before danced around inside me and I stood a few steps away with my arms crossed and my legs far apart giving a slight, tense wave, who would have imagined that we had just spent all night tangled in each other's arms and the bite marks on his lower back were from my teeth during lovemaking? I probably I looked like just another fit young man saying goodbye to his chum after a night of drinking beer and trading stories about women. I didn't know if that was funny or sad.

And my flat was different when I walked back into it. It smelled of things that had never been there before, things I wanted to keep. Never before had I had someone come to my place, let alone stay the night. It was as if I had crossed over to a new zone in adulthood and I very much wanted to hold on to it.

It was my first weekend off in a long time and I spent it sleeping in and reading, exhausted from a very long week of work and wanting the time to pass quickly until the next time we saw each other. When I was not sleeping I lay in bed replaying our time together over and over in my head. My bed still had the scent of his body but it seemed to be fading with each passing hour. And when my mother phoned, I was transported to a different place and my lover's presence felt like something I'd imagined.

"I called you last night but you were not answering," she sounded tired and anxious. Her voice was hoarse but I couldn't say if it was from being sick or having just woken up.

I took the phone to the sitting room and turned on the TV as I spoke to her, trying to calm myself down. The pleasures of the night before were long gone.

"Did you just wake up?" I asked.

She cleared her throat. "No, I feel like I'm getting a cold, I think. Listen, I was thinking, why don't I come down to Durban this next weekend if you're not working?"

The sitting room was hot now, the sun having fully landed, its heat radiating off my walls and floors. I stood up and walked over to close the blinds half-way and then turned towards the kitchen, thinking maybe I could find myself something to eat.

"Ah . . . I'm working next weekend actually," I said finally.

"What about the following weekend?"

There was a pause. I pushed the glass in my hand against the fridge door and let it fill up with ice, aware that the machine was making too much noise for either one of us to speak. I hated lying to my mother, but I wanted first to see if Sediba could come and then I could leave the weekend open for him.

"The whole weekend? You're working the whole weekend?" My mother was also pouring herself some water on the other side.

I put a cube of ice against my lips then moved my tongue around it, tempted to crush it with my teeth and make an irritating noise that would force her to let me off the line, but I only sucked it instead. Are we ever adults around our parents?

"Mama . . . I may have some time off. Why don't I let you know tomorrow? I'll know my schedule better then."

She sighed with palpable relief. "OK, OK."

"You sound exhausted. Too much work at the shop?"

"Agh . . . I should sell that place. It's part of the problem. I'm always busy."

"Mama you love being busy." I had never before heard her complain about being busy.

"I do. I did. A woman shouldn't be too busy for her home . . . for her marriage."

"Mama . . . " I didn't know what to say. It was so unlike her to make such an intimate statement that I felt as if I'd walked in on an adult conversation.

There followed an uneasy pause as we were both trying to undo the previous minute. She surely regretted it, because the next thing her voice rose and she was almost cheerful when she said: "*Haai* man! *Eish* . . . tell me about you. What's new? Hm? How's the hospital?"

I leaned back and proceeded to tell her about my patients. She always liked hearing about their personal stories while my father was more interested in their medical conditions. With my mother I had to mention that they had traveled from a distant rural village to the city, their children had hurt themselves while under someone else's care, or their husbands seemed detached. That was what kept her engaged. So I kept talking about what I had found interesting, and the more I spoke the less she spoke, and the less she spoke the calmer I felt.

I put down the phone thinking that under no circumstances did I want her to come for a visit—even though I couldn't shake the feeling that coming to see me was some sort of life-line for her. But if I let her come, the things I kept hidden from her might come out, fierce beasts lunging at her, forcing us both to *see* who I was and what I wanted. My parents had not returned to my flat since they helped me move in. Whenever they visited Durban I went to meet them at their hotel or at a restaurant of their choice, where we sat together for a meal, happily pretending that my almost being a doctor was the only thing worth talking about. I feared at these times that we might have a run-in with a man I had been with, a knowing look might pass between us, exposing to my parents this other life.

At work Andrew was quick to remark that he'd noticed a change in me. We were three days away from the weekend and it would be another two days before Sediba returned. Andrew and I were sitting with some students behind the new wing of the hospital building in the area designated "Staff Only." While I was enjoying a break from the rain and the burst of sunshine, my thoughts were terribly scattered. I only caught bits and pieces of what Andrew was grumbling about.

"I mean, it's weird, you know? In America I was just considered black. No one ever, even for a *second*, called me anything else. And . . . here I'm called Coloured." I could see Sediba's arm across my midriff. "It's such a mess . . . " There was Sediba's grin, his eyes narrowing when he laughed. I was impatient for him to be back. Even as we kept in close touch, calling each other every night, he seemed farther and farther away as the days went by and I felt more and more irritable.

"My dad told me all the time. He said: 'In my country, I don't see anyone thinking you're just Black.'"

I must have looked as anxious as I felt because Andrew stopped speaking and took a forkful off my plate, which startled me because it was so out of character. We were not the kind of friends who shared anything but a lift from home to work and a beer once in a while. I looked up in surprise. He was happily chewing a mouthful of my green beans and smiling, his eyes daring me to get annoyed. When I didn't say anything he said: "Dude, if you're not gonna eat it, someone should."

I shook my head and smiled. "I was . . . actually, I was going to eat that and I am a bit distracted, I'm sorry."

"I know I'm talking with food in my mouth," Andrew couldn't help apologizing for himself, something I was not at all used to, having gone to school with some of the most arrogant guys I knew. "My mom would be pissed. Eating and talking is one of her pet peeves."

"I've never heard anyone say that before: 'pet peeves'?"

"Yeah, it means things you absolutely can't stand, like bad restaurants or constant misuse of apostrophes."

We both laughed but Andrew now pushed away his plate and folded his arms, looking at me with a slight frown, as though I were a puzzle he was trying to put together.

"Now, back to you. Why aren't you eating?"

"Oh," I picked up my fork now and regained my interest in my food. "I must have had too much for breakfast." I steadily avoided his eyes.

"Mmm-hmm." I started to fidget.

"I've noticed a change in you this week. You're cheerful, something I've never known you to be."

"Oh, come on!" I snapped. I was annoyed, because I had always thought of myself as quite a joyful person in spite of everything. If I had been good at anything so far in my life it was putting on a good face. I could get rowdy with friends when all I wished for was to curl up and cry in a corner. I could laugh at jokes that sounded like thinly veiled contempt about my sexuality. I was good at being jolly.

But Andrew's inquisition remained undeterred.

"I'll tell you what I'm thinking," he leaned forward and started to whisper. "Either you're in love or you're just plain gettin' some."

He laughed heartily either at his observation or at his impression of a southern American accent. |

"Ha! You're mad then,coming up with bizarre theories. Come on." I widened my eyes, tried to look incredulous. "I am stunned, my friend. Stunned! I'll have you know I'm in a good mood because my mother just said she's coming to visit in a few months," I lied. "She doesn't travel very much anymore, so this is big. But thank you for giving me a life I don't have." I forced a laugh and stood up to throw my brown paper wrapper into the dustbin. I had had this feeling before, this fear that someone was on to me, that they were *aware,* and it made me feel as if I were slipping into the ocean and there was nothing to hold on to. People had cornered me—I remembered my high school friend Beast in particular and his low voice, his icy and determined stare—and I had felt as if I were losing ground. It was best to walk away, I had learnt. You didn't stare down the inquirers because it made you look defensive, but you also didn't stay and fidget. You laughed and walked away, you pretended they'd just told you that in spite of the research, they actually did believe the earth was flat. You made *them* look silly, not yourself.

But Andrew was different. Whereas guys like Beast had maintained their stare and stood firm, Andrew laughed with me and followed me, saying as he walked past me, "I bet I'm not wrong."

It was strange what small things it took to make you feel found out. Even stranger and still a mystery to me was how I could work so hard at hiding something and still have the odd person not only find out but be so very sure of what they thought they knew.

Later when Andrew drove me home after insisting and I relented because I realised it was his way of apologizing for intruding, we kept the topics on patients and the hospital. We were laughing about a gift an attractive young patient had given him—a pretty glass vase that she instructed him to put in his dining room "where everyone could see it."

"You know it's against the rules to phone her, don't you?" I was saying, when Andrew, who was looking straight ahead, said: "Wow, who is *that?*"

When I looked I saw Sediba leaning against the bonnet of his car, arms folded, head turned all the way up and looking at the sky, like a child who had just spotted an airplane. He had come a day earlier. I felt as though I had just walked into an airless room. I opened the window and took deep breaths.

Andrew said: "Oh, look at you!"

"What? Look at me what?"

"Who is he? Do you know him? I mean, hell, I'm a straight man but even I can see that guy is hot."

The thing about Sediba was that his looks and the way people stopped to stare had hardly changed. He was still that quiet boy in a blue and white scarf sitting cross-legged in front of his parents' house. It wasn't so much that people thought he was handsome, but that he had an air of importance about him, a strong and intimidating presence. That day he was wearing a beige and black fedora with a pair of sunglasses. People always felt a little bit out of his league, like he was from a grander place than the one they lived in.

I shrugged and tried to sound nonchalant as I stepped out of the car, with, "Oh, he's a childhood friend. Why don't we talk tomorrow?"

"I'm not on tomorrow," Andrew said, and then to my dismay, turned off the car and opened his door.

"Where are you going?"

"To meet your childhood friend," he said as if it was the most natural and polite thing to do and I was the odd one for being surprised.

He hurried up to Sediba, who seemed to only now be noticing us. I frowned a bit at Sediba and nodded my head in Andrew's direction.

Andrew said, "Hi, hi I'm Andrew," his hand flying out eagerly to shake Sediba's. He fixed his shirt and I knew right then that he was feeling uneasy.

Sediba held out his hand and then added to the handshake by placing his left hand on top of both their hands and smiled into Andrew's eyes.

Andrew was impressed. He looked Sediba up and down in true Andrew fashion: shamelessly, without any attempt at hiding his admiration. But Sediba was used to people staring. He smiled politely and asked questions to divert attention.

"So do you work at the same hospital? How do you find it?"

While Andrew chatted away about patient load and trying to learn isiZulu, Sediba kept the conversation flowing by offering bits and pieces that were really nothing if you thought about them but to the listener felt like he was disclosing intimate details about his life. It was the intent eye contact that fooled.

"Kabza and I grew up together. We moved within the same pack. You know how wild township boys are. We drove our mothers mad. You know what I mean. Anywhere you grow up, all boys get up to a lot of nonsense, right?"

Andrew was nodding away, absorbed, growing more and more comfortable. I reckoned he felt more of a connection in those five minutes with Sediba than he had ever felt with me, and being the guy who always craved a good talk, he was getting ready to settle into long conversation. Sediba was so good at this that he even made me believe what he was saying, that we had actually always been friends, that we had run around "within the same pack" instead of moving in circles, avoiding each other.

Finally, it took was a pleading look from me for Sediba to swiftly glance at his watch and gasp, "*Eish*! I really should watch the time. *Kabza!* Let me give you the things your mother sent and then be on my way."

And with a look of disappointment Andrew said, "OK, then. I guess I'd better run."

Shadows were growing longer, the light becoming faint in the horizon. Sediba and I watched Andrew drive away, and then we looked at each other with a knowing look. The walk up to my flat felt long. We were running up and practically sprinting to my door. My shirt was half off before he closed the door behind him and both of us were kicking our shoes off and very nearly tore each other's clothes off, kissing and pulling impatiently as we fell to the sofa.

"That was the fastest I have ever done that," Sediba said when we finally sat up, panting.

I kissed the smooth skin on his clean-shaven chest, my lips moving against his sweat.

"It was?" I said, genuinely surprised. For me, quickly and quietly was the only way I had ever had sex before him.

"I don't know," he said, kissing my forehead. "I like taking my time."

I sat up and looked at him. "Didn't you ever have sex in a hurry? Because it felt so . . . urgent?"

Sediba shrugged and stood up to head to the washroom. "Only with people I didn't know. Anyway," he paused to look back at me, "I don't think you want to know about that, do you? Me and other people?"

I didn't reply. I was curious but I wasn't sure how much exactly I was willing to hear.

In a moment, there was the sound of the tap water running and the washroom door clicking open.

"Andrew seems nice," Sediba called out from behind me.

"He's fine," I said, "but he talks a lot. Talks about his feelings every day, all the time!"

When I turned around, he was leaning against the wall behind me, still naked as I was.

"What's wrong with talking about your feelings?" he asked, with a slight frown.

I was annoyed now, not wanting to talk about Andrew. Andrew needn't be coming into my home now, I didn't need to feel I was sharing my intimate moment with him.

"It's not a guy thing?" he asked.

I shook my head. "It's not something you do, as a guy, no."

Sediba chuckled. "Not macho?"

It stung, the word *macho*. It brought back his blue and white scarf and my practicing to sit and stand with my legs apart. I shut my eyes and let the thought slip out.

He said, "He's your friend. My friends and I tell each other our feelings."

I looked away from him, pressed my fingers pressing against my eyes. The truth was, I just didn't know where to begin, talking about such things.

Sediba said, his eyes narrowing: "I like to talk about how I feel."

When I didn't respond, he added, "You're allowed."

"What?"

"To tell me how you feel."

When I looked around me I noticed that apart from the clothes there was something else on the floor: food. Sediba had brought bananas, apples, mangoes and some green vegetables: spinach and beetroot bulbs were scattered on my carpet and a cabbage had rolled under the table.

"What's this?" I said, making my way around the room as I picked them up.

"What's what?" he said, watching me with a smile.

I held a mango and stroked its smooth skin with my thumb but my eyes didn't move from his body. "All this. What's all this?"

"It's called food. You have none in your house." His arms were folded, one ankle crossing the other.

"I don't cook."

Sediba didn't move or attempt to cover himself. He looked very comfortable and grew more amused as he watched me getting aroused.

He said, "That's too bad."

"What's too bad?"

"I don't cook either," he said, and then he was saying something else but I couldn't hear what—I only heard the mango in my hand fall and roll away behind me. Now my hand was in his and he was leading me to the bedroom. "No rushing this time," he was saying.

Those first few weeks in Durban with Sediba were glorious, peaceful. He would drive down on Saturday evenings, taking Mondays off—even the ones when I was working—and we'd spend hours in bed, sometimes reluctantly venturing out to the beach or a restaurant. Neither of us liked clubs, so we never tried going out at night— we were not interested in being around other people, and I secretly dreaded running into men I'd only known through one-night trysts. He always brought food and we attempted to cooking it together. We burnt potatoes and overcooked the rice; we over-salted the meat and put the wrong spices in our seshebo. I think we made things worse by tasting before serving the food, always adding more salt, more pepper, more oil. Almost every time we couldn't help but come out with dish after dish that was overcooked or overspiced. It was a mess. But then we sat at the dining table with its two chairs, looking out at the sky, the fading sunset, the multicoloured rooftops, happily eating our mistakes. My flat was filled with smells of cooking, fresh fruit, and another person's clothes, which I borrowed and wore or buried my nose in when it had been too long between our meetings.

I was more content in that time that I had ever thought possible.

Sediba's love for Kwaito had prevailed through the years. He would take whatever CD he was listening to out of his car stereo and bring it up to the flat so we could listen to it together while he cleaned and I cooked or he cooked and I cleaned. The thing he loved the most was to turn on a new Arthur, Mdu, or Boom Shaka and get my opinion on them. We were together when TK Zee came out with Dlala Mapantsula and he insisted I listen to the song between my shower and getting dressed, as he danced around the room wearing only his boxer shorts, saying: "These guys stand head and shoulders above the rest."

Even when his visits were short, because I had been working a lot and we only had a few hours before he had to drive back up north, our days felt long and slow. As we got more comfortable with each other, we started talking a little about the sex we had had before we started seeing each other. I was surprised at how honest I could manage to be while still staying mum about the bulk of what I had done, the shame of my past loneliness still a sore memory.

Mostly we spoke about the things we could laugh about.

I told him about sex with a straight guy in Cape Town who kept saying, "Seriously, I'm straight" almost throughout. I told him, "It should have turned me off but it just made me laugh and made want to have more sex with him."

Sediba would lie on his back, sometimes laughing so much that he'd have to turn over and cough a little bit. He told me, "I once had sex with this guy who wanted me to wear a hat that Basotho wear. He had one in his bedroom that he kept for boys like me, I guess. He had lived in Lesotho for years and had something going on about those hats, told me about all his Basotho lovers. It was so odd. Not sexy at all, I'll tell you that."

Other times, when we were more serious, he'd say, "I can't believe how many people trust me with their secrets—some of them quite disturbing—and I could never say something as simple as, I'm going to Durban to see my boyfriend. They come in and sit in my chair and tell me about their sadness and their hopes and I can't just say, when I drop the phone, 'That was my boyfriend.'"

I thought about how my job required people to open up to me about embarrassing things too. The two of us took care of people in our work and they had to trust us but could never find out who we really were.

Except for keeping us secret, everything felt easier. Suddenly knowing that there would be someone waiting for me at home made my days go quicker and I went back to the days of loving medicine, of feeling that I had the skill and patience it required. Because my isiZulu accent was so bad and I constantly mispronounced words when speaking to patients, sometimes I would wait for the nurse to speak for me, to translate for the Motswana doctor. But now I was feeling bolder and speaking my broken and atrocious isiZulu and watching the patient squirm at my attempt—or be amused. I didn't mind anymore. Sediba, whose father had been born and raised near Durban, spoke isiZulu very well, and he would teach me a few things about my pronunciation, which made me feel less intimidated by the language. Of course when you think that he was teaching me a lovers' language—words I was never going to use with my patients—you can see why I came to love hearing him speak it. Even the secret of us, in those days, was more delicious than painful.

I had more patience. I was less restless. Even Andrew talking about his days growing up in the United States I happily listened to, and offered my two cents worth. His parents seemed like they had tried, I would tell him, considering the political climate they were raising him in. "No," I would reassure him, "you don't have to call yourself Coloured because that's what someone of your skin colour and hair texture is called here. You can call yourself whatever you want."

He wanted to call himself black.

Not before or since have I felt happier or more at ease with myself.

Yet there was the nagging feeling of something being wrong at home. My mother phoned more than she ever had before, giving me updates on her days. She would tell me how much money she had made, how her employees had behaved, whether or not her car needed cleaning. Mundane details really, and I only minded a little bit, until she started with how she had gone to the hair salon and chatted with Sediba's mother, who appreciated how much time he was devoting to her poor, sick sister in Durban. She suggested that Sediba and I spend time together while he was here. "He should have a break from the aunt. Honestly, it must be so difficult for that poor boy to be doing all that work. His mother tells me he buys food to bring every time he goes. He was always such a good boy."

Sometimes while she was speaking I picked up my remote and turned on the TV, watched it with the volume down. I didn't like to hear my mother talking about Sediba, and I didn't enjoy the panic that led to a headache, sweating and nausea every time she suggested I spend more time with who she didn't know was my lover.

I had always been a rather impressive liar—if lying could be called impressive—but I never did enjoy its violent effects on my body. After some time I was so determined to stay enveloped in my bliss with Sediba that I answered the phone less and less.

I suppose falling in love makes us selfish and oblivious to the rest of the world. I had observed it in other people but never in myself before. Now I forgave everyone I'd ever known their blissful absence while in the cradle of a love affair. I understood.

In those weeks of working hard and then falling happily into the arms of the man in my life at the end of every week, I ignored the first sign that my mother's world was crumbling.

And then I returned home one rainy Monday afternoon to find myself unceremoniously yanked back into my parents' lives. I had rushed back to my flat with great anticipation. I was tired, done with the week and anxious to shut everything out. I had planned only to spend the next few hours making love and talking to Sediba. He had spent the day on the road and then seeing his aunt, before coming to take a much-needed nap at my flat.

It was more my mind that was tired—an emotional sort of exhaustion and not so much in my body. Earlier in the day I had lost a patient who had come in stable but whose condition had quickly deteriorated. I hated it when that happened, it unsettled me more than was necessary and reminded me there were parts of my job I had yet to master. I suspect it's a side effect of always hiding something: you become obsessed with wanting to know what will happen next—you hate surprises. So I preferred feeling that I could almost always make accurate prognoses at my first meetings with my patients.

I found Sediba still asleep—not even startled by the sound of the door closing behind me. He was always a deep sleeper, something I envied. After hanging up my coat I picked up the newspaper he had been reading, folded it and placed it on the table in front of the sofa. I stroked his forehead with one hand and the fine hairs on his belly with the other—something I liked to do to wake him up. He awoke with a start, pressing his fingers against his eyes.

"You're back," he said, taking my hand in his and smiling into my eyes. I kissed him slowly but when I pulled back something about the look on my face brought a slight frown to his. "Bad day?"

I nodded and he made room for me to lie next to him and put my head on his chest.

"This young boy died suddenly. I didn't expect it . . . " my voice trailed off as he stroked my arm.

"*Eish . . . askies.*"

I liked coming home to a spotless house with the windows open and the fresh scent of a distant lemon tree that I knew was outside though

I had never seen it.

"Do you want a glass of wine?" he asked and I nodded but when he started to stand up I held onto him a little bit longer before letting him go.

"What did he die of, the boy?"

"I suspect complications from AIDS. He just came in and collapsed. His mother said he hadn't been doing well for a while, hadn't left the house, but today he'd been able to walk outside and make his way to the hospital."

Sediba was standing at my kitchen pouring us both a glass of red wine and listening. I said: "Did you bring that?" and he smiled at me. "I wanted you to try it, my mother loves it."

I sat up as he handed me my glass and put his own on the table and then sat next to me, heat rising between our touching arms.

"He didn't look well but he didn't look like he was about to die. I was surprised . . . I hate being surprised."

Sediba kissed my cheek gently and said: "Drink your wine." I obeyed.

"Your mother called."

My heart raced. "Did you answer?"

He frowned. "No. I didn't answer. Why? I would have, but I came in just as she was starting to leave a message."

"No, I wouldn't want you to answer," I said.

"Why not? She knows we're friends now, doesn't she? I've come to visit on my way to seeing my aunt. What's wrong with that?"

I shook my head at him, incredulous. "What if she suspects . . . you know?"

Sediba looked annoyed. He picked up his glass, drank, and stood up to go to the kitchen.

I said, "Come on, you don't want your mom to know either."

"My mother knows." His voice was flat, I couldn't decide if he was sad or angry.

"Your mother doesn't know!"

"She knows. We don't talk about it, but she knows."

When he saw the curious look on my face, he added, "We work together. We live on the same street." He picked up the bottle of wine. "This wine. We share this wine once a week or so after work, just me, my mother, and father in their sitting room, chatting about our days." I blinked away my envy. The life he was describing was as unimaginable as snowfall in Kasi.

"She's never seen me with a girl except my friends—like Thuli— and she never asks me about girlfriends. Every Saturday she says: are you driving down this weekend?" He looked me in the eye, no trace of joking: "She knows."

I felt my hand shake and I put down my glass and stood up.

"About us?"

Sediba looked confused for a moment and then shook his head.

"She knows about me, not about us."

"Oh," I exhaled.

"Nobody knows about you." He said it almost to himself, looking away. I ignored his bitter tone.

He then asked, "Are you hungry?"

I didn't know what I was feeling, pressing my thumbs against the armrest of the sofa, my eyes unable to meet his. I started to walk over to him in the kitchen but changed my mind. Sitting on the sofa seemed like the better option.

"What do you mean nobody knows about me?" I spoke into my glass, not wanting him to see how awkward I felt.

"You should phone her back, she sounded awful."

"What do you mean?" I looked up at him. He shrugged and pointed to the answering machine with the blinking red light. I went to the kitchen and turned it on.

Kabi . . . how are you my child? I've been phoning and not finding you. You must be tired from working so much (a heavy sigh). *Anyway I'm coming to visit you. I think I'll come soon. Just phone and tell me when you're not busy and I'll come. Or I'll come anyway, it doesn't matter if you're busy. I have to leave here. I have to go on a mini-holiday, just a few days.*

There was another heavy sigh and then the machine beeped to signal the end of the message.

"I don't know what's wrong. She has been phoning nonstop."

That wall that I had grown up with—the one I could not reach around—was going up. All I could do was say, "It's like when I was in Cape Town."

"What happened in Cape Town?"

I saw shapes shift in front of me and had to shut my eyes to feel less dizzy. I could not talk about Cape Town. Cape Town was the thing I had buried alone in the middle of the night and washed my hands. Cape Town was the shame I couldn't revisit.

I said, "She just . . . she phoned me a lot there."

Sediba said, "It's hard for her that you're not there. She's told my mother when she's at the salon."

"She worries too much about me but, but I think she's fine."

Sediba stood up and came to sit on one of the white stools at the kitchen counter.

"Maybe it's not you she's worried about."

"What do you mean?"

"Maybe it's her own life . . . ?"

"What? The shop? My father working too hard? What?"

Sediba looked away and kept quiet.

I said, "She's probably bored," but Sediba continued to twirl his finger around a key ring on the counter, saying nothing.

"I'm going to shower," I announced, unable to control the anger in my voice.

He too sounded exasperated. "Just phone your mother back."

It was not our first fight, of course—that night before I left home was the first time we fought—although it seems unfair to him to call it that. I had experienced this before: the need to walk away, countered by a pull towards him. Getting into the shower and getting cleaned up took great effort. I needed to say something but couldn't find the right words, so being ever so stubborn in my anger I pulled myself away from him and turned the water on.

I expected to find him sleeping or quietly harbouring resentment, but when I toweled off Sediba was lying in the bed with a broad smile.

About an hour later I closed the door with a sleeping Sediba in bed and went to phone my mother from the kitchen. She sounded dazed, not remembering why she had phoned or what she might have wanted to say.

I said, "You wanted to come? I don't think next weekend is such a good idea."

She didn't seem to mind, to my surprise. "*Ag*, I just wanted to see you soon, it doesn't have to be next weekend. Do you know how much food we've sold this week?" She regretted her tone on the answering machine, wanted us both to forget it. "They've announced we'll have a blackout after the storm so people are stocking up. People always stock up on food this time of year anyway—it's the end of the year, they'll have a lot of parties and—"

"Mama," I interrupted, suddenly recalling Sediba's statement: "Maybe it's her own life . . . "

"Yes? What's wrong?"

"Your message sounded . . . " Words escaped me. "I thought you said you had to go on holiday or something."

My mother gave a cough and said, "I think I have a cold. You know how a cold can make you feel exhausted."

There was a lull in the conversation. I would hear my neighbour's radio. I suspected the guy was a night owl because whenever I couldn't sleep I heard faint sounds of his music. I picked up a glass from my cupboard—appreciating that Sediba had done my breakfast dishes before taking his nap earlier.

I hated the feeling of going to bed when there was still light outside and then waking up when it was dark, so now I walked around the flat turning lights on, half listening to my mother while distracted by Whitney Houston singing one of my mother's favourite songs. I told her: "My neighbour's playing 'Didn't We Almost Have It All.' " It was the sort of music my mother liked to hear all the time on weekends after work, listening to it on Metro FM with a glass of wine in one hand

and a cigarette in the other. My mother and Sediba's mother were two of the few women their age I knew who smoked. It was a wonder they were not better friends: each running her own business, each impeccably dressed and with Setswana accents that made them sound at once sophisticated and rustic; their habits were unconventional.

I thought I heard my mother sniffle on the other side but when I asked, "Are you . . . ?" I couldn't find the word "crying" because it was my mother and you didn't ask.

To change the subject, I asked about my father. "Is he working too much?" I had spoken to my father two days before and he had sounded exactly as he always did: busy and interested in my work. My father never asked about anything other than my work and I appreciated him for this.

My mother replied, "He's doing the way he always is," each word lower than the previous, her voice heavy and dragging.

When I dropped the phone that feeling of things being wrong gnawed at me, not letting me settle down and not allowing me to think. I considered going for a jog but of course it was too late and too dark. I started to walk over to the cupboard, thinking that I would make myself some tea, but instead I turned towards the bedroom. I climbed back into bed and held on to Sediba.

Home

IT WAS A FEW MONTHS into our relationship that Lelo got married. Even as I wrote down the date in my day planner, my hand shook a little and I had to put the pen down to steady it. After Sediba had told me about the wedding, I stood near my sofa as if forgetting to sit, staring down at the coffee table while he stood with his back to me, looking out the window, the way he tended to do sometimes when he was deep in thought. Neither of us said it, but we were terrified. We would have to go, of course. Lelo was one of our oldest and dearest friends. This was an obligation, not a matter of picking and choosing what we felt like doing.

We would have to be *there*, with everyone, remaining a secret again as we had done just before I left home that first time. We would have to leave our cocoon.

"I'll arrive on the Friday," I said softly. "There's always something on the Friday."

"I'll see you when you arrive then," Sediba said, and it felt as if we were already practicing our deception.

This was all we needed to say about the matter at the time; I turned to go and fetch us something to drink from the fridge and we proceeded to do what we always did, carefully side-stepping the topic, not wanting it to seep through the contentment of our world away from home.

When he left that Monday evening I sat at my dining table staring at the bottle of beer in front of me, wondering what we would do, how we would be. I considered first the practical things: I would have to hire a car, since I hadn't yet bought one. There had been offers from my parents to buy me one when I graduated, but I was tired of being soothed with things my parents could buy, so I had stalled them both. For the wedding they would of course expect me to sleep at their house—although if I stayed out all night with my friends they'd think nothing of it. I had barely visited since first leaving home, and when I did visit, it was for so brief a time that my mother would say, "It hardly counts . . . " She was right, it was merely a pop in. Durban was not only my refuge from Cape Town; it was also my hiding place from home.

I spent the week contemplating what the weekend would look like, unable to make plans with anyone, because whenever Sediba and I spoke on the phone we continued our sidestepping, and our silence around it grew more uncomfortable with each visit.

It became so painful that by the time I had to leave and make my way up north, I had decided to pretend that I was merely going to see my friend; that there was no problem at all with us being together up there, with our parents and friends somewhere nearby. As I packed my bags and went to pick up the hired car, I fantasized about driving straight to Sediba's house, unpacking my bags there and spending the weekend at his place instead of my parents' house. In my mind I would arrive to a home ready for me with pretty sheets and good food. I'd walk into it as I did my own house and my parents would think nothing of it—they'd only expect me to come by and have one meal with them.

In an attempt to slash through the tension, I phoned Sediba before I left and joked, "So I hope you've laid out your best sheets and have the beer cooling in the fridge because you know I have a long drive ahead. I'll need a cold beer and a comfy bed when I arrive." I could almost see him smiling on the other side.

"It'll all be ready for you," he half whispered. It was always obvious when he was with a customer because he spoke in what I called his "professional" voice. He might as well have been ordering a product.

But this always led to me tease him more: "And I like a hot foam bath and my feet rubbed . . . " He let out a slight giggle. "I'll be right back," he was saying to someone and then I could hear the noise fade behind him as he stepped outside.

"OK. OK," he was more serious. "When do you get here, *na*?"

"To your house? Six long hours."

Sediba went quiet. I heard the match scratch and strike across the box. He only smoked at work when he was having a tough day. He inhaled sharply and said, "Stop joking. You won't even see my house." There was a long pause as I looked around my room, wanting to throw my clothes back into the wardrobe and drawers and forget about the wedding. I so desperately wanted it all to be over already.

He said, "So we're going to be eighteen all over again, hey?"

I could hear him exhaling, blowing out smoke. Something odd about cigarettes: I liked how they tasted on someone else's breath. Sediba had the same thing: he liked the taste of them on my breath, so these days I only smoked when he was around. I wanted to tell him how much I did want to see him, his home. I wanted to go together to the wedding, sit together and hold hands. And so I could not respond to his question. It felt unsafe, talking about it on the phone at this point. I thought I'd scream out the things that filled me with dread and it would not be fair—he was at work.

He sighed, exasperation blowing through the phone.

"Drive safe, yah?"

"OK. See you." I dropped the phone, furious and helpless. I had six long hours to look forward to and a whole weekend of pretending I barely knew the man I loved. The old exhaustion seeped in, settled in my chest even before I had left my place.

Here is the thing that happens when a man is in love with a woman and that woman loves him back. Here is one of the most important moments in a man's life: there comes a moment when the two sit together and the man says: can my people come to your people? The moment you see on television, where a man asks his girlfriend's father for her hand in marriage, doesn't happen with my people. This is bigger, involves a lot more people, an entire clan. You send your uncles and aunts to meet your girlfriend's aunts and uncles. There are negotiations about what's to come, what the woman is worth—how many cows, how much money—whether or not the man is up to the task of taking a wife. The man must ask a woman if her people are ready to receive—to welcome—his people before he asks them to go. Growing up as a boy in Kasi your mother always speaks of that day; the day she will have to ask the uncles to go and speak on your behalf. So like everyone else's mother, mine had dreamed of this day and I knew she still looked forward to it, that she'd want me close by at this wedding, want me to see how it could be for me—for us.

What this all did was turn into balled-up resentment towards Lelo, his future wife, our parents, and our friends. I hated the occasion before it had even started and I hated even more that Lelo, my friend who was getting married to the woman he was expected to marry and not the one he was in love with, got to dance around the township being congratulated and showered with praise. He was marrying Masechaba only because his mother approved of her more, because she was going to be a lawyer, and his other girlfriend, Lerato, was considered unsuitable because of having two brothers in jail. He had been with Lerato longer and in my opinion he had always liked the idea of Masechaba more than Masechaba herself. On the other hand I understood the power of making choices based on what our parents did or didn't approve. I was in no position to judge him.

Still, I was bitter for it—a feeling I needed to keep in check since I was meant to stand alongside him and wish him well in less than twenty-four hours. I spent the ride home thinking of ways I could find to see Sediba alone, because that would at least quiet the wretchedness of the weekend.

When my car finally pulled up at our gate, I saw that instead of having to step out and call on the intercom I could drive through because someone had left the gate wide open. Both my parents' cars were in front of the double garage doors. I parked behind my mother's, assuming my father would be driving out soon, since he was not usually home in the afternoons. He must have come for a quick meal, I guessed. I took a deep breath as I walked, my shoes crunching loudly against the pebbled walkway.

As I approached the door, I heard voices coming from my parents' bedroom on the floor above, followed by a scream. Aus' Tselane appeared suddenly and stood still at the door, clutching a pile of the washing in her arms and looking frightened.

"I'm here!" I exclaimed stupidly and ran to kiss her.

"*Ao*! You've arrived, *na?*" She forced a smile.

"Are they fighting?" I asked in a guarded, conspiratorial whisper. She grimaced and stepped around me, and hurrying away.

"Are they?" I asked again but she didn't answer.

My mother looked cheered up as she appeared and threw her arms around me, kissing my cheeks happily.

"This time you have to stay the whole weekend!" was the first thing she said.

I went straight to the fridge and opened it, looking for food.

"If you're hungry get Tselane to make you something. Keep her busy." She clicked her tongue. She always spoke of Aus' Tselane with disdain; I wondered why she kept her as her helper if she could just as easily find someone else in the endless sea of people looking for work.

"No," I said. "I'll just make myself a sandwich."

My father came out with his arms outstretched and pulled me into a warm embrace.

"Sorry son, I have to run back to the surgery," was his greeting. "Come tomorrow before the wedding and I'll show you some changes I made."

My father liked to take me back to the surgery every chance he got, a way of reminding us both that someday we would work side by side. I think he didn't believe it would actually happen—he didn't think I would ever return, so whenever he could he'd pull me in, ask me to come take a look as though selling me the benefits of coming back. And because I knew my own reservations, knew that he did in fact have reason to worry, I felt ashamed as I reassured him, saying, "*Eng*,

Papa. One more year."

In another home, a child might have mentioned the screaming and asked what was wrong, but in our house there was a line I couldn't cross. We walked around not saying things, stepping over and around what we saw and felt and carrying on as if we had never come across our own feelings. So I asked the right questions.

"Has it been hot here?"

"No," my mother said, taking over my sandwich-making.

"It's rained all week but it's going to be a nice weekend for the wedding."

And so we went on. I longed for Sediba's voice and my friends' laughter, so as soon as my mother said she was going down the hill to the shop, I hopped into her car and went to look for my friends.

Trunka's house has always been one of the township's central spots. It's one of the first houses you see when you drive in, partly because it's painted a shiny white with contrasting black on the window frames and partly because it's always buzzing with activity. There's always someone sitting and drinking or buying food. I had spotted people around there when I drove into town, so I knew if I wanted to go and find people Trunka's would be the first place to go.

In the car my mother played her Aretha Franklin CD, her elbow on the open window, her head resting wearily back.

"Are you tired? You look tired."

"Ag, adult problems," she said, taking a deep breath and a sharp turn at the main road. No parent ever considers his or her child an adult, I suppose.

"You and Papa are busy, huh? All this work! The shop and the surgery. You should go on holiday."

She snorted, shook her head, and turned up the volume and Aretha sang: "Everything is going so much faster, seems like I . . . am watching my life and everything I knew . . . "

She swayed her head back and forth slowly to the beat, her hand reaching out to pat her newly-braided her at first but then resting there a while longer. I watched the road. Old houses had been turned new with brighter colours and larger gates. The township is always changing faster than anyone can keep up, but what stayed the same in every township was the children playing on the streets. You had to slow down and swerve to avoid brick goal posts and stop and wave an apology because you had just driven over a well-drawn game of fish on the ground. Watching all the playing I remembered my childhood and the day Sediba arrived. Who would've thought I'd now be in love with the boy in the polka dot scarf?

"What's on your mind, baby?" My mother turned the music down and we were rolling up the windows to keep out the dust. "Patients?" she asked. It reminded me of how she spoke of my father. Whenever he was quiet she'd say "probably patients" and wave away his contemplative look. I nodded then, not wanting to bother her, knowing she was asking only to move us away from talking about her and my father. Knowing also, that she was aware that I had heard them yelling.

"Do you want to see your friends?" she asked, already turning towards Trunka's house. As we approached, Sediba's mother was crossing the street and my mother and I waved.

My mother sucked her teeth and said, "This one. She acts like she has the star child." Aus' Bonolo, Sediba's mother, came around as we slowed to a stop. She was as impeccably dressed as I remembered her, her hair in a beautiful round bun and her nails a deep, elegant, purple.

She came around to my side and gave me a kiss on the cheek. I noticed how she had the same large, beautiful brown eyes as her son, which gave my heart a bit of a start.

"*Yoh*, Kabi! You look so handsome! When did you arrive?"

"This morning," I said after swallowing.

"I'm sure Sediba doesn't know you're coming. He's been so busy he doesn't know what's going on with his friends." She leaned in and said to my mother, "You know we're doing all the people for the wedding."

My mother said, visibly toning down her annoyance: "Mmm. I thought you might be. I was going to come to you but I decided to go to town. I thought you'd be busy."

Looking genuinely sorry, Sediba's mother said, "Oh, I would have taken you. I would have made time . . . " But my mother had made her point and she was turning the car back on. I felt sorry and embarrassed. My mother had never liked Sediba's mother. They were so full of themselves, she'd say. It puzzled her that they were doing well but chose not to move up the hill or into town. I think she was always expecting them to join in the competition but they never did.

"OK, Bonolo, I have to get back to the shop, we're also very busy," she said, and Sediba's mother turned to me. "Kabi, I'll tell Sediba you're back. I'm sure you'll all see each other all weekend anyway, *neh?*"

I said: "OK, Ma," and we zoomed off.

My mother dropped me off at Trunka's house. As I stepped out of the car my mother turned to me, her hand on mine. "Don't even worry about your friend getting married. Our . . . your—your time will come."

Trunka was busy, running around getting things ready for the weekend. He gave me a light hug and a pat on the shoulder before continuing with what he was doing, unloading the lorry and stacking the beer crates on top of each other against the wall of his back rooms.

I joined him and helped, and asked, "So where are the other guys?" really only wanting to know about one.

"Running around. You won't believe where Lelo is . . . "

I knew what he meant. Lelo was with Lerato and probably the son he kept an open secret, bringing him to see his friends but not bringing him to his mother's house. We laughed but only a little because I think we both recognized the sadness in Lelo's situation. I shook my head, silently pushing down my disapproval. I had come here to celebrate, not to judge. Later we shared a beer on the cool veranda and Trunka caught me up on what was happening around the location.

"He's not like a man getting married," he said about Lelo. "He's running between two women's houses. *Eish. Mara* these are men's problems. Women don't understand."

I drank my beer and watched the road.

"And Sediba . . . "

I inhaled and held my breath.

"What's new with him?"

"He has a woman in Durban, I think. You know how he is, so private. But I suspect he's serious because every weekend he's out of here, driving down. I asked him if he wants to marry her."

I gulped down my beer and picked up another.

"What did he say?"

"He says he hopes so."

My back went hot. So Sediba talked about his love life these days.

"What else does he say?"

"Nothing. He won't say anything until you ask. We don't even know her name. Probably a Zulu girl with nice clothes, like he has. But we all agree he looks happy these days. He didn't for a long time, but these days . . . "

Gulping down my drink, I stood up. "*Eish Jo*, let me run. I'll come back later," I said, but Trunka was already distracted with the line forming in front of the tuck-shop. He ran off to help.

When I walked back up the hill I briefly thought about going to check on Sediba but stopped myself. It wouldn't be a good idea, no matter how much I wanted to see him. Instead, I tried phoning him again, but he didn't answer. It was like this overnight: he was not answering his phone, which led to an SMS argument. I'd write: "Do I not get to see you?" And he'd respond, "I have so many clients." Which was not really answering the question.

My parents were in and out of the house and never in at the same time. Aus' Tselane kept busy with the washing and the cleaning and seemed especially subdued. I went to the wedding feeling dejected and angry.

Traditionally there is a "bringing out" of the bride where we, the wedding party, take her through the streets singing wedding songs— songs that call out neighbours and friends to come see her, to celebrate. Being Lelo's best friends, Sediba and I had to be in the party, the group of men accompanying our friend to fetch his bride. It was one of the most anticipated weddings in town because Masechaba is a gorgeous woman. Big round eyes, high cheekbones, skin the colour of dark, burnt oak. She was one of Kasi's hopefuls: the people who are proof that we are better than the rest of the world thinks we are. And after Lelo had studied law and was a gainfully employed man, Masechaba's mother had warmed to him. Two cows and a hefty sum he had paid for her. This wasn't just another wedding around here, it was one we were all meant to remember for a long time.

It had gone on between them for years, on and off, even after Lerato had had her baby by him, even when it was clear to anyone who knew them that Lelo and Lerato were mad for each other, and the passion between the two of them couldn't be denied. There was something about Lelo, I suppose, that Masechaba couldn't shake. She was devoted to him and either pretended not to see or simply didn't care about Lerato. And it was obvious when she stepped out of her parents' house, went out into the world as someone's new bride, that she was radiant and content. As is tradition, she had been kept in a room away from prying eyes. So there was a collective gasp as we all caught our first glimpse of the glowing bride. All agreed that Lelo had found the perfect woman, that on looks alone this was a beautiful match. When we stepped behind the bride and groom and started singing, Sediba came rushing up the street to join us, buttoning his jacket, spreading a painful smile.

I danced along with the crowd, keeping my eyes away from my lover. We went up and down the streets, neighbours coming out of their houses to join us, car horns hooting, baritones and sopranos lifting the spirits of all who had come to see, old women who were Kasi's praise poets stopping us every now and then to extol the bride. I have always loved a good township wedding. The biscuits baked by the women in the neighbourhood, the meat cut by the men and cooked by the women, the ginger beer, everyone singing and dancing until the sun goes down: they never disappoint. But I couldn't enjoy this one. This was the most painful one. My friends had reached the point where they were paying *lobola*, taking wives, making their mothers proud. I had been hiding out in Durban acting like there was nothing expected of me, but back here, my sense that I would disappoint and break my mother's heart was like a noose around my neck. I wanted to leave.

There was a moment, I think, when a praise poet said something about the sanctity of the marriage bed and my eyes met Sediba's and a lump got stuck in my throat: he and I would never have this. The aunts and uncles, the grandmothers ululating and sharing praise poems—talking about the woman's beauty, the man's duties and the happiness of the ancestors at the meeting of two people in love.

This would never be us.

Later we stole a moment and went back his house. We were pulling and grabbing each other, our movements too hurried and somewhat aggressive until he put both his hands on my wrists: "Stop." His voice was soft. "We're not like this. We're not . . . letting that shit in here."

I nodded because I couldn't find my voice and we flopped onto the bed with our clothes still on and our eyes on the ceiling fan. Through the open window, Hugh Masekela's trumpet floated in loud and clear, haunting. Someone was playing Stimela, music from a more determined time. The kind of song that makes you feel like a hopeful little boy. When Sediba held my hand I had to squeeze his and clench my jaw to stop myself from crying. "I hate this place," I told him. "I hate it. I'm never coming back."

He turned to face me. "You have to come back."

"No."

"It's home. You have to come back because . . . because I'm here."

When I looked in his eyes I could see that he was angry. And I was scared.

Separately we left his house and at the wedding we sat at opposite ends of the table, working at keeping our eyes and minds on the music, the people, the food—anything but what we were feeling. When our eyes did meet it was brief. The enormous white cake obscured our view of each other with the likenesses of the bride and groom at the top.

The wedding tent was large and white, hot inside and packed with every close relative of the bride and groom, plus us, the friends who had accompanied them. The older neighbourhood women wore aprons over their traditional brown wrap dresses and fussed over both the bride and the meal. They'd come in fanning the dishes, making sure the flies stayed off the food in the heat. My mother still had her apron on—you had to let everyone know you had taken part in preparing the feast.

First she came in and put her hands on my shoulders: "Did you eat?" she said and put a plate overflowing with rice, peas, carrots, cabbage, beetroot, potatoes and slices of beef in front of me. I saw Sediba's, Trunka's, and Base's mothers do the same.

"Did you see Tshidi?"

Tshidi from my high school days, who was friends with Masechaba, was at the wedding. "There are some high-class girls here," she added. I flinched. She hadn't used that term in a long time.

"Yes, Ma. I replied." I lied but thankfully it seemed to make her think I didn't need more encouraging.

When she left, Base whispered, "Look, there's Sediba's person." He pointed to the opposite end, at two women who were pulling up chairs near where Sediba was sitting.

One of them had beautiful long braids that looked freshly done, and the other one had short, straight hair. I had never seen either of them before.

"Who's that?" I tried to be casual.

Base said, "The one with the braids is Alice. She wants Sediba. I'm not sure if they're seeing each other . . . "

"But Sediba has someone," Trunka said.

Lelo had left his bride talking to her friends somewhere and was coming around towards us, catching the tail end of our conversation. He said, "But maybe he wants a Maimela person too. Durban is far!"

Everyone laughed but I didn't. The exhaustion came back, settled, and I had to sit up and talk myself out of it.

The two women sat down next to Sediba. I looked at him but he wouldn't look in our direction. So I sat, stewing, contemplating returning back to Durban before the night was over.

Back again at his house we had a fight.

"I'm sorry."

"Diba," I tried to remain calm, "Is this a break-up? What's going on??"

"I'm sorry," he was saying, throwing his arms in the air. "It's weird here. It's . . . my parents are here. Your mother is . . . all our friends are here. All week I've been listening to this excitement about the wedding, people asking when I'll be getting married-"

"Diba, are you pretending to have a girlfriend now? You?"

"No! No. I'm not. She comes up to me, we chat about nothing, I walk her out, but I've never had anything with her. Ever. At all."

"This is hopeless . . . ," I started to say, because as afraid as I was, I needed to say it. It felt hopeless. There would have to be a time when we both acknowledged it, when we both gave in and tried—a lot harder this time—to be the men all our friends were becoming.

But Sediba didn't want to see it that way. "It's not hopeless. It's weird here. I know, it feels weird here."

I let him pulled me close. Right then I thought: for now, I'll pretend it's simply awkward and not utterly discouraging. Just for now.

But then hours later I was sneaking out of his house to go lie in my old bed at my parents' house, feeling like I was, in spite of all my efforts, returning to my childhood.

For me, things shifted after that wedding. I couldn't quite get back the contentment I'd been feeling before Lelo's wedding. I'd walk around consumed with jealousy, envy, resentment towards my friends back home. It felt unfair that who I was could never fit into the place I had been brought up in. More upsetting and daunting was the sense that my life with Sediba couldn't go on. He was a proud and self-possessed man and I knew without him saying so that he intended to come out to our friends and community at some point. I couldn't see myself standing next to him, openly admitting that I was his boyfriend. The thought of doing that, of the look on my parents' faces, was terrifying. When he wasn't with me I'd feel myself holding back tears, imagining having to let him go. When he was with me, sleeping peacefully at my side, I watched him for a long time, overpowered by a sense of impending doom. Sometimes I would get up and walk around my flat, drink water and stare into the night. I contemplated waking him, asking him to tell me that I was overreacting; that we'd never have to end things.

Then one night even he couldn't sleep through my misery. I was generally quiet but maybe subconsciously I had wanted him to wake up, carelessly dropping a glass into the sink. When he appeared at the bedroom door I tried to smile.

"What's going on?"

"I'm just getting water."

"I mean, what's going on," he leaned his head against the doorframe. "Why can't you sleep all the time?"

"Ah . . . I didn't think—"

"Yah, I noticed." His sigh was heavy. "What's wrong?"

I shrugged. "It's always odd, going back. Seeing my mother, seeing everyone feels kind of weird."

He looked at me for a long time. "Yah, I see that."

"I don't know, you know. It's weird to see you and not *be* with you."

Sediba ran his palm over his face.

"Come to bed. We're here now. You can *be* with me," his grin was infectious.

I could see he didn't want to talk about it, that he too was stuck. It was like that time when I had tried to apologize when we were back in Kasi. He couldn't, for some reason, get into it. It only got me more worried.

Cape Town

YET HE WAS OBVIOUSLY TRYING in his own way to work out how we could stay together.

"We're going to this wedding," Sediba told me, as I was getting ready for work two weeks after Lelo got married. We were walking around each other as we got dressed, trying to hurry so that he'd have time to take me to work before starting his long drive back home. He pulled his t-shirt over his head and his forehead wrinkled as he focused on deciding which pair of pants he would wear. I pulled on my usual pair of black jeans, which I insisted looked professional because I couldn't be bothered to buy or wear formal pants. Sediba had agreed they were better than trouser pants, which he hated and called old, so that cemented my decision.

"We're going," he continued, "because these are good friends of mine and I want you to meet them. Also, we won't have to avoid each other like at the last wedding." He had remained friends with the guys he had met at varsity. Unlike me, he had gone alone, without high school friends and he'd had a true fresh start, not taken pains to hide his sexuality. Refusing to keep moving between two or three worlds, wearing different hats for different friends, he had met people who were also gay and stayed with them—friendships that were now still solid. He had mentioned once or twice that I'd like them or they'd like me, but they were scattered across the country and there hadn't been an opportunity to meet them all until now, when his friend Scott was marrying a guy Sediba hadn't yet met. It would be a first for both of us: a wedding between two guys, both White.

This was the first time in two weeks that he had mentioned Lelo's wedding. The memory of that weekend still stung. We tip-toed around the topic, and when he said "the last wedding," his voice lifting the words as if with the tips of two fingers and then suddenly dropping them with disgust. I stopped buttoning my jeans and watched him.

He sat on the bed and tugged at his shoelaces, not really tying them, just pulling with impatience.

"We're going. It'll be fun, you'll see. Different."

I'd been the one waking up at night restless, but his anger about Lelo's wedding came out in quieter, less detectable ways. I could feel it when he stood still at my window, staring outside with his jaw clenched, or when he stared at the floor instead of watching TV. I could see it in his eyes when he hesitated at the door, jangling his keys, not wanting to leave. The only times that he had seemed visibly upset before had been when he argued about politics with Trunka, Lelo, and Base, the four of them divided between PAC and ANC. Seeing him this way now was unsettling. I stood a few steps to his left, holding my breath.

"You're . . . angry," I said.

He glanced up at me briefly, not really seeing me and then back down, back to the thing he was doing with his shoelaces. When he was finished he put both his hands at his sides on the bed, his shoulders arching as he took a deep breath.

"You know what Trunka said to me?" I went to sit behind him, staying quiet. "He said it only took Lelo one week. One week and he was back at Lerato's house. As soon as Masechaba goes to school in the morning, Lelo is back at Lerato's house. He's bringing paper work home, going into work later because it gives him time with Lerato in the mornings while his wife is at school."

I said: "Well, he always did say he'd never leave her. Remember? Before he got married he always said how good she was in bed and he could never leave . . . " It was unlike me to repeat something like this and I felt shame slither through me like a quiet snake through long grass. We didn't talk about the guys at home and their sex lives. Sediba looked at me for a moment like he was taking in a stranger, and I turned my palms up to say I didn't know what to make of any of it.

"Good in bed?"

"Diba . . . "

I didn't really want to be talking about Lelo and Masechaba or what he was doing with Lerato. I didn't want to remember. But Sediba turned to face me and asked me the question as if seriously expecting an answer: "And if that's how he feels, if he likes sleeping with her, why the fuck did he get married to someone else?"

I panicked. I was not used to dealing with an angry Sediba. My mind said the thing to do was let him say what he needed to—be quiet and let him talk. But then he stopped talking, sat up straight, took a deep breath, and after a bit stood up to go and look in the mirror.

"Let's go, then," he said finally. "Let's get on with the day."

I stood up and followed him out of the flat and to the car, where he got in and then out again, saying, "Can you drive for a bit, I need to think." I took the wheel and we drove silently through busy streets and mild traffic jams, the radio off.

When he dropped me off, he said again, more calmly this time: "We're going to this wedding." I nodded and squeezed his hand. Usually he'd try to kiss me and I'd say: "Not here, my patients and colleagues . . . ," but that day when he leaned over I moved forward and quickly kissed him before his mouth reached mine, like I was apologizing for standing by while other people did things like get married to one person while sleeping with another. Having grown up in a house with my silent parents, I had been taught to be quiet about anger, resentment, and contempt. I had been taught it was unrefined to express these things.

I stood at the hospital entrance and watched as he turned right and headed towards the highway, feeling somewhat helpless. We were going to this wedding and we were going together.

All week, whenever we spoke on the phone, I avoided asking him how the other guys were. He didn't seem angry when we spoke—he

never did when he was away from me. He liked to save certain conversations for when we saw each other, that he found it impolite to
discuss on the phone certain things, private things that should only be
said face to face. Sediba would always be the boy from the family who
made you want to straighten your tie and shine your shoes.

When he came to fetch me that weekend he was wearing a very
flattering black ivy cap with his favourite dark blue jeans and white
t-shirt. I noticed that his belt was new. Sediba was a bit of a shopper.
He liked to treat himself to little accessories: a belt here, a hat there.
Nothing too big or expensive, but he'd often go out after a long week
and find something small that complemented an item in his wardrobe.
He strolled into the flat, cheerfully giving me a kiss as he always did
when he greeted me and then throwing his keys on the coffee table.
He was obviously looking forward to this trip. I hadn't seen him this
cheerful in a while.

"Our flight leaves in two hours and I still don't know what I'm
going to wear tonight," I said. I was nervous about meeting his friends
and I was nervous about us going out together, to meet people and
sit together where everyone knew that we would go back to the same
room and sleep in the same bed. I was not ready for that, but I suspected that saying so would throw a dark cloud over our weekend.
And even if I were not ready, I wanted to have a good time. An escape
from everything I knew sounded quite tempting.

Sediba took my hand and led me to the bedroom. "That's why you
have me, isn't it? You're in this for the free fashion advice, right?"

I grinned. "That's the only reason I'm in this." And like that I felt
more at ease because there was a return to the Sediba I enjoyed, the
one who could make me laugh in an instant.

We played around in the bedroom, with me choosing the clothes
that I knew he'd disapprove of and laying them on the bed, pretending
I was seriously considering them while he closed his eyes and shook
his head, insisting, "You'd be lost without me. You're lucky I came
when I did. In fact I'm staying with you just to make sure you don't
repeat any of these fashion mistakes," and I'd say: "Please don't ever

leave me then!"

By the time we got serious and looked at our watches we were having to throw our things together in a rush and dash to the airport. I had never been on a trip with anyone other than my parents and friends before. It took me a moment to realize that I was starting to feel anxious not because of this trip, but because every time I stepped on a plane my body remembered having to take a seat between two people who rarely spoke to each other. I had to adjust my mood and start looking forward to a great weekend. Sediba looked relaxed and content, resting his head against the back of his seat by the window. "Don't be alarmed by some of my friends," he said with an easy chuckle. "They've never met someone I was seeing so they might ask a lot of questions. They're all a bit curious."

I was jealousy. I didn't have any old friends who could look forward to meeting him. Andrew remained curious about Sediba, dropping hints about us all going out together with Angie, the woman he was now seeing, but I kept postponing the date and avoiding the subject whenever I could.

"What are they curious about?"

"Well, I mean I've gone out with one or two of them but never very seriously and I don't normally offer details about what's going on with me."

I nodded. I hadn't thought about that but of course it made sense that I would meet someone he had been with. I still didn't like to ask Sediba about boyfriends—I could laugh about a story or two but liked to imagine that he, like me, had had nothing but brief encounters before I came along. I suppose at some point I had decided that I was the first guy whose bed he had returned to over and over again, and as always happens when one needs to keep a fantasy going, I hadn't given him a chance to tell me otherwise.

He was running his finger along the outline of the window frame when he added, "I guess they're curious because I didn't offer much about myself before and now I've said a quite a lot about you. You know, more than I've said about anyone else." His eyes darted from the window to me and then back.

Satisfied delight rippled through me. I grinned at him.

"I'm sure you've done the same with your friends," he said.

I shifted in my seat then and reached for the in-flight magazine. "I really haven't kept in touch with my old friends," I told him.

"You and your school friends were so close. All going to UCT together and staying in the same res?"

It was nice, at least, to be sitting next to one old friend who remembered a thing or two about my high school years. Sediba had not forgotten me talking about the guys from school. I thought about my old friends and how, once we were at UCT, our paths had hardly crossed. I wasn't even sure where they all were now.

"It's been a while."

I didn't look at Sediba because I couldn't face his curiosity. I was dodgy about Cape Town and I knew it. Every time he brought it up, I'd say: "Ah, that feels like so long ago now," or "*Eish, Jo.* Cape Town was crazy," knowing exactly what it sounded like. I was implying that it was so much fun I didn't even know where to begin talking about it. Sometimes to myself, I even pretended that it had never happened— that I had gone from Maimela straight to Durban.

This time, as always, he let it go. Yet it was always coming. The threat of the Cape Town conversation was always looming, darting out at odd moments and I aimed to tuck it into small corners every time. When she came to bring our meal, the stewardess's eyelashes fluttered at Sediba. With her fingertips she brushed her hairline, calling our attention to a bun of beautifully wrapped locks. She was quite attractive and obviously used to easily getting attention. Sediba smiled back politely and thanked her, barely acknowledging her flirtation. I winked at him after she was gone but he didn't seem to want to joke about it. Throughout the flight she would come and give him special attention, asking if he needed anything, but when I looked at him his eyes were on the magazine or out the window.

After he had handed her his empty cup and she lingered near us a little bit longer than necessary, her eyes on him, I teased him with a whisper: "I think someone wants your phone number."

He rolled his eyes and glared at me. "Doesn't she see that I'm with someone? I mean if she were with her man, would I flirt with her?" He clicked his tongue, the anger, and bitterness of the previous few weeks resurfacing.

"Come on. Not everyone can tell," I offered.

He turned his whole body towards me. "Exactly. That's the problem."

I felt accused of something and couldn't respond. He waited but I only shook my head. "It's not me you should be angry with," I said.

Sediba closed his eyes and turned back to face the window, ending the conversation.

We started our descent over Cape Town, picture-perfect mountains in the distance, the stuff of postcards and tourist magazines. But closer, just beneath the wings of the plane, were the squatter camps: endless fields littered with cardboard and plastic homes spread alongside the perfectly maintained roads. I gripped my armrest. My temples throbbed at the sight of Devil's Peak in the distance, my knee shook slightly and I tried to resume my breathing.

"The Cape contrasts," Sediba said. "Millionaires fly over squatters, plastic and cardboard homes near some of Africa's wealthiest."

I shut my eyes and grunted, wanting very much to hold his hand that minute. It seems stupid now but I hadn't anticipated the wave of wretchedness that gripped me at the sight of Cape Town. Maybe I had thought only of the wedding and meeting new people, and that had me fooled into thinking I was going to a completely new place. And I had never been to Witsand. It was one of the many coastal towns in the Cape that I hadn't yet visited and from what I heard it was a small tourist place, quiet in the winter and far removed from the bustle of the city. It sounded idyllic. Perhaps in my imaginings I had neglected to land in the city, heading straight to the beach town instead. Now here I was, forced to confront my first few varsity days amidst mountains and a view of UCT. I had a fleeting memory of myself stumbling and falling, my head spinning from too much booze.

If he noticed that I was a bit shaken, Sediba took it for excitement and nostalgia. When we had settled into our hired car he said, "Do you miss it? You look like you've got a lot on your mind. You haven't said much since we landed. Feeling nostalgic?"

I exhaled and put my hand on his thigh, feeling a bit more at ease now that we were alone again.

"I'm just remembering," I said and opened my window.

After we'd driven for a while, he said, "You know, someday I'd really like to hear about Cape Town. You talked about it so excitedly before you left and you were so looking forward to it. *Eintlik* I was surprised when I heard you'd gone to Durban. Even that day when I first saw you jogging I thought I had made a mistake. I thought for sure it couldn't be you."

"*Eish* . . . I had to leave Cape Town. Too much partying and too little studying. I almost flunked, so I left. My parents were kind of furious with me."

This was at least partly true, I reasoned. I looked at the directions on the map, shrugging off the thoughts of Rodney, the drugs and the day I packed my bags and walked out of the residence with no one there to say goodbye.

———

It is quite a seductive coastal drive along the Atlantic side of the Cape. The towns further north are littered with shops and crowded with tourists and sunbathers, but then you go further south and it starts to feel like you're leaving everyone behind. It's the sprawling white sands that first hint at the change in pace—so white and clear, you almost think you're the first people to get here. The land looks untouched. I had always meant to do some exploring but never got around to it because I was either too hung over or too busy catching up with my studies.

Sediba looked over at me, and when we drove into the smaller roads and reached a stop sign, he leaned over and kissed me. He was purely excited, but for me both panic and excitement rose in my chest, at odds with one another.

"I think you'll like Scott. I've never met Daniel but I'm sure he's nice. Scott always had good people around him."

"So where did he meet Daniel?"

"Here in Cape Town. I think Daniel went to UCT or something." He was trying to focus as he drove so we didn't miss our turns as we moved farther and farther away from the cluster of houses at the entrance to the town.

"Are you sure?" I started.

"He did say it was secluded. It's a private beach or feels like it or something like that."

Suddenly we were on a dirt road and couldn't see the water anymore. We were climbing, going up a hill between patches of grass, before we suddenly found ourselves facing a large red brick house. The road seemed to end, as if it were created especially for the house. We went up its driveway, which became a circle at the end, reminiscent of the grand English country homes one read about in novels.

"This is it," I said.

"You see how Whites screwed us on the land issue?" Sediba said. "This is how the 1913 Native Land Act looks . . . in a nutshell."

We stepped out the car and stood there for a moment, taking in the estate. There was some noise somewhere in the back of the house but no one was at the front. A few cars were parked around the driveway, not enough for a party yet. The guests were not meant to arrive until later that evening for the pre-wedding supper.

Sediba started walking and I followed. Round a bend we saw the sprawling green grass of the backyard, overlooking the beach. To our left stood a smaller, white unit—which in the township would be called a "big house." It was older, built in the style of the old Cape, with a white wall and a tiled roof. Further down and nearer to the beach, before the grass curved into what I assumed must be stairs, they had built a round outdoor braai area, white like the smaller house and sheltered with a thatched roof. Around the braai area were a few people lounging on chairs, chatting and drinking. A stone path led down to them but I stood at Sediba's left, hesitant.

"There he is!" He called out just as a guy our age with a white shirt and white pants started coming our way, calling out, "Sediba!"

"That's Scott," Sediba said and to my great surprise, took my hand with the delight of someone about to introduce his favourite person in the world. "Come," he was saying. "Come."

I felt the instinct to pull my hand away but stopped myself. Anyway, he was gripping it so firmly and so happily that I was suddenly swept up in his joy. Scott was half running now, waving his hands in the air. The people behind him were staring, curious. It didn't escape me, of course, that we were the only people there who were not White and I wondered if that would be the case all weekend.

Scott threw his arms around Sediba, before turning to looking me up and down, eyes narrowing: "Oh, no! You are not supposed to be this gorgeous. We're supposed to gossip about you and you're giving us nothing." He was leaning over now, brushing his right cheek against my left.

Sediba and I laughed. There was something so easy but also so vulnerable about Scott, that I took to him right away.

"All of us have been dying to meet the guy who tamed this one," he said with a flick of his thumb at Sediba. "We were hoping you wouldn't be gorgeous, so we'd at least say nasty things about you since he wouldn't settle with any of us." We were both laughing and looking at him run his forefinger up and down in the air. "Tell me something bad about you. What's wrong with you?"

"I don't know . . . I'm a bit of a clumsy lover."

"Yes! Thank you. Just a pretty face. Are you really horrid? Because that gives me something to talk about." His expression was mock hopeful.

"Awful," I said. Sediba folded his arms, a little embarrassed but obviously quite pleased that his friend and I were getting on fine so early on.

I hadn't realized that as we were talking someone had come up towards us and now he had draped one arm around Scott.

"Oh! Ah . . . " I started but wasn't sure what to say.

"You've met?" Scott looked from me to the guy I had met once as Danny at Rodney's place.

He was standing with a satisfied grin across his face, looking quite clean-cut, and also attired in a white top and a pair of white linen pants that suited the relaxed, beach atmosphere. I wondered if they had planned matching outfits for the wedding as well, which struck me as being a bit silly. The Danny I had met had been less relaxed than this one. This guy looked at ease but there was also something else, apart from his longer hair, that was very different, but I couldn't put my finger on it.

I looked over at Sediba, whose narrowed eyes were full of curiosity.

"Danny," I said finally.

"Kabelo," he said with an easy laugh. "I remember you."

"Yes . . . me too." It was embarrassing, seeing the first guy I had ever had sex with as I stood there with my current boyfriend. It made me want to find a hole and climb into it.

"We met at one of Rod's parties," he explained casually, responding to Scott and Sediba's curious looks before offering Sediba his hand. "You must be Sediba. I've heard a lot about you. Scott thinks you're his only hope of looking stunning tomorrow."

Sediba laughed and I wanted to join him but the laughter got stuck like a piece of dry bread in my throat. Had Danny, now Daniel, not mentioned Rodney, I might have gone on maybe one more minute without thinking about it. The possibility of seeing him might not have come crashing down at that moment, ending my two minutes of a good time. I wanted to ask about Rodney but was too afraid I might find out that he'd also be coming.

"Yes," Scott was saying. "I feel better already."

The conversation was coming to me in little spurts, like the dial on a radio moving and stopping along several stations and barely making sense.

"I have two shirts like you asked . . . " came Sediba's words. Some laughter, and Daniel was saying something about "go whale-watching . . . morning . . . " "Are you OK?" Scott was saying. "You guys must be exhausted. Let me get you settled in the guest-house . . . " Then Sediba's hand was squeezing mine and we were following Daniel and Scott towards the small white house. I tried to remember to breathe, to listen more and be part of the conversation. I tried to imagine that Rodney and I—if we were to meet here—would be nothing but very happy to see each other.

On the way to our rooms Sediba and Scott fell into step and Daniel stopped to let me catch up and walked alongside me.

"So howzit Kabelo? How've you been?"

"I'm fine thanks," I said. "So I'm trying to decide what's different about you," I was speaking with a lowered voice, not sure if Sediba was or wasn't catching bits and pieces of the conversation; not wanting him to.

"Well, is it maybe the fact that I'm not high?" Scott said and belted out a laugh that mimicked Rodney's a little bit. I didn't remember him being so expressive. There was something very cool about him when we had first met, like he was being careful about how much he was giving away. Now he just seemed like he'd open up about anything if you asked.

"I don't remember you being high," I said.

Daniel stopped and looked at me. "Everyone says that. I don't know, I think I was always the guy who could take drugs and look normal. Maybe I had a high tolerance. Anyway, the difference is, I'm off drugs. Well, the heavy ones, at least. What about you? I remember you enjoying the booze and weed!"

I was irritated that he was making no effort to lower his voice. We were at the door of the cottage now. Sediba and Scott had stopped and were watching us.

"I heard about Rodney's parties," Scott said. "Didn't think of Sediba being with a bad boy." He hit Sediba playfully on the shoulder.

I was so mortified by the comment that even my attempt to laugh it off fell flat. A strange little chuckle came out instead, making me look and feel terribly awkward.

Sediba said, his eyes upon me, "I want to hear more . . . "

"We used to go to parties thrown by a mutual friend," I offered, believing now that Rodney would very likely be here. He had said how close his and Danny's families were. And as if he'd heard my thoughts, Daniel said, "Well, Sediba will meet Rod this weekend."

I took a breath and let the air stay in my lungs for a while. Sediba was still eyeing me curiously as we followed the guys into the house. He put his hand lightly on my shoulder, wanting me to look at him, but I only gave him a brief glance.

It was quite a lovely cottage, with mostly bare white walls and a polished cement floor. The door opened onto a sitting room with large French doors facing the water. Next to the sitting room was the kitchen with a rectangular wooden table and four chairs. A passage led to a bedroom on the same side, also with French doors opening onto a balcony overlooking the beach. White curtains rose and fell as the sea breeze blew in through the open doors. The duvet cover was white and so were the pillows. The overall feeling of the place was neat, clean, and minimalist. I wanted to stay longer than we had planned.

When Scott and Daniel finally left, Sediba flopped onto the bed while I stood at the open doors looking out to the empty beach. I had decided that I wanted to spot Rodney before he spotted me and work out how to approach him.

"So who is Rodney, an old lover?" I turned to find him propped up sideways on his elbow, head resting on his hand.

"He's an old friend. I'm not excited to see him." I walked over to him, took off my shoes and lay beside him.

"What's wrong?"

"I should tell you about Rodney."

"What about Daniel?"

"That's just a little bit embarrassing. One-night thing. Rodney's . . . well . . . I don't know. The Rodney thing is more than just a little embarrassment."

He reached up and stroked my cheek. "This is the Cape Town stuff, hey? This is the thing you don't talk about."

I nodded. "I'll tell you. For now let's just say I don't want to see Rodney."

"And Daniel was a fling then?"

"Brief, one-time thing. He seems so different. So much more . . . comfortable than the last time I saw him." He was now on his back, facing the ceiling and I went to lie on his chest. "And Scott? What was that about, how you wouldn't settle with any of them?"

Sediba chuckled. "Don't all gay men sleep with one or two of their friends? It's a small community."

"I never had a community," I sounded bitter and immediately regretted it.

"The parties were not a community?"

It occurred to me then that that was exactly what the parties were. I barely remembered most of the people's names and I would never be invited to anyone's wedding, but that was what we were: a small, dysfunctional gay community.

He rubbed my head and said, "I like this hair cut. The guy did a good job." I smiled up at him and he kissed me. I loved that he knew when I didn't feel like talking. We lay in silence, listening to the crash of waves, dozing off to the sound of it, the laughter and chatting around the braai area fading into the distance.

There were lots of activities planned for the weekend: a boat ride and then a braai later the evening of the day we arrived; sundowners on the beach followed by a dip and then of course a brunch after the ceremony. The events would go on until late Sunday afternoon when everyone was expected to leave. There was an itinerary laid out on the kitchen table along with a book of instructions about the cottage saying where the towels were, tips about conserving water and so on. It seemed we'd only have an hour or so to recharge before each event.

Sediba had worked like a mad man all week, rescheduling clients and overbooking so that he could feel OK about taking a few days off—such was his work ethic. He hated disappointing his clients and leaving his mother with more work. I lay on my back listening to his breathing until a knock on the door woke me up.

Barefoot and feeling refreshed, I got up and went to the door, assuming it would be Scott. When I opened the door the light hit my eyes so harshly that I had to squint and step sideways to avoid the glare. The woman standing before me was obviously not here for the party. She must have been about my mother's age and she was wearing a maid's uniform: crisp white dress with a light blue collar and an apron to match. Her hair was tucked neatly under a bonnet matching the uniform. On her feet were old worn-out running shoes.

"Molweni," she said politely. I said: "Molweni Ma," and stepped aside to let her in but she didn't move. She explained in isiXhosa that she was there to bring fresh towels and handed me a stack. I took them and thanked her before politely smiling and closing the door.

"She's the only other Black person here then," Sediba remarked as we were getting ready for the evening festivities.

"It's going to be uncomfortable. I was sort of glad she didn't see us together."

Sediba stopped fastening his belt to look at me. "No," he shook his head. "We're not doing this, not this weekend. I'm not here to hide. We don't know her, we don't have to hide."

"You know what I mean. It's like having a parent here."

"What's uncomfortable is that Scott's family is keeping up with this ridiculousness, putting their helper in a uniform—that's what's embarrassing." He walked over and put his arms around me and said into my eyes: "*We*, are not embarrassing."

I wanted to say something about him not saying the same thing the week of Lelo's wedding, him hiding just as much as I did, but it was nice, standing there in a lovely room with a beautiful view. I didn't want to spoil it.

So I decided I was going to have a good weekend if it was the last thing I did. There would be no one here expecting me to find a wife, and for that reason alone, I wanted to enjoy myself. As we walked to the beach for the boat ride, Scott and Daniel came over and handed us glasses of champagne.

"Everyone should be sloshed before a boat ride," Daniel declared.

And we all raised a glass to their future, with Scott putting his arm around Sediba and adding, "And lifelong friends!"

I'm not someone who enjoys boat rides. Not even with the hope of spotting whales—it was the time of year when record numbers of whales are seen as they migrate, and that beach is known as one of the best for whale-watching. The constant rocking made me feel sick and I was eating salty crackers to settle my stomach. Sediba kept checking on me and then going back to talking to friends, laughing about this, that, and the other thing—old inside jokes they all shared.

Doing my best to be polite, I chatted briefly with a guy who wore sunglasses for the duration of the boat ride, even when it was not so bright anymore. It was unsettling not seeing his eyes because I had never met him before. He said his name was Abe and he had a set of very expensive-looking binoculars. Every now and then he'd push up his sunglasses and glue his eyes onto the binoculars. All he was interested in was whales, saying, "I'm an avid whale-watcher" more times than he needed to. He didn't seem to mind that I was silent, leaning over the railing with my eyes closed. He was full of information about the whales though. If I had paid better attention I might today be able to say a thing or two about whale migration.

We finally docked back near the house and I was the first to hurry along the boardwalk so I could return to the cottage to rest my head. Sediba stayed behind with his friends, who were all welcoming and eager to get to know me, so I was sorry to be feeling ill. I could see they all had genuine affection for Sediba. They would ask his opinions on their clothes or on their hair, and they asked about his mother, his business, and about me. I was glad for him to have this, but I was also painfully envious of this other world, the world away from Kasi where he seemed very much at ease.

I had my shoes in my hands as I walked down the boardwalk and onto the beach, slowing down to take deep breaths and let the nausea fade. I must have been deep in thought, listening to the birds' *koh-hoh* and the swoosh of the water, so that I didn't see Rodney until I was just steps away from him.

His hair was shorter, cleaner cut, and his face a little fuller. The way I remembered him, I couldn't have imagined Rodney in formal black pants and a button-down white shirt, as he was now. The only thing that was the same about him was that the pants were a little too big and he was as skinny as ever. He had rolled up the pants like someone getting ready to wade into the water and the sleeves of the shirt were pulled up and buttoned just above his elbows.

He was sitting on the sand, a tall glass of a clear drink in his hand. He looked up as I approached and said—as cheerfully as one might upon seeing a very good old friend—"Oh my God! What the hell are you doing here?"

I stopped and for a moment felt nothing but pure joy at seeing him.

"My God, Rod! Look at you!"

We embraced warmly. He stepped back and looked me up and down. His hand went up and he ran it from the back to the front of my head.

"Howzit man? You look very hot with your hair like that. You look like a grown up." He chuckled.

"And you also—except your hair is shorter."

"Oh, I would never have thought—yuss, look at you. Are you a doctor now?"

"Last few months of community service," I told him. "What about you?"

"Oh, I gave that rubbish up. I have my own gallery now. Went to art school, opened a little gallery. It's really more of a tiny work studio than anything, but I love it and I don't have to be a doctor."

"Wow, Rod . . . " I was searching for something to say when the group from the boat reached us. I don't know what it was about me and Rodney—maybe how close we were standing or him still rubbing his hand against my hair—but something about it made Sediba come and stand so close that our shoulders were touching. It felt less romantic and more protective.

"This is Sediba," I said to Rodney. They shook hands.

Rodney said, "Wow, hi. I heard about you from Scott but I didn't think . . . I didn't know of course . . . "

"I know, I didn't realize when he said 'Daniel' that it would be Danny."

"I don't call myself that anymore," was Danny's response from somewhere in the background. "Past life."

"Past a lot of things," Rodney said and the two of them laughed like they had just shared a joke that no one else could understand.

As everyone started walking again, Rodney and I stayed back and fell into step with each other. Sediba walked ahead with Scott but kept glancing back at us curiously. Rodney and I were talking about nothing serious, he catching me up on his gallery and I asking questions about it, but still I felt guilty about us staying apart from the others. So when plates were handed out I went to sit next to Sediba and we ate together, listening to Scott and Daniel's playful banter about how they met. Everyone was laughing and having a good time. At one point Sediba looked at me and said, "Are you all right?" I think his question related to Rodney, because he had known how nervous I was about Cape Town. I nodded and then, rather unexpectedly, he reached back and put his hand gently on my lower back. I smiled, looked happily into his big, round eyes.

In a while I saw Rodney go off from the group and sit at the top step leading to the beach. Sediba was talking to a friend of his about what it meant to have a business in Kasi instead of the centre of town, when I slipped off and went to sit next to Rodney.

I took off my shoes and lowered myself next to him, leaning my arm against the railing. We sat looking out at the water, the sky a much darker colour now and the water barely visible. Our shoes at our sides and our feet rubbing against the sand on the wooden steps, I realized how much I had missed Rodney and how, much of the time, I could not find my way past the guilt. Rodney looked pensive.

"This beach feels new, undiscovered." I spoke first. He smiled at me and then turned to face the party behind us.

"So who's the guy?" He was spreading his pretty, mischievous grin now. I found it both lovely and reassuring.

"It's Sediba. He's someone I've known a long, long time."

Rodney hit me playfully with the back of his hand. You'd think we had not gone a day without seeing each other.

"He seems . . . *smitten*."

This was not a conversation I was used to having. I didn't have friends who asked me about my love life or who even saw us together. It was uncomfortable even as it felt good to be that free to talk about Sediba. I rubbed my hands against the railing and Rodney laughed out loud—a haunting sound that had me flinching, unable to look at him.

"What's so funny?" I tried to sound relaxed.

"I think he's not the only one . . . ha! Look who's in love." His laughter rose and floated above us, traveling now to the party behind. I turned to find, as I had expected, curious glances, people stopping mid-conversation, their glasses held mid-air. Sediba looked as if he was expecting me to share the joke. I turned away to face the rising tide.

Rodney said, "So does he know how you feel about him, or are you still keeping secrets?"

I was not so daft that I didn't realize I had been asked two questions, each as loaded with accusation as the past was weighed down with resentment. I inhaled and wondered if the tide would be too high that evening for us to go for the planned dip. I knew what to say, it was only taking me a moment to wade through the feelings swirling around inside me. I tried to get to where I was going, to what I wanted to say, but I was moving towards my point slowly, my mind fretful.

"I'm so, so sorry Rod. I'm sorry I just . . . just left without getting you away from those guys. And I left Cape Town without saying 'bye." He rubbed his forehead and exhaled.

"Ag, man. We were so young. I was never even sober enough to say my own name most of the time."

We both let out a chuckle. Overcome by a blinding sorrow, I put my hand on Rodney's shoulder, looked him squarely in the eye and said, "Rod, really, I'm really sorry I just left you. I got so scared. There were serious drugs in the house. I thought of police coming . . . I panicked and ran. I'm really sorry."

Suddenly Sediba's voice said behind me, "Sorry to interrupt. I brought some drinks."

Startled, I stood up and took a martini from him, but when he handed one to Rodney, he declined.

"No thanks. I'm staying away from the booze tonight."

I frowned in disbelief. "You?"

Rodney let out a short laugh. "You'd be surprised how much has changed Kabz. Anyway, I'm going to find my DJ." As he went, he said, "Cheers, Sediba."

"Let's go and hear the speeches. These guys are funny," Sediba said to me. I followed him, reaching over to put my hand in his briefly.

We sat listening to the speeches telling us how Scott and Daniel had met, how they were meant to be together. Rodney sat next to a guy with long, wavy hair who talked into his ear and made him giggle. I wished so many years had not passed and that I could tell him more about Sediba and hear about his boyfriend. I felt sad about the loss of our friendship, now more so than I had allowed myself to admit since moving away. But it was all right, I reasoned, because now he was here and we could chat and laugh. I hadn't expected to ever see him again.

And Rodney, without drinking or smoking zol, seemed a different person. It was he and his boyfriend who were the first to wade into the water that evening. Apparently someone had had the idea of doing something mad like having all the party guests dive into the ocean at sundown with our clothes on. It was good fun. I stood laughing and chatting with people but not going in, just handing people towels as they ran out, their clothes soaked and sticking to their skin.

From across the way, beyond the many wet heads on the beach, Sediba eyed me with an amused smile and started walking towards me.

"These people are mad," he said in Setswana, holding the front of his shirt between his fingers. "Do you know how much this shirt costs?"

I laughed at this, just as Scott came running behind us. "Sediba, did you just say your clothes are too nice to go in? Did he just—he just said that, didn't he?" Scott asked me. I nodded and we burst into laughter.

"I didn't even have to hear you say it, I just knew it," Scott said.

"No, I will go in. I just have to change!" Sediba said, and grabbed my hand and pulled me away. "We're changing, and then we're going in!"

"Maybe Kabelo wants to go in anyway!" Scott called out behind us.

"No, he's wearing my pants!" Sediba shouted back and my sides were hurting from laughing so much. Everyone was running in and out of the water, splashing each other, throwing each other into the waves. The moon hung low, and so did the stars, which collected just beyond reach, and the sky curved, enclosing us in a sparkling dome. I was tempted to forget that we had not come to stay.

Sediba and I had gone running from the beach but when we reached the top of the stairs leading to the house, we slowed down. It was quieter up here. The lights around the outdoor entertainment area were still on as were the ones at the main house and the cottage. These lit the path for us so we stepped on the large stones and followed them to the cottage. The place had already been cleaned by the helpers and looked as if there had never been a celebration, as if the people running in and out of water had nothing to do with the house above.

I noticed that Sediba and I were becoming pensive at different moments during this trip. We spoke about the usual things, but then we would both drift off, neither of us speaking for a while. There was also a new—or old—kind of tension between us. We would exchange a knowing glance, or our hands would brush against each other; he made gestures like holding my hand or he'd put his hand on my back as we sat with the others. The air between us was charged with a new, younger sort of energy. I felt, in short, like a man newly in love.

And so as we left the beach that evening we were not saying anything, only listening to the clip-clap sound of our sandals on the stones. I thought how happy I was and wondered what he was thinking, but did not want to disturb the peaceful silence.

When we reached the cottage, he turned the key in the lock and pushed the door open, standing aside to let me walk in first. I switched the passage light on as I went in, and we kicked off our sandals. I could feel his eyes on me as I walked down the lit passage to the bedroom, slowing my pace and moving my hand along the wall. At the door I took off my shirt and turned the light on, then back off, remembering that we might be seen from the beach. He slipped his arm around my waist, the inner part of his forearm sliding softly against my bare skin. Then he kissed the space between my shoulder blades. I pulled out of his grasp and went to draw the curtains together.

Later we lay next to each other in bed letting the air cool the sweat off our bodies. I had left the French doors open and only closed the screen, so there was a light ocean breeze coming in. We were silently watching the curtains fly low above the shiny cement floor, the bedside light now on. I could feel his ribs rise and fall at a gentle pace against mine. We had by then lain this way many times, but there was something a lot more exciting about this time that made it feel different. Perhaps it had something to do with this wedding weekend feeling like an escape, a sort of honeymoon away from our real world.

Sediba's lips came to caress the outer edge of my left ear as we both started drifting off to sleep.

"Should we go back to the beach?" I asked, but his breathing had fallen into a slower rhythm. I wanted to stay there a long time and not ever go back to where we had come from.

When we woke up I could feel something different in the air. There was a thick cloud of fog as we were getting ready, but it gradually cleared and the water was calm. Maybe everyone feels this way on the morning of a wedding because I noted that I had felt the same way when Lelo was getting married, though this time, without the usual early morning buzz of the township, the calm was more intense and there was an unbearable sorrow around me that I could neither shake nor explain. Is this why people cry at weddings? Is there a feeling of letting go of something?

I had been the first to bathe and shave while Sediba was sleeping, so when his turn came I was already dressed but couldn't bring myself to do my tie. Instead, I stepped barefoot onto the balcony and looked out at the water. That old feeling of standing at the end of the boardwalk looking at ships in the horizon came flooding through me. I realized that I was standing in the position that my mother had always stood in, my forearms resting on the railing. The night before, on the boat, someone had mentioned that somewhere to our left—although it was not visible to me from the balcony—was the Breede river. I wished that I had binoculars now so I could see it. What I could spot in the dunes just ahead was the Blue Crane—one of perhaps three birds that I can identify. Apart from the most well known, the owls, peacocks and the seagulls and so on, the ones that didn't take an avid bird watcher to spot, I know a Blue Crane. I think, of course, this is because it is our national bird. It was the bird's legs that always fascinated me, long and twig-like, they are delicate and graceful. The one I saw, not far from where I stood, was with a chick, whose body was still so fluffy that I wanted to reach out and touch it as they steadily made their way across the grass.

"Are you ready?" Sediba said, startling me. He came over and quietly fixed my collar, apparently deep in thought himself.

I suppose the birds had led me to think about my mother. I had told her that I was going to an old friend's wedding and even as I said that I wondered what would happen if she heard that Sediba was also off to Cape Town for a wedding.

I asked him as he tucked the tie under my collar, "Where did you tell your mother you were going? Did you say it was two guys getting married?"

He exhaled and turned to face the water like me, his eyes following the bird and her chick.

"My mother doesn't ask questions like your mother. She doesn't probe." I watched him slip his hands into his pockets and briefly shut his eyes. He said, "She doesn't know it's a gay wedding, no. But the thing with my mother . . . like I said before, she knows things without me telling her."

I didn't have a chance to ask anything else because now people were gathering near the entertainment area. It was time for the pre-wedding gathering and we had to go down. I hurried to put my sandals on. "I feel funny in a suit and sandals," I said.

"I know, but it's what they asked everyone to do." And he too put on his sandals and followed me out to the gathering.

Along the path down to the beach stairs had been laid pots of red and white roses. The entertainment area had been transformed into an elegant outdoor dining space, with lines of red and white ribbons—punctuated by similar-coloured balloons—hanging above round tables that were covered in white cloth. It was an enchanting scene, with classical music playing through speakers placed on a wall behind the tables. Three men and three women, all black, walked around in black and white uniforms, serving hors d'oeuvres and champagne. I felt uneasy seeing this, but was ashamed to realize that I couldn't tell if it was more uncomfortable to feel that we were living in a different world from the helpers or to feel that I was being seen with a man by my elders.

Sediba whispered, "Here we go."

"Yah," I said. "I know." But I got the feeling that we meant different things.

We joined the party and accepted drinks while we waited for Scott and Daniel to come out. I couldn't make myself meet the helpers' eyes. When one handed me my champagne, I cringed as I took it, barely acknowledging him. Sediba, on the other hand, smiled and greeted him in isiXhosa. I had never met the man before but he was elderly and the same kin tone as my father. I couldn't face him.

Down the stairs we went and onto the beach. We were chatting and mingling when the music changed to Mendelssohn's Wedding March. From the big house Daniel and Scott came walking out, hand in hand, in blue and white suits and sandals. As we turned to look at them, Sediba slipped his hand onto mine.

Scott's mother and father were there, but from Daniel's side only his mother had come. The day before, on the boat, I had heard Scott tell Sediba something about Daniel's father "refusing to be part of this."

We were asked to stand in a semicircle, each of us holding a handful of rose petals while the grooms stood at the edge of the water, being married by a minister who performed the ceremony in a professional yet relaxed manner. Scott and Daniel had written their own vows although they half-cried through them, talking about being each other's great love.

Afterwards we all joyously clapped hands and threw petals at them and they turned to face us and thanked us all for being there.

There would be a little wait before we sat down. People were milling about, exchanging stories about how they knew the grooms, talking about how beautiful the ceremony was. Some tore off from the group, taking walks or going back to sit near the house. Sediba asked that we walk along the beach for a moment. I was happy to walk away, having had my fill of the crowd and wanting some space.

Our feet got sandy, our footsteps sinking as we walked at the edge of the tide. Sediba was pensive again and I was in a bit of a jolly mood, walking in every now and then to let the water wash over my feet and then back out alongside him. He didn't stop to wait when I branched off, his head to the ground and only occasionally glancing at me. Then finally he pulled me to him and said, "Stay."

I asked him what was wrong.

He stopped and took my face in one hand, his fingers caressing my cheek. I leaned and rested my head in his hand the way I liked to, and he gave me a peck on the lips.

"It was nice, wasn't it, *lenyalo*?" His voice was both solemn and sweet—calm.

I chuckled at his use of the Setswana word.

"It was nice, why?" I asked.

He started walking again, taking my hand in his and squeezing it. He said, "You know, I mean I think you know . . . " He inhaled sharply and stopped.

"What do I know?" I could feel my heart racing, he was acting so unlike himself. It was so out of character, this sudden starting and stopping, this loss of words.

He started walking again and continued, "I mean I think by now it's quite obvious, *Jo*. It's obvious I'm in love with you." His eyes flitted from me to somewhere past me, towards the depths of the ocean.

Something heavy and unmovable came and settled on my chest. I was, in my mind, gasping for air although on the outside I must have looked relatively calm.

"Diba, you know I feel the same way." I told him.

He took one long step forward suddenly and started walking backwards, facing me. Something flew into my eye and I blinked rapidly and reached a finger to the corner of my eye to wipe it off. He stopped, came closer, held me still and blew the dust out of my eye. We stood there, the tip of his nose touching mine, our foreheads together.

I spoke quietly this time, "Diba, what's wrong?"

He wrapped his arms around me and pulled me in, but said nothing.

"Diba?" I whispered, but he only kissed me—so slowly and passionately, it was as if we were alone in a room with the door shut and we had all night, but then he let go and said, "Come on, let's go eat."

We turned around and I followed him at a brisk pace and we said nothing else.

We were seated at our table with two other couples, two women and their male partners, and I tried to start the conversation.

"So what did you think of the ceremony?"

I posed the question to the woman sitting immediately to my right. Her name was Carol and we had been seated next to each other, I think, because we were both medics. One of the guys was a designer so I think that explained the seat next to Sediba. The thing about Kasi weddings is that there are no seating arrangements. You sit next to whomever you choose. This was more formal, requiring more effort. Everyone seemed polite. They were all searching for things to say. We were all strangers, except to our partners.

Carol answered right away, "It was lovely," without offering more.

The man with the strawberry blonde hair and piercing blue eyes seated to Carol's right seemed to give it more thought, "I don't know, I thought it was a bit . . . much, to be honest."

Carol, his girlfriend, stuck her elbow in his rib and her cheeks went flush.

"Dominick! It's your cousin, you could be nicer."

"I don't get this marriage thing, frankly. Gay or straight," was Dominick's nonchalant response.

Carol took a deep breath and with her fork, rearranged the peas on her plate.

"This is an issue between us. Going to weddings brings it up, I suppose."

We all put food in our mouths, hoping to make the awkward moment pass as quickly as possible. But Dominick was not giving up.

"What do you guys think? I mean, you're lucky you're guys and there's no pressure. Girls always want to move into it: 'when are we getting married?' 'I'm getting older,' 'I think it's time.'" He was, thankfully, not imitating a woman's voice.

"Well," the woman to Sediba's left chimed in nervously, her voice cracking. She was not comfortable speaking to strangers. "I think Scott and Daniel were both ready. Daniel's one of my best friends. There was no pressure."

Dominick waved his hand. "I wasn't talking about them . . . the pressure thing, well, listen. I'm just saying that men don't hassle each other to get married, that's all I'm saying. Right?"

He was looking at me. I shrugged but Sediba pushed back his seat and folded his arms like he was feeling quite comfortable getting into it with him, like it was actually something he'd given a lot of thought and was glad someone was bringing it up. "I don't think it's a girl thing. I think people in general just want more commitment, that's all. It's about every couple, the way I see it."

I think because he felt a bit slighted—because he had counted on support from the guys and was surprised that Sediba appeared to side with his girlfriend, who was now biting her lip and turning her shoulder away from him—Dominick decided to attack.

"Well, then how do you define commitment?"

"What the two of you decide works, I guess," Sediba told him looking as if he was giving it some thought. But I knew he wasn't thinking about it, he was just slowing down the conversation. "It's up to both people."

I was about to say that commitment was just staying together or something like that, something not very well thought out, when Scott and Daniel arrived at our table. They had been going around greeting guests, happily taking pictures and just overall looking like they were having the time of their lives. It brought on a nice feeling, seeing two people so happily showing off their togetherness. I had to fight the creeping realization that I was maybe feeling envious of their carefree manner, watching them being openly loving with each other in the place they both called home. Whenever the thought came up, I had to reach out with another thought and swat it like a fly.

I was hoping we'd move on to another subject at our table, but Daniel asked, "So, when are you two doing this?"

I knew as soon as he said it that it was the wrong—or even the worst—question he could have asked us. We had come here—or at least I had—to pretend that Lelo's wedding hadn't happened, that we were doing just fine, now Daniel's question sent a chill down my back because it was like digging up a buried weapon.

I leaned back in my seat and smiled, trying to look really relaxed.

I replied, "Well . . . we're just . . . this is really new."

Under the table, I felt Sediba's hand find mine and our fingers entwine. I held on to him.

"But look at us," Scott said with a grin and a dramatic sweep of his hand in the air.

"We've only been together a few months—"

"Four months!" Daniel interjected.

"Four months," said Scott, "and look at us today."

His eyes were dancing, excited like a child's seeing something shiny meant for him, going from Sediba to me and back to Sediba.

"I remember the way you sounded when you first told me about Kabelo. Come on. I'd say, actually, you guys should have gone first!"

Sediba leaned back the way he had done earlier when Dominick spoke about commitment, his hand staying with mine under the table. He said, "You're making Kabelo nervous. Don't make my boyfriend nervous."

I felt a mixture of things. A bit of relief, and then some panic, and then some excitement. I always liked it when Sediba called me his boy-friend and I was relieved that he didn't take the discussion any further, because he was right, Scott and Daniel were making me nervous, but I was also panicked because I could see from the way Scott was reaching for the bowl of sweets in front of him and the way Daniel leaned his head against Scott's shoulder that they were only getting started with this.

It was like the Daniel I had met as Danny that one time had come back into the room. There was something showy about him as one side of his mouth curved up, eyes mock-pensive, as he said, "A township wedding. I'd go to that. It could be a real cultural experience."

Before I even looked at him, I knew what Sediba was feeling. He cleared his throat and in a cheery tone said, "Ha! A cultural experience in your own country, bra! That's the beauty of South Africa, hey?"

Daniel backed away, but Scott had something to say about this, and I could see why Sediba liked him so much.

"It does sound odd to think we all know each other, but we don't know each other, really. It's appalling that I've never been to a township even though I've grown up here."

What he meant was that it was appalling that you could be White and have Black friends, have lived your whole life in the country and still not know what a township looks like.

"Has there ever been one?" Daniel was swimming in a different direction, evidently—or going back to where we had left off.

"One what?" I asked him cautiously.

"A township wedding. Has there ever been one? Have two Black guys ever gotten married?"

"I've never heard of one." As soon as I said it, Sediba reached again under the table and clasped his hand to mine. I wondered if I had had too much wine and champagne because I had to shut my eyes and then open them again to refocus, my thoughts like inaudible whispers. I wanted to take off my glasses and clean them but thought it would make me look uneasy.

Daniel's eyes were moving back and forth between Sediba and me, as if they were waiting for a story.

"Well, like I said," Scott said finally when neither one of us spoke. "Maybe this would be the first one."

Daniel snorted. "I'm sure all the ANC supporters would be horrified." He couldn't help but hit on the hot buttons—as though his mouth were moving before he could stop himself.

Sediba's grip on my hand tightened. He said, "Well, no actually. It was the ANC that brought these laws in. If it weren't for the ANC, what you just did today wouldn't be legal right?" His gaze focused on Daniel as though daring him to disagree. Our table mates had already stood up and danced through a song or two while we were having the discussion, but now they were back and settling into their drinks.

Sediba and I waited uncomfortably for Daniel to respond. Then Scott reached over and kissed Daniel's cheek. "*Ag*, my love. You know how I hate politics. Daniel's the anthropologist here so he's all about cultural norms and differences and what not. Right?" He put an arm around Daniel's shoulder.

"I suppose you're right," Daniel said but he was looking at me and not Sediba. "I suppose they're not entirely rotten. When I think of them, I think of how much violence the country's had since they took over."

"I see what you mean," Sediba said, letting go of my hand. "But there's always been violence. Just that some of us were protected by the state and some of us were victims of violence from the state. Violence is nothing new."

Daniel looked for a moment as though he did not comprehend, and then, when I thought he was starting to and I was hoping he'd say something, he waved a hand dismissively, like he was shooing away the whole topic.

A relative came over and scooped the couple away and then it was Dominick's turn to gloat, saying, "See? Marriage is a hot button for all of us. Regardless of sexual orientation." He was drunk by then, so he pronounced the words *sexual orientation* like they were a phrase he was reading for the first time in a book—like he was finding them odd and wanted to make sure he was saying them correctly. We all laughed lightly at this, finding it refreshing to move away from the tension the topic had brought.

Later, while we were driving back, after a somewhat tense goodbye from Scott and Daniel, I joked, "Shit, I hope this doesn't mean we're not invited to their next big thing. They do throw a good party."

Sediba chuckled. I put my hand on his neck, rubbed my fingers on his bald head and my thumb on his chiseled beard.

"Like that Dominick guy said, it's a hot button for everyone, hey?"

Sediba glanced at me and then at the rear-view mirror, before showing his indicator, slowing down, and pulling into a lookout spot. I felt my chest tighten.

"What are you doing?"

He didn't answer but parked the car near some picnic benches. We could see the ocean and a deserted beach from up there, and there was no one else around. As I sat watching him, he turned to face me, looking as though he were examining me. I felt the heavy weight on my chest again, and then, oddly, I remembered Andrew telling me, "You have such kind eyes. I think people think they can tell you anything." I tried now to imagine that that was what Sediba was seeing.

"Is it stupid? The whole marriage thing. Do you think it's stupid?"

"No. I don't think so. I don't think it's stupid."

I was nervous and he could tell. That's why his hand reached for mine.

"I used to think it was dumb, you know? For us? For gay people . . . I thought it was just dumb. But now . . . Lelo's wedding . . . " He shut his eyes as if pushing away the memory. "Then Scott's."

"I think . . . I think I'm beginning to think it's possible. Not so dumb." I took off my sunglasses and put them on the dashboard with my free hand.

"It's not dumb. But is it possible? For us? I don't know. I mean, we don't come from the same world as Scott and Daniel. You know that."

I tried to smile, to lighten the meaning of what we were discussing.

Sediba let go of my hand and opened his door, pausing with his hand on the steering wheel before stepping out. He left the keys in the ignition and the door open and walked over to the nearest table. The car was making that ding-ding signal, which drove me mad, so I took the keys out and followed him to the table, not closing my door either but the wind had become stronger and it blew one door shut. I sat next to him and we looked out over the dunes, momentarily lulled by the ebb and flow and the sound of the tide. After a while, I reached over and touched his hand lightly.

"It used to seem impossible but not anymore," he said, continuing as if we had never stopped talking. "I used to think it was even ridiculous, the thought of two women or two men getting married. But now . . . "

"Diba . . . " I lowered my voice, tried to sound as calm as I possibly could, given that my head was throbbing and my heart was racing. "I understand. I do, really. I mean being there was beautiful. The ocean, the food, and the little cottage . . . I know. It was romantic. I felt it. But it's like being on holiday and then you have to get back to your real life. Scott and Daniel are from a different world. Same country but different world—"

Sediba had shut his eyes shut and his head was shaking.

"I loved being free too," I said. "I liked us being together openly. It was—"

He hopped off the picnic table. He put his hands to on his head, looking away.

"Kabz—"

"It's not that I don't understand. Don't think I didn't—"

He turned around suddenly, an urgent look on his face. "Kabelo! I'm in love with you. I mean, really, really . . . Every morning I wake up and I'm surprised that you're not lying next to me. Something happens at work and I think: I have to phone you. I mean it's ridiculous. Now I sleep badly when I'm not sleeping next to you. What is that? I don't know when that started happening, but I know—" He stopped and took a breath. His eyes were upon me, pleading. The heavy feeling again rose within my chest, so forceful that I had to sit up straight, put my hand on my chest to press and calm it. I looked at him and as all his words slowly came in and settled in different parts of me. For the first time I understood that perhaps this was the only reason he had brought me to the wedding. I could have met Scott before, and if we had really wanted to, we could have taken a similar trip together. We both had the means. But now I could see that this weekend had been about more than going to a friend's wedding. It had been about me seeing that it was *possible*—possible for us to imagine a more open future; for us to be out in front of everyone, openly affectionate and maybe even to get married. In all my life I had never contemplated marriage. I never imagined what came after being with someone. I was not even sure being gay could mean being in love. These things that Sediba was saying were big and new and frightening. I was in love with him—I probably had been in love with him longer than I realized—but I had never thought that I could do anything more about it.

I stood up and walked to him, took his hand.

"Diba, I feel the same way. You know I feel the same way. But that doesn't mean anything out there, to other people. Think about Maimela. Think about Kasi people and the things they would call us. Our families and friends would be horrified! If I move back, who would come to a gay doctor? Remember that guy, that hairdresser who lost his business because of the rumour that he was gay? Then the gay rumour turned into the AIDS rumour and no one would go to him? We couldn't . . . it's not possible."

"Even with me?"

"What do you mean?"

"It was OK to hide and not tell my mother anything. I was OK being a gay man and being quiet about it, thinking I was at least sparing people the part of me they couldn't look at. But I can't with you. It's different with you. It feels screwed up to hide *this*. I hated Lelo's wedding. Everyone got to walk around with their girlfriends and boyfriends and you and I couldn't even look at each other! Why? Because we're not a man and a woman? Fuck! It's legal. It's as legal as Lelo's marriage."

I was caught between wanting to run and wanting to comfort him. I reached for his other hand.

"We've talked about this, Diba. We know what we can and can't do and how people are, what they expect. I'm not saying I can't be out with you but . . . I am saying it's just not possible. It's not up to me."

He sighed and put his arms around me, resting his chest on my shoulder.

"We've talked about not being seen. OK. But this has changed. We're not boys anymore and we're not just . . . it's not simple. I can't hide with you. Anyone else . . . I can't with you."

We stood there with our arms around each other and me feeling that something very fundamental to who we were had gone and shifted whether we admitted it or not, and I had no way of turning back time and putting it back in the right place. Over the weekend I had thought we were as sure of things as ever—but as always, whenever people started to talk about their feelings, I felt lost and unsettled. Since leaving Durban I had refused to think about us breaking up, but I just couldn't see any other way. I couldn't come out in Kasi, It would break my parents' hearts. I couldn't even begin to imagine doing it.

I thought of my mother and her reaction. I'd always seen my attraction to men as nothing less than a betrayal of my parents, and when Sediba said that we should be out, that we should be together openly, I was terrified of what that would do to them. I believed that I owed them some sort of compensation for not fully being what they expected of me, I thought working hard to make them proud was the only thing I could do to make it alright. And so I didn't think I could give Sediba what he was asking for.

That conversation was the moment when I decided finally that I had to end this. It wasn't fair to keep him thinking that I could be what he needed.

I already resented Lelo for being able to do what was right, what was expected of him, and now I had this growing, unreasonable resentment towards Scott and Daniel. I kept thinking: wouldn't it be nice, just to be able to put the two worlds together?

Every now and then, for some time now, Sediba would ask me what I was planning to do after my year of community service. "Do you think you'll live with your parents for a while?" He'd say, attempting an air of nonchalance, but not quite mastering it. We'd be doing the dishes and he'd say, his back to me, "Don't you think it'll be weird living with your parents again, next year? I mean if that's where you're planning to live."

I'd skirt around the subject the way I'd learned to do all my life, pausing to pretend I was really giving it some thought, when all I was doing was trying to find a way out. The day after we returned from Cape Town he sat up straight on the sofa, propped his back against a pillow and made it hard for me to escape without a clear answer.

"You know that I love you because I tell you."

I nodded, stroked his arm and said nothing.

"I'm really looking forward to us living closer, because I know what's going on with you, how you're feeling, that you love me when I'm with you. I don't know it from you saying, I know it from being close to you."

His manner indicated that he had no intention of letting me escape this time. I turned off the TV and sat down so that we were facing the same direction and he could no longer see my eyes. He moved to caress my neck with his lips.

"I don't know where I'll be living. I mean, it's so busy . . . "

"You have three months. It's getting to be time. Wherever you go, it won't be this far though, right?"

He reached down and held my hand.

The windows were letting in cooler air at this time, but I was feeling hotter. It's not that I didn't like hearing him say he wanted me to live close to him, I just felt uneasy at the thought of being so close to a time when I would have to make this life-changing decision.

"I think so," was all I could manage to say.

Sediba swung both feet onto the floor and got up. He paced back and forth and I watched him nervously.

"After all this time, I still don't know what you want."

"That's ridiculous, Diba. Come on."

"No, I don't. What do you want?"

"I want you!" I yelled at him. "Obviously."

He stood still, arms folded, feet planted firmly on the floor and looked me in the eye. "You have me. What do you want, from here on, with me?"

"Diba . . . come on. Stop. So I haven't made firm plans. It won't be so hard. I'll find something."

"Where? That's the only thing I'm asking. Where?"

"Can you please just come back and sit next to me? I don't like the way you're talking. I told you, I want you, that's all."

He furiously put his shoes back on and then he was marching out, before he changed his mind and came back to stand in front of me. "Well," he said and then took a deep breath. "I'll tell you what I want. I want a life with you."

"A life?"

"Marriage, a house, maybe even a child."

I gulped. "Diba . . . *come, on!*"

"Look, it's what my parents had and I've always assumed . . . Listen: it's what I want. I can't change that."

"Diba . . . "

For a while we just stared at each other before he left the room to cool off.

It had been a good opportunity to be honest but I had been a coward. I couldn't think of the best way to tell him that I was sorry, but I was never going back to Kasi.

Two weeks later I saw for myself that my mother was unraveling and I suspected, with a dread that tore every part of me to shreds, that she was going to take me with her to her own special hell. I knew it when I spoke to her on the phone and I knew it when she arrived unannounced at my doorstep with only a small bag in one hand, wearing no lipstick and her hair tied back in a stiff ponytail. She said, with great effort to appear nonchalant, but betrayed by her own tears, "Your father and I will get a divorce."

It was only one hour before Sediba was due to arrive. I swallowed and pushed away my shameful thought but it kept coming back: how was I going to get rid of her? Her sadness engulfed the room, taking away the joy that had recently floated in and filled my home. Her face was the picture of the house I had grown up in: glum and desperate. Her scent—jasmine and roses—was so powerful and captivating, so heavy that through it I could hear a sad Motown love song on a lonely Sunday afternoon back at our house. When her eyes lifted she was looking in my direction but not quite at me, so consumed was she by her own misery.

I hurried around the room trying to tidy up even though there was really not much to do and I was just busying myself to keep my panic in check. She sat on the sofa and stared outside without saying a word.

"What . . . what happened? Did something happen?"

Without turning to look at me she said: "Ag . . . I told him he had to explain it to you." Then she took off her shoes and put her feet on the sofa.

"I haven't been here in such a long time! I like it. I like what you've done with it. It's so tidy and pretty. And look at this," she pointed at the paintings and photographs on the wall. "You decorated it so nicely."

My mother was not looking at me or seriously taking in my place when she spoke; then she was staring at something outside. Her voice was so flat that I couldn't stand to hear its sorrow. I brought her a glass of wine. "This is a really good one, from Stellenbosch. I know you'll like it."

She took it without looking at it.

"Sit down. Sit down next to me. Let me look at my only child."

I sat and then waited for the smile that came but was so fleeting that I thought I might have imagined it. She took a sip.

"Do you like it?" I asked her, anxious.

"Hm? Yes it's lovely. Listen. Your time here is almost over. You have to go and start working somewhere else. You have to do your work somewhere else, right?"

"Yes, Ma."

"How do you feel about doing it here?"

The question felt like a trap, although I couldn't understand why, exactly. I said, confused, "It was always the plan to go back to Maimela. I know the area, the language. I could be close to papa and that way when I do eventually work with him I'll know all the patients really well." Why was she asking? She had known the plan from the beginning. And of course Sediba was already upset about this very topic.

"I'm thinking of moving here. If I did, you could be close to me." She smiled, but it was a pleading look, desperate, and it made me want to flee the room.

"OK," I forced myself to appear at least a little bit enthusiastic. "OK. We could do that, but Mama, tonight I have to go out. I'm supposed to see friends now, maybe you can go and lie down and we can see each other when you wake up? You look very tired."

I was thinking that I would go outside and wait for Sediba and tell him that my mother was here—that we couldn't be alone in the flat this weekend and that I hoped he understood.

Luckily my mother liked the idea of going to sleep and I stepped outside to wait for Sediba. I sat down on the steps downstairs facing the gate and waited with a heavy heart. What would I tell him? He couldn't drive back now or stay at his aunt's. He hated staying there. We had had made plans to drive down the coast. The last time he had said, "You know, just because we hate clubs doesn't mean we have to stay in. Why don't we drive down the coast and see what's there? Stop for lunch and things like that." I had looked forward to it all week. Now I tried breathing slowly to calm down but I couldn't. I stood up and paced up and down the small garden area in front of the building.

Finally he arrived, using the spare card I had given him to get through the gate. He smiled and waved at me as he turned into a parking spot and felt I the dread rise and rise and rise until I couldn't breathe and ran over to him, panting with panic.

"Hi," he leaned over to give me a hug. "I almost kissed you right here," he said.

I stepped out of the embrace.

"What's wrong?"

"My mother is here."

"Oh. That's OK, we'll just say that I'm visiting."

I said, "No!" and it came out more forceful than I had intended.

He was completely taken aback. "No?"

"No. She's miserable. Depressed. She wants to stay here for the weekend."

"That's fine." He was opening the boot now.

"That's fine? Where will you go?"

Sediba folded his arms and threw me another look of astonishment.

"You and I are going down the coast. You can tell her that we're just going for a drive. We'll return later today and I don't mind staying with my aunt for one night."

I bit my lip and waited, trying to find the right thing to say but it was not coming to me.

"What is wrong? Do you want me to go and then come back?"

I nodded. "I need to think."

Sediba took my hand and squeezed it quickly before letting it fall. "Fine. Think. I'll be back later."

"Thanks," I said but when he leaned forward I took a step back.

"Not outside," I said, and he held up both his hands.

I waited for him to get in the car and reverse it. When he reached me, he stopped and winked. "As long as I don't leave here without . . . ," he said with a grin. It was an attempt at a joke and I appreciated it, so I chuckled in response. When his car had disappeared down the road, I ran up the stairs, back to my mother.

I found a completely different woman.

My mother had touched-up her makeup and was standing at the bathroom door, one hand on her hip, the other behind her. Her lips were now painted a glossy reddish brown, her black eye liner was darker, bolder. She had even decided against the ponytail, her hair now brushed back, flat, its tips touching her shoulders. There was no trace of the subdued woman who had walked in a few minutes before.

This woman was more livid than sorrowful.

"Are you with someone? Going out with someone?" she asked.

"What? Why do you ask?"

"Are you?"

I was gripped with panic. Had she seen me and Sediba outside? I was trying to think, how could she, you couldn't see the entrance to the flat complex from my room. There were two buildings in this complex and mine faced the ocean while the other faced the street. She couldn't have seen us. Had she walked out? Seen him hug me?

"Not . . . well . . . I'm . . . I'm dating—"

"Why do you have two toothbrushes and two shaving kits?" From behind her, as if she had been saving it for effect, my mother pulled up one of the two kits. It was actually mine and not Sediba's.

I had read a lesbian woman's story once, where she said her mother had found out she was gay when she walked into the room and she and her girlfriend were sitting across the table from each other. They were not holding hands, they were not looking at each other in any special way—they had only been sitting and eating and the mother just guessed. You never know what it is about you that will reveal your secret. I had always imagined it would be something dramatic like being caught kissing or in bed. In the end it was only a shaving kit—and my lover had not even been there.

My defense was feeble. "Why are you looking at my things?" I took the kit from her. Back in the sitting room, I tried to think of ways to appear indignant, but this was my mother and I was no longer a young teenager without the experience of how cruel life is outside of home. I needed my mother, I didn't want to fight. I needed her to say it was fine, that she'd be all right with it.

She had opened the windows and there again came that whiff of lemons from the tree I hadn't yet seen. I had a passing memory of Sediba's arms around me and my head on his shoulder, taking in that scent. My mother came to sit across from me and leaned her elbows on her thighs. I could see what was happening here: whatever she thought was going on with me had helped take away her own misery for a moment. She had something to take care of now. There was my mother's old sense of purpose.

"I want you to tell me something. You said you were dating, but you have two shaving kits. Why?"

There was no way out of here. I could open every door I had known to let in a little air but there was no door to step through. There was nothing to do but say what was really going on. I didn't want to, because I didn't trust her to stay calm and tell me it was all right, that the nation's constitution says blah blah blah . . . I was at the top of a table and I had to tip it, let the rope pull me up by the neck. It had been many years of running but this was the end. I thought of Rodney and wondered for the first time if he had sobered up for his conversation with his mother or if he had been high on something—if that was why he had been bold enough to tell his mother that he liked sleeping with men.

My mother folded her arms, legs crossed, one red high-heel shoe dangling back and forth like it was a red pendulum above my sitting room mat. Her eyes were narrow and her lips pursed into a reddish-brown O, waiting. I picked up the bottle of wine that I had placed in front of her and took a long swig from it, wiped my mouth with my palm, and surrendered.

"I'm gay."

I felt the room spin, the wine glass blur and suddenly there were two glasses. I shut my eyes and pressed them with the heels of my palms.

"Now you know," I said, my best attempt at appearing nonchalant failing me.

I didn't—couldn't—look at her. For a moment neither one of us spoke. When I opened my eyes I had an uncontrollable need to grin, a need in me that often comes out of nervousness.

My mother picked up her bag and put it on her lap, her face towards the window as though contemplating a great mystery. I felt cold and then hot all at once. My body couldn't find a comfortable position on the chair. A small bird came and sat at the window and quickly flew away as if sensing danger on the other side of the glass and I wished I could do the same.

Finally, when it appeared she had thought it all through, she threw her bag down and spoke. "*Sies!* A doctor, behaving like a dirty street person? A doctor? A gay? My own child, a gay? *Sies!* You're a gay? What kind of thing is this? Is this from your White friends? Is this what you think is white? It's so . . . it's not proper, Kabelo. Even if you want to be White, Kabelo, this is repulsive, *mara.* Hao! *Sies!* A gay? A gay?" The more she spoke the word, the more I felt repulsed by it—I saw myself the way she did for that moment: disappointing, dirty, vile. She spat out the words and left them on my floor. *A gay.* The ground shifted. My head ached persistently.

What is there to say when someone expresses such blatant contempt? I couldn't defend myself. I only looked down at the floor, my face in my hands.

I suppose soon it became clear that she would get no satisfying response from me, so she marched out of my flat and slammed the door.

And then just as quickly she was back. She opened the door and stood there, no intention of coming in. She had forgotten something, I thought. I stood facing her, waiting. Perhaps she had come to say it was all right, she was under a lot of stress, it was work; it was this thing with my father, times were changing—no matter what, I was her son. She loved me anyway. No such luck. She said: "*Bona* Kabelo. Do me a favour. Don't come back to Maimela if you're still practicing these things. I didn't raise you to shame me."

And that was the very last thing my mother said to me.

Today I remember the phone call about my father's death, but the one about my mother's comes to me every now and then as a jumbled mess of voices and words muffled by crying in the background. My father phoned from home, Aus' Tselane wailing in the background. When you're a medic you always think: I should have seen the signs. You look back on the time you were in class and you learned about these particular symptoms and you feel completely stupid for not having noticed them as they happened to you in your world. I wouldn't have guessed that my mother would kill herself. That she would go silent for weeks, be cold and distant for some time towards me, that I would have guessed. But kill herself? No. A psychiatrist I worked with once told us, "I often think a lot of anger goes into suicide."

I remember the flat was cold and unlit when Sediba came to sit with me, just before I made my way up north, having heard the news. I wouldn't go with him. I had done enough to my parents, I felt. He was getting ready to leave when my father phoned. I had been in a state and had stayed up all night pacing around my flat while he woke up now and then and begged me to come to bed. I had left the windows open, my phone was on the floor, and I had not eaten or slept.

"I'm so sorry," he was saying. "You're going to be fine."

"Why do Black people say 'you're a gay' instead of just 'you're gay?'"

Sediba shrugged and flicked away the insignificance of my question.

"Maybe she had an underlying problem. Maybe it was . . . " I was speaking in a whisper, my voice hoarse from shock.

When I looked up he was staring at me, his eyes so desperate and pleading that I couldn't bear it. He couldn't find me—couldn't pull me close and comfort me. I kept darting away from his arms, moving in circles, stepping out of his embrace when he reached me. He wanted the person he knew to come back to him and sit with him in the room, but I needed to run away. Finally he was exhausted.

"Do you remember the first time we met? When my family moved in?" His voice was quiet and sad. I nodded, still not looking at him. I was curious where this was going. He stood up and came to sit next to me, so close that now all I wanted him to do was hold me, but he didn't.

"I remember all your friends—I didn't think they'd become mine later—but all of them were amused by me, the way people always had been. But you weren't. You didn't laugh when they did. There was something so reassuring about the way you looked at me . . . and then Lelo said I sat like a girl and the look you gave him," he chuckled, rubbing my neck gently, "you were so angry he said that. I'll never forget it."

I got up to turn the light on. When I returned to the sofa I sat farther away from him. I said, "I was afraid of you. I didn't know then but I know now."

The gulf between us seemed bigger and my whole world felt lonely. He wasn't gone yet but I knew he would be soon. I knew I would have to let him go, finally, and the knowledge brought with it a staggering sadness, so overwhelming that I started breathing faster, afraid of what this meant for me, for my life.

"You were afraid of yourself," Sediba said. He moved closer and started to kiss me. It was so sad a kiss that I returned it wholeheartedly, feeling helpless and reassured all at once. But then he started inching his hand up my shirt and I heard my mother's voice saying, "*Sies!*" and I was afraid that every time he touched me I would hear her voice again. So I caught Sediba's hand and firmly pushed it away. When he pulled back he stared at me, his eyes begging.

I sat up and shifted away. I heard the wind whistling furiously outside, and one of the windows slammed shut. There was a storm brewing.

I said without facing him, "Look, Diba, this thing . . . we have to end it."

He didn't sound surprised. "We're in love," he said, matter-of-factly, "We can keep going. Can't we? Because we love each other."

"But it just broke my mother's heart. Just because we want it doesn't make it OK, you know. And where would we live, eventually? In Kasi? Come on. You know we have to end it."

"I think we can find some way. I think you're grieving and—"

"I can't ever live there like this. Knowing what I did to my mother and having people look at me like, like I have no shame."

He sank his head into his hands. "I love you."

I said, "I love you too," but my voice was so hoarse that it came out in a slight whisper. I had upset him more.

"Oh, now you say it. *Now*, Kabelo? All the time I hear, 'I feel the same way.' But now, today, when you're letting me go . . . "

He had called me by my full name. It sounded strange and formal and distant.

"You know I do—"

He walked away. One moment he was in the bedroom, the next at the window, staring out into the evening. "I don't say anything. There are things . . . I don't say anything, I just let you be. I know how you are and because I love you, I don't even . . . and the way you just let people think . . . I just hope that someday it will change. Every time I come here I hope to . . . " he stopped suddenly and then he walked towards the door. Through my teary eyes the room looked blurry.

"What do I let people think?"

He paused, turned around, shook his head.

"What? What do I let people . . . "

"Always. Like we're doing something shameful. That stewardess on the plane . . . " He wanted to hurt me, I understood.

"Where will you go? You just arrived. I'm sorry. Let's just . . . let's look at it as taking time off. I just need a little time. I have to go back for her funeral. I just need a little time, I think."

His face twisted in anger, his chin trembled, his eyelids fluttered furiously. "Do you? Just some time and then you're fine? We're fine?"

I hung my head. "It was never going to be . . . we're not . . . *allowed*, you and I. It's not like we could do this forever—"

"Because?" he snapped, madly throwing his arms up in the air.

"Come on, *Jo*. You know where we're from. We sort of knew we'd get caught—"

I think it was me calling him *Jo* in the middle of it, like we were back to being pals—like I had already moved on, that enraged him.

"*Caught? Caught?* Because we're two children at a forbidden game?" I opened my mouth to speak but it took a while before the words formed and finally came out. By then the door was open.

My voice was clearer now the second time I said it: "I do love you too—"

"Fuck you, *Jo*," and the door slammed behind him.

Home

MY MOTHER'S FUNERAL was as hideous an affair as these things are meant to be. I couldn't tell you who attended. People kept trying to feed me and I kept going to my old bedroom to look at the clock and then out the window to see if I could spot Sediba in the crowd. Every few minutes, there I was: clock, then window. Clock, window. I hated the priest, who prattled on about all kinds of things—none of them having anything to do with my mother. I thought he was suggesting that God had taken her to do better things in the afterlife or something like that. It was distressing to find out that I was capable of so much rage.

My father and I exchanged the usual empty pleasantries. I was unsettled to find that if he felt sadness, it lay very deep inside him. So deep, he obviously had trouble accessing it because I couldn't find it in his eyes.

When everyone was gone I stood in the backyard looking at my mother's garden, wondering about her thoughts before she died, still puzzled by why she wanted me to stay in Durban. Why had she wanted me to be away from my father after so many years of us planning to work side by side? I couldn't get an answer out of Aus' Tselane, who was the least comfortable person at the funeral. She was so nervous that I couldn't get her to sit down and talk calmly—and I certainly was not about to ask my father, a man with whom conversations were limited to about three subjects in his life.

At last I saw Sediba outside, with all my friends, all huddled in a corner, talking. In the backyard I had to make my way through crying mourners before I reached them and when they all hugged me he reached out his hand without looking me in the eye. "Sorry *Jo*," he said.

Lelo, behind me, asked me something about the *wie-sien-ons*, the party you have after a funeral to celebrate someone's life. When I turned around I found that Sediba had slipped away and was gone.

I boarded a plane the very night after we buried my mother and went back to my flat. To my surprise my father had been quite encouraging about me going back, saying, "We all need to carry on. It's what she would have wanted," the way people confidently make pronouncements about the wishes of the dead. I was quite anxious to leave, and headed for the airport.

I think that I stayed in Durban not so much because I wanted to or she had wanted me to. I stayed because I just couldn't make myself move.

Durban

ONE OF THE MOST PAINFUL MOMENTS in my life—during that period after my mother's death—was discovering the different types of loneliness. There is the kind that eats away at your insides and pushes you to go out and find something to fill the void even when you don't know what that something is. Then there's the kind that keeps you walking around in your dreams finding the thing you lost but with the faint knowledge that you will wake up and the thing will be gone. That kind of loneliness is worse. It had me waking up all sweaty and thirsty and cold so that I was forced to listen to nothing but the sound of restless dogs howling at the full moon. I would recall what the superstitious say, that dogs only howl like hyenas when they've just seen a ghost.

I lived in dreams where he was still with me and cursed the howling dogs many nights. I woke up feeling empty and yearning for him, but also guilty because the dreams were never about the loss of my mother.

I started feeling lucky to have Andrew, who brought me food at lunchtime and chatted on about his family and his problems, and for once I was happy to hear him because I didn't want to think or talk about myself. Until, out of the blue one day, he said, "I'm really sorry about you and Sediba. I mean . . . I see . . . I can see that you've been really sad. I haven't seen him around, I figure it's more than . . . well, more than your mom. The thing you're sad about."

His eyes were so kind and so gentle that I didn't have the strength to deny it, correct him or be the way I had been before. I nodded and bit my lip to stop myself from letting out the familiar sadness that smothered and cursed me every day.

I poured myself into my work, trying very hard to enjoy it, learning as much as I could and spending as little time in my flat as possible, and when I did, I overslept. I picked up the phone a hundred times, sometimes even letting him answer so that I could hear his voice and then dropping it. I was like a fourteen-year-old with a crush. This was no way for a grown man to behave.

Finally one day he said into the phone, "Talk to me or don't call."

I went into a routine that I couldn't break. Every evening was the same: I would come home from work and, being unable to stomach the stench of loneliness tucked in every corner of my flat, I took a long, slow walk around the two rectangular buildings where I lived and contemplated the life I once had.

The blocks were both painted an impossible blue—a colour someone might liken to the sky but only out of a need to place it: the African sky is never that faded, chalky shade. Standing on the pavement near the parked cars, my feet touching the bold yellow line separating the parking area from the pedestrian path, I looked up and counted the windows until I got to mine. There were only four floors and my flat was at the corner, its windows always open to let in the scent of that lemon tree tucked away somewhere in the neighbourhood. I imagined that the place held a life of laughter and smells so enticing you would never want to leave.

And why not? It had all been true not so long ago and I liked to think it could happen again. I liked to separate the memory from the dreams, which were teasing and spiteful. The memory—because I picked and chose—could be a sweet, gentle caress, but the dreams I had no control over. They were a medley of objects and faces carrying scorn and the burden of guilt.

I resisted sleep, putting it off for as long as the senses would allow, all the while bargaining with the body: one more sip of wine, a bit more water, one last memory. In my right hand there was always a cigarette glowing; I enjoyed the smell but didn't want to taste it, fearing it would remind me of tastes and feelings that would very surely break my heart. In this and other ways I played games with memory, allowing it to take me here but ducking from there, shutting my eyes to places too painful to visit.

He stayed with every part of me. This could not be helped. I thought of him at every turn, with every slow step and every pained breath—the cigarette burning away and sometimes burning my fingers because I was not paying attention.

Every night I willed him back into my life and at times even convinced myself that after I climbed the eight flights of stairs—forty-eight steps exactly—I would arrive at my flat to find him standing, waiting for me. How many times had I opened my door almost expecting him there only to be greeted by the emptiness of my life. When I finally drifted into sleep I dreaded the moment when I would wake up and try to sort through the sounds and pictures in my mind: was it real? Had there been someone sleeping beside me? Why was the other side of the bed cold when he had just been there? That loud car hoot on the street had gone on throughout the dream but was it still a dream if I could still hear it?

I had to convince myself that I was fine, that in reality people's faces did not change back and forth, back and forth like in a magic trick.

It was at this time that I met Sizwe.

The initial diagnosis for Sizwe was acute pneumonia. Andrew had been on his last hour of call when Sizwe arrived. When I came in, Andrew briefed me on his condition, telling me he suspected it was AIDS-related, adding, "And also, he's a she."

I liked Sizwe from the moment we spoke. He asked in Sesotho, "Dr Mosala. Are you Mosotho or Motswana? I lived in Jo'burg for three years, that's how I learned Sesotho. My girlfriend is Mosotho. Was Mosotho."

He had a dark scar running the length of his right forearm and his head was swollen from what he said was "a fair fight."

"Why do you say 'was'? You broke up?" I asked him as I examined him, my stethoscope landing on a thick bandage, covering tightly bound breasts.

He looked me in the eye and his face changed from friendly to a warning glare. With his wheezing and exhaustion he shouldn't have been speaking but he insisted, "I'm a man. I don't want questions about my chest."

I nodded and continued. Then he coughed up some more phlegm and shook his head. His words came out in a lower whisper this time. "We didn't break up."

I didn't ask him to explain, only told him what was wrong and what we needed to do. He was drowsy from the medication at this point so I wasn't sure he heard me. I remembered the young man who had died suddenly a few months before, when I had gone home and told Sediba about it and he had held me and given me a glass of wine. It was raining when I left the hospital that night and I jumped onto the first taxi I saw, managing to catch it just as it was about to close. The hospital was buzzing as it always was at every hour, patients restless and out for a smoke, taxi drivers standing in groups, chatting and waiting for passengers. A steady stream of visitors going in and out of the buildings.

As the taxi drove on, I was thinking about Sizwe. I had had many young patients before, many who had died the same way, but there was something about this one—maybe it was the determined way he looked at me, I don't know. I felt he had looked right into me. There was something *knowing* about his eyes. Like he recognized me. He was wheezing and in pain but was determined to appear brave.

At home I sat at my table with a glass of wine in one hand and the phone receiver in the other. I briefly considered dialing Sediba's number, as I did every evening after work and every morning when I woke up. I took a sip and sat still, watching the city's glowing lights below, my heart aching for times I could neither hold on to nor go back to.

My father would still be at his office, I knew, so I dialed.

"He's so determined," I told him about Sizwe.

"People often are in the last stage of their lives," he replied. I could see him settled into his chair, picking up a pen and writing notes on my case and making a point to ask specific questions—a quiz disguised as regular conversation. I enjoyed this part. It brought out the scholar in me.

"So I haven't tested him but I'm sure that it's PCP and I think he knows too."

"You have to—"

"I know, Papa. I know. I just, you know . . . I want him to have just three more weeks."

"Ha-a. You know we don't get to decide that. That's not for us to decide."

"It breaks your heart . . . " I started, but stopped when I heard the faint sound of a pen or pencil scratching the crisp, dry surface of paper. Here I was going where my father had taught me never to go, so I sensed a teacher's frustration in a student going rogue.

Yet I could not help but continue. "I know we don't, but Pa, you should see him. He's so young. Sixteen or seventeen. Strong, in spite of it, and determined. He occasionally asks me about myself."

My father cleared his throat and made an excuse about work. It was the classic Mosala strategy: if you delved too much into feelings, we got on with work. So we said our goodbyes and he dropped the phone first. I held on, dialed Sediba's number fully and dropped it before I heard the first ring.

How do I describe what happened with Sizwe? It was brief, my encounter with him, as I was not the only doctor seeing him. Yet every time we were in the same room, interacting, I felt a pull towards things I couldn't always clearly name. Perhaps it was when he said, "You don't look at me like something's wrong with me." When I told him that well, something was wrong with him, that he was very ill, he said, "You know what I mean," his finger pointing to his chest. There was something about him that reminded me of myself, but whenever I saw him I kept thinking, I've never been that hopeful and open, why would he remind me of myself? Perhaps he was more someone I might have been, under different circumstances. A bolder, more liberated young person.

He wanted to sit up when it would have been better to lie down, he wanted to speak when it took every bit out of him to speak one word audibly. His lungs were sacks of fluid ready to give up. Yet every time I walked into the room he perked up and we chatted briefly before he dozed off from exhaustion or the medications. He told me, "I watched this show once where there was a man wounded and his girlfriend believed that if she kept talking to him he would stay conscious. So when my girlfriend was sick, I kept talking to her, telling her I loved her—every day—thinking it would keep her alive." He gave a chuckle and coughed up phlegm.

Andrew and I disagreed about him. He kept saying: "He. She. I have no idea."

"He wants to be addressed as a guy."

"But she's clearly not."

I was tired and irritated by him and his suggestion we take the bandage off. "It's up to him," was all I could manage to say. "It's his choice."

It was the night before I got the phone call about my father that I saw Sizwe for the last time and I really could see then that he didn't have much time. I had checked his DC4 cell count and it was well below fifty. He had moments of lucidity but they were fleeting. His mother sat beside him, clutching a rosary, and whenever she opened her bag, white tissues flowed out like flowers unfolding. She spoke about how determined her son had been. "Always, always he insisted we take him as he is. Never apologizing . . . I was only happy he found someone who loved him."

I sat with them, checked his vitals but mainly just kept them company, before going home. I had told the hospital to phone me if anything happened, so when the phone call came, I thought at first that it was about Sizwe. It was about my father.

Home

Aus' Tselane went back to her family for a few days, and said she would return the day before the funeral. This seemed rather strange, given how devastated she was by my father's death. She refused to give me a plausible reason. "My sister's child is very sick," she said, but something about this didn't sound right. I stood at the door of the spare room, the guest room when I was growing up, and watched her pack her clothes into a small black bag.

After all these years, I observed, she had not accumulated much beyond a few dresses and two pairs of shoes. I leaned against the door-frame as the thought brought down the weight of sadness on my back.

She looked up at my puzzled face and said, strangely, "Your father insisted I move out of the backroom, so that's why my things are here." I was lost in a fog of confusion and weariness, so I only shrugged and said nothing. I saw from the tightness in her jaw and her brisk moves from the wardrobe to the bag that she meant to leave and leave she would. So I put my arms around her and walked her to the taxi, half resenting her for leaving me alone. We stopped at the side of the road and I pointed my finger up—the sign for town, where she would go to catch a taxi to Phalaborwa—and when it stopped I picked up her bag, waited until she was seated by the driver's side and handed it to her.

"I'll be back," she said and forced a smile. "You'll see, I'll be back."

I shut the door and waved her away. All I could do was go back home and try to tell myself that with the help of neighbours I would be fine and that I had to be fine: it was all upon me now.

My father had sold my mother's shop only two months after she died, because he couldn't manage both the surgery and the shop. I had protested, asked him if we could at least rent it to someone else instead of having it completely leave the family, but he had said, "No. It's too much for me. I have to let it go."

In fact a lot of things had changed around the house.. My father seemed to have worked at erasing my mother's touch: the rosebushes in her neat and pretty garden had been replaced by wildflowers that I couldn't identify; the front iron gate, which had been white, had now been painted black; all the interior walls were in pretty, playful colours like yellow and pink. Even the kitchen cabinets had been redone, with pine in place of white finishes.

And the changes didn't stop at the house. My friend Base was now thinner, slower, showing definite signs of being quite ill. I knew what was wrong and it was too painful to think about. At first I had looked at him with more shock than I had intended, and then had to look away, regretful. Maimela hardly felt like the same place.

Then of course, I was now to be the doctor and the surgery and all everything that came with it was awaiting me.

The day after I arrived, Sediba came in the morning with Base and Trunka, wearing overalls and a cap pulled down to almost cover his eyes. I was walking out of the house, on my way to buy food for the mourners as they walked in. My heart leapt at the sight of him, his arms lifting the pot and his face turned away from me, obviously in an effort to not meet my eyes. I said: "*Heita!*" and all three of them said it back, and then I had to move around them to get to the car, my arm briefly brushing against Sediba's back. He stopped for a moment and said, "*O Sharp, Jo?*"

In front of our friends I couldn't put my arms around him and rest my head on his shoulder. I turned around and looked at him, my hands in my pockets but said nothing, before getting into the car. It seemed to reverse almost without me, and once out through the gate I put it in gear and sped down the hill.

When I came back to the house about an hour later, Sediba was not there. The guys had mowed the lawn and helped set up the big cooking pots and left. A few men and women from the neighbourhood had arrived, cleaning and making preparations until darkness fell and I was alone again.

I sat at the kitchen table in my childhood home wondering how long I would continue to feel this alone. The walls and the furniture seemed to stare back at me, as if to inquire who this stranger was and what I wanted from someone else's home. Probably what I found most disconcerting was that I just couldn't find traces of my mother here. Nothing about the house had her fingerprints on it. Perhaps my father had been angry too—maybe he had decided that if my mother had been too angry to be with him then he would erase all parts of her from his home. Maybe that is what killed him, I reasoned. I wanted to talk to Sediba about it. I looked for him everywhere. I woke up hoping to see him and went to sleep terrified that I may never have another minute with him. I re-arranged the times that we had been together, revised the arguments we had to make myself feel like I had done it all right, to give myself a chance to do it over and do it properly this time.

I did the same thing with my father. In my mind I had come home more, spent more time at the surgery the way he had sometimes requested. I saw myself telling him that I had someone now, even if my mind protested, I forced it to see a father who was pleased for me and accepted the man I was.

All night long I paced, going to sleep for a bit and then waking up again, wandering around the yard the way I had done in Durban. Only this time I was not dodging sleep, it was the other way round. I kept wondering when morning would come and save me from my loneliness. It was during one of these nights that I thought of Sizwe: how I sensed he knew about me, what he had said about keeping his girlfriend alive.

Maybe Sediba had needed me to tell him I loved him so that he could live here. Maybe being with me had kept him alive here. I certainly knew that when he loved me it had kept me going. All my life I had been treading water, afraid of sinking into something terrifying.

I had feared when my legs would give up, when I would be crushed by my own secret. And then he came and loved me and suddenly, for months, I was surfacing, being pulled up into his scent, his skin, the look he had on his face when he was about to kiss me.

I had forced him to leave and now was wandering alone at night, looking for a way back to him.

I was grateful for tradition. Neighbours arrived at sunrise ready and eager to prepare the house, cook the food, and clean the yard.

Maimela was devastated by the loss. Every day someone came to me: an elderly lady would take my hand in hers, a man would put his hand on my shoulder, and there would be some recollection of something that my father had done or that the person had said to him. We would stand there with tissues or handkerchiefs, bringing my father back to life with our words, seeking small comfort in a memory.

I had always thought, while living in Durban, that the problem with being in a place where no one has known you as a child is that you constantly have a feeling of floating, alone, unanchored. When people don't know or love someone in your family and when they haven't known you as an infant—when no one knows your roots—your presence might be disconcerting for locals. They always look at you with some suspicion. In their faces you always see the question: Who are your people? What is your story?

Being at home, I felt what I had not felt in Cape Town or Durban. I felt like the neighbourhood, the dry heat, the smells and the sounds were cradling me. My always-weary body now had a bit of renewed energy, a feeling that I could have the strength to bury my father properly. People around me all pulled together to give him the send-off that we felt he deserved.

Still, there remained the nagging feeling that their love, support and respect might all fade once they found out the man I was.

I gave myself the week to think about what I would do next, because I had no intention of leaving this time. It was hardly a matter of choice: I had to take over the surgery, there was no one else to do it. Plus, I had *seen* things: I had come across signs pointing to where I needed to be. My father used to tell me that once you knew someone needed help you could not walk away. "It's your duty then, when you see illness, to stay and do what you've studied to do."

The local cemetery, vast and stretching as it was, was filling up. I had heard that they were opening a new one.

"There are lines to go in for a burial every weekend," my father had told me. "As soon as people start knowing that there is some help, they will come to us, this will get better."

So I would stay. I thought of Base and the large, dark lesions, deep purple against his brown skin. His laboured walk, his ongoing fatigue.

I had to stay.

We normally take a week to prepare for the burial. We wait for relatives who come from far away and have nights of remembrance, cooking and drinking and speaking to the ancestors. But I had arrived on the Tuesday and I planned the funeral for the Saturday, because I couldn't keep the surgery closed too long. I understood that people didn't stop being ill because someone had died. I remembered my father working the week of my mother's death, going in the mornings and coming back to the house to work with the neighbours in the afternoon. As a child he had cut short our holidays to get back and keep the surgery open, because many people didn't have the means to get on a taxi and take their loved ones to the hospital where they would have to deal with long waiting lines.

So I set to work in the mornings while all my friends took over at the house. Trunka was especially helpful. The man has the best organization skills that I have ever seen: he could run a large company, given the chance. It was easy to see how he could have turned his father's tuck shop into the successful business that it now was. Watching him inspired me to do the same for my father's business. I wanted to feel as proud of myself as I felt admiration for him.

Still, going into the surgery was no easy task. The first day was the hardest: I went in unsuspecting, thinking I would just go in and see a few patients and then run back home to work on the preparations for the funeral, but things got very uncomfortable very quickly. As soon as I saw the building, a corner house turned into a business, with red brick and white windowpanes, I wanted to turn back and run away. A great sadness flooded my body and taking the last few steps from the street into the place was like making my way up a mountain.

My father had opened his surgery before I was born, so he had been in it all my life. He had taken a six-room house at the far corner of a busy street that included small township businesses: a bottle store, a dry-cleaners, and two general stores, one of which was my mother's. All the business people had known and respected each other for many years. The idea that I was now meant to be one of them was rather daunting. In my mind I was still ten years old, going into my mother's shop to help at the till and then to the surgery to play in the waiting area, asking people if I could help with anything. I still remembered the older patients patting me on the head, telling me stories.

Now I was to be the doctor behind the closed door and I had to give people the same service that my father had given them for almost three decades.

Even unlocking the door was difficult. My father's keys were held together by his old Chiefs key ring—Chiefs being his favourite soccer team. The waiting area had changed. Long leather sofas had replaced the fabric chairs of before. In the four corners stood potted plants on side tables along with magazines. Informative posters decorated the walls: AIDS, heart attack symptoms, prostate health, the importance of breast-feeding.

The secretary's desk was now a long wooden table and the tiles were white as they had been before but looked new. In his office, my father had left his white coat hanging over his chair behind the desk and his stethoscope behind his door, where he had kept it when he was at work. It had gone in his leather bag when he left the office. The whole place was in pristine condition, not unlike the way I remembered it. My father had always been insistent on high standards, as he called it, in his work place.

I steeled myself when I picked up the stethoscope, willing the lump in my throat to disappear as I swung it around my neck. I could almost hear his voice, telling me, "The people deserve the best care."

I had drifted through my work in Durban preoccupied with my own loneliness. But all parts of a person's life need to come together and make sense for one to feel grounded. It had been only in those weeks when Sediba and I were together that I had been more present, more available to my patients but the rest of the time I had sleep-walked through my job, doing my best and being efficient but rarely enjoying myself. Part of that was because hospitals overwhelmed me. I found the pace too hectic and working alongside other doctors, while it allowed for more learning, was a challenge to someone who had spent much of his life envisioning working in one surgery with only one other person. There was always a bit of competition here and there, something I was never very good at handling.

I am also the kind of doctor who likes to see people go home. I've found that there is more of a sense of helplessness when patients are in a hospital bed, surrounded by other sick people. They are generally more hopeful when they can see their doctor and then go back to the comfort and familiarity of their own homes.

On that first day at the surgery I realized how much I looked for-ward to those moments of being alone and quiet after each patient. I swiveled in my father's chair like a child, remembering the times when I would come and visit as a youngster and declare: "*Le nna* I want to sew people's hands," and he'd say, quite seriously, "Then you'll have to go and learn how to do it."

Everyone who came in my first morning wanted to talk about my father. Some cried through an exam and I had to sit back and wait before I listened to their breathing or took their blood pressure. Many of them were elderly. They had known my father when he was a young doctor himself and he was the son who had grown up right in front of them. They had loved him through it, attended his wedding to a beautiful young bride and were there to welcome their newborn son when I came. They expected the same of me. I was the grandson they used to send to the shops to buy snuff or bread. The men shook my hand and the women patted my shoulder with pride. "*Tjo!* You have grown!" They exclaimed. "I remember when you played marbles in front of my house."

"You look just like your father at your age. He was so serious and always worried about us." Mma Mathibe, the woman who sold cold drinks out of her house when I was a little boy, pinched my cheek. "Ei, ei, ei! But you are handsome. Sit! Sit down and tell me when you're getting me a grandchild." For a moment she was the one standing and I was the one sitting instead of the reverse, like I was the one being examined. She had left her house on bad knees and an aching back and walked the distance to the surgery for a specific reason: a duty to fulfill. She put one hand on top of another, clearing her throat. Her words were given gravity by the stern look that suddenly fell over her face. She said, "Listen, *ngwanaka*, just because your parents are not here doesn't mean you don't have someone to take you to ask for *magadi*, do you hear me? Any time you find yourself a nice girl, come back and tell me and we'll take you to ask for her at her parents' house."

I winced at the thought of going to ask for *lobola*, reminded again of people's imaginary accomplished, adored young lady who was about to waltz into my life. My armpits started to sweat. I laughed and stood up quickly, asking Mma Mathibe to roll up her sleeve as politely as if I were asking for a drink of water at her house.

She was not fooled. "I know you're shy. You always have been, ever since you were this tall"—she stretched her arm to the side, palm up to demonstrate my little boy height. "You were just like your father. Always quiet, thinking. Your eyes looking in the distance. Well, now it's time to stop looking in the distance, *akere?* You are a man now and you have come home. And we, also, we are here and we will be your parents. *Akere?* We were always your parents. Today, we come in because the ones who raised you are gone."

I nodded, a tear escaping in spite of my willing it to stop. I had come home. They needed a wife for me.

Still, of all the things people said to me, the most painful to hear was, "I feel as if he's standing right in front of me." I had never really worried about filling my father's shoes until I put on his coat and heard them speak to him through me, making me feel like a guest filling in for someone whose return we should all be waiting for.

I worked steadily through that first day with barely any time to eat and had to phone Trunka and ask if they minded watching over things at the house a little longer because it looked like I would take all day at the surgery, aware and regretful that I was taking him away from his own business, but he assured me he didn't mind. He had help, he said. He had people he was paying at the tuck shop. When I walked outside for some fresh air, I was stunned to see the line of people extended outside the gates of the surgery. It was a scene reminiscent of elderly people waiting for their pension at municipal offices in the apartheid years—or voting days. Those who knew an opportunity when they saw one were walking up and down selling peanuts, chips, and water. I pulled out my phone and asked Trunka where I could find someone to employ temporarily for help at the surgery: we needed to bring in extra chairs, water, that sort of thing.

The funny thing is that in the end most of the people had come to pay their respects and were not actually in need of a medical check-up. When I left in the early evening I was exhausted. I had left the car at home so I would have to walk through the township, cross the main road, and trek up the hill—all along greeting and speaking to people about my father. I took a deep breath and put away the coat and stethoscope, straightened the papers on the desk. It was not until I was picking up my father's bag from behind his desk that I noticed, at the far right corner of the desk near the windowsill, a picture of Aus' Tselane. At first I thought, well, she worked with us for so long and they were so close, it made sense. But there was something in her face that kept me staring, that made me sit down. She was looking at the camera as if she and the person taking the picture shared a delightful secret.

She was in a sundress with thin straps and unlike most times her hair was not tucked under a head wrap. Tight messy curls flew freely around her head, blown by the wind. Her face was turned towards the camera, like she was looking back, sneaking a glance at someone. I sat at the desk for a long time, composing myself. I looked at the old black and white clock on the desk and picked up the phone to dial Sediba's number—and as I had done so many times, I only got to punch in the first few numbers before I gently put the receiver back in its cradle. Leaning back on the chair, my body again felt the heavy weight of shock. I wished with every part of me to speak to him. I wondered if the place would feel even lonelier than Durban. Here I was uncovering other people's secrets while holding on to my own with no one to speak to.

It was as if I had been looking at a crooked picture and now finally someone had straightened it. It brought a better understanding of so many things: Aus' Tselane's nervousness when I came back the day my father died, her need to go and mourn somewhere else, away from the scrutiny of a disapproving township, the changes in the house, and most of all, my mother's unraveling. I hadn't had a clue.

Everyone had lives that people they loved could never know about. My respectable township father had broken his wife's heart right in her own house, and I hadn't known a thing about it.

I wanted to run to Sediba's house the way we used to run up to my flat together. I wanted to peel my clothes off and climb into his bed and tell him about my day and hear about his, the two of us cocooned in our secret. But I didn't see him. Even as I walked from the surgery to my house I never got a glimpse of him, nor did I get a message from him. Still I kept hearing about Sediba everywhere. Whenever I returned home someone would say, "Thank Bonolo (Sediba's mother) for sending her son in with those potatoes." Or, "Sediba brought the meat this morning with his father." He was the phantom friend, coming in and out of places just after I left or right before I was to return. I became convinced that he was skillfully avoiding me and it made me feel helpless, angry, and hurt. I had thought for sure he would come and speak to me earlier but now wondered if his anger crossed out his love for me.

I went into the surgery every morning and tried hard to come back by midday. Everyone seemed to forgive me my absence at the house, saying, "No, no. People need you at the surgery. We'll take care of the food and the house. You go and work." I was embarrassed to see that I had become something new in their eyes: a grown and highly regarded man, one they needed to take care of the way people tend to take care of grown men. I wondered if this new man might earn a bit of understanding if they knew that he was in love with the hairdresser and not one of their girls—even if the hairdresser refused to see me.

———

So then it was not until the morning of the funeral that he came to me.

I was supposed to be getting ready but my heart was so heavy and the weight of it seemed to spread to my limbs so that I was not able to move very much. I did everything in short, almost timed spurts. I stepped out of bed then lay back down. I took a bath, came back and lay back down. It was after I had put on my underwear and a t-shirt and was lying back down that there was a knock on the door.

"I'm getting dressed!" I called out wearily. Already there was commotion outside the room. The women and men had arrived early and they were buzzing about all around me but because I had barely left my room, I couldn't have said who was there and who was not. I had no interest in stepping out of my room again and in my mind the day seemed to stretch so far ahead of me that I was convinced it would never end. I had not even opened the curtains to let the light in, wishing they would all leave and go to the wretched cemetery without me. I even worked out a scenario in my head where the house went completely quiet, the funeral happened without me and I only got to hear about it days later.

I had said that I was getting dressed, but the door swung open anyway, creaking on its hinges and then it closed. It was odd but I didn't look behind me. I lay still on my back, my eyes closed, assuming that the person had opened and then shut the door, leaving me alone. But then I heard his voice: "I brought you a tie."

I gave a start, came up on my elbows, and turned my head to see a beautiful man with a tapered beard and a bald head, wearing a black suit and a white shirt. He was leaning against the wall to the left of the door, holding up two ties—one in each hand—and attempting a pained smile.

I slumped back down and looked at the ceiling, the sadness and anger overwhelming me.

"You brought two ties."

"You get to choose."

"I have ties," my voice was slow with grief.

Now he walked forward and opened the curtains. The light blew in with a force that only morning light possesses, making me shut my eyes to let them adjust. He came and sat to my right on the bed.

"You have one tie. And, it won't go with a black suit," he said, putting both ties across my belly.

I looked up at him more closely, searching his face for signs of something promising. He returned the look in that intent old way that I had become used to and I found this encouraging.

"Put the tie on," he said, now looking away.

"Did you know my father was having a thing with Aus' Tselane?" I spoke with a bit of feigned nonchalance. He said, without looking at me, turning his attention to the open window instead: "You still sleep with the window open."

I snorted. "I guess you did know."

"I wouldn't call it a thing. I think it was much more than that."

I covered my eyes with my arm and sighed again dramatically.

"I guess everyone has their secrets."

"I wouldn't call it a secret."

"It would have been nice for you to tell me."

He was still not turning to look at me, something I was beginning to find disconcerting.

"No," he said examining his hands. "It was not my place. Strict orders from my parents. And it would have hurt you . . . so, no. I wouldn't have done it."

"Fucking township secrets." I spat out my words.

He gave out a short, bitter chuckle and then straightened his tie.

In the silence that followed I sat up and came close to him. I put my nose on his shoulder, taking in the scent of lilac on his skin. Its familiarity jarred my senses, jolted me back to things buried in safe places that refused to remain safe. I put my hands at his sides, at his waist—more for balance than anything—and held on.

"Fuck," I whispered, " . . . I miss you." He did not move.

When I slid my hands around to his stomach he said, softly, his voice sounding like he was very gently pulling himself away from something from which he had little control, "Put your clothes on. They'll be waiting for you."

I hesitated before standing up, my hands refusing to let go. I waited for him to shift his body, to nudge me away, but he stayed still. Slowly I moved, my feet touching the floor as if testing water temperature at the beginning of the season. Then the floor was warm and comforting from the sun's heat. I walked over to the wardrobe where my suit was held up by a wooden hanger and started getting dressed. First I pulled on the pants and tied the belt and then I pulled off the t-shirt. When I was buttoning my shirt I looked up, and through the mirror I noticed Sediba with his hand on his chin, elbows pressed to his knee, watching me.

My hand stayed on my chest, fingers caressing a button. We had been here before, many times. One of us getting dressed, the other sitting or standing, witnessing the ritual with great fascination, watching the naked body and then the fit of the clothes on the body you loved. We had cherished this routine. And the one getting dressed would slow down as if giving the other a chance to take it in. This had all been in a different place and now was a different time. We were together but apart. I wanted him to stand up and bring me my shoes or fasten the last three buttons the way he would have done before and I sensed that he wanted the same but was not sure what to do, so ever so slowly, he looked away.

I threw the tie around my shoulders and took my shoes to the bed, where I sat down and started putting them on.

"I hate ties," I told him as I pulled my shoelaces. "I was hoping not to wear one."

Now he laughed with a bit more delight like he was hearing an old joke. He said, "You can't. Not today."

I was so pleased to hear his laughter that I sat up straight and looked him in the eye.

He reached up and fastened my tie, neither one of us speaking. When he was done we sat next to each other, watching the light dance across the floor as if this were any ordinary day.

"I want to stay in here," I told him. "I can't go and bury my father, Diba. Who buries both their parents in one year? Well actually, everyone these days."

He shook his head. "No, everyone's burying their children these days."

I remembered Sizwe's swollen nodes, the wheezing, his hands too heavy to swat a fly landed on his nose. I saw his mother and the handbag of flowing tissues; red lipstick bloodying the soft white paper.

"That's true. Many more to come, I think." The images now came tumbling like dominoes. They were of people I had seen just that week. Base. The children of neighbours. Older women, despondent. Young girls, pretty and smartly dressed, sitting cross-legged on the dusty ground because their bodies were too heavy to stand. The symptoms I recognized before even they did. There had been a wave of young people coming in that week, saying things like, "I didn't come before because I thought it would go away."

We were heading into the pit of death and I needed someone to hold my hand.

Sediba was looking curiously at the bags I had come home with. They were stacked against one another just below the window because I couldn't be bothered to walk across the passage to the spare room and tuck them into the wardrobe. Now he turned his whole body to face me and asked, "Are you staying?"

"I . . . I have to. It was always my father's plan, as you know. Even if my father isn't here. Or especially now that he's not here." But then I wanted to be talking about something else, so I put my hand on his and told him, "But apart from that, I want to."

He looked at me more closely, eyes filled with longing and grief, his hand not shifting away. He said, "Everyone will be there today. I will be there all day."

I dropped the weight of my body back onto the bed. Slowly, hesitantly, Sediba came down to lie beside me. I didn't move, only because I was afraid it might end too quickly.

"Thank you for calling me about my father," I said. "I waited for you. I waited for you all week. I thought we could talk."

He replied, "Just talk?"

I didn't answer.

"Is there such a thing, with us?"

We lay side by side, his forehead on my right temple, his arm across my middle, his breath coming and going gently across my face.

He said, "After this, after today, I have to tell you something."

I nodded, wishing we could both just fall asleep right there.

Aus' Tselane came back as they were carrying the coffin out. She stood lurking in the background, head covered in black cloth and her face veiled in black lace. Anyone who saw her knew that she was hoping to go unnoticed. I kept trying at least to have our eyes meet, but she was dodging me, possibly having guessed that I was now in the know. I hadn't had the courage to step into what used to be my parents' bedroom; the door was shut the way she had left it and I hadn't had the will to open it and go back to confront more of my father through his things.

It was possibly the largest funeral I had been to in the township, even bigger than my mother's with all the society women who had come. Because my father's care had covered such a large area at a time when there was a great shortage of doctors, many had come from very far to pay their last respects to a man they had not only trusted but also quite loved.

My father's coffin was carried into the church by his friends, mostly men who had worked in their own shops on the same street. Out of the church the pallbearers were my friends. Sediba was in the front with Lelo, and Trunka and Base were behind with two other childhood friends I had not been particularly close to but who had cared enough to stand when the priest asked for pallbearers to come forward. At the end of the church service I had moved forward to help but was gently told by Sediba's mother—hand on my back—that it was against custom to carry your own father's body after death.

I spent the day biting down tears, trying to appear stoic but not removed. Each person's words blurred into another person's song. Speeches turned into biblical parables growing into hymns spoken instead of sung. I think it rained but I couldn't say with certainty. Old women introduced themselves as distant relatives, following the Setswana tradition—or is it only a regional habit?—of explaining what my father called them and what I was meant to call them: "When your father looked at me, he said: young aunt. When you look at me you say: great aunt," and so on. I forced smiles and shook hands both damp and calloused, bodies coming and going around me, men patting my weary back and women with dry lips coming to kiss and caress my cheeks. I smelled alcohol on sympathetic breaths and snuff on noses coming close to kiss my cheeks. Through it all I bit my lip and coughed away the lump in my throat but when the coffin was lowered and I was asked to throw down my handful of dirt, I froze and looked up at Sediba, who stood next to his mother, their arms locking. I froze, wanting him to tell me what to do.

He took a step forward but his mother stopped him with a hand on his shoulder and signaled to his father, who came around instead and with a hand on my elbow, gently nudged me forward.

"Come son," he said. "It's time."

With a trembling hand I threw my fistful of dirt on the coffin. I think when I closed my eyes he thought I was about to faint, so he gripped my elbow suddenly, giving me a start.

In a line my friends came forward, each pouring down their handful of dirt, afterwards brushing off their hands back and forth as if washing off a sordid act.

They all moved to give me hugs but Sediba, when his turn came, gave me a quick pat on the back—a gesture that almost made me laugh, it was so ridiculous.

Afterwards we all went back to the house, washed our hands out of the large bowls that had been arranged along the gate by women and men who had stayed behind to prepare the house and the food for the mourners.

Walking back into the house after the funeral I was struck again by the emptiness of it, the enormity of the loss of my parents. Why was it, I wondered, that the week before the funeral always gave the illusion of the person still being in the world? It is always after the burial that you really start to feel that they are never coming back.

After lunch, when the mourners had left, my friends and I gathered at Trunka's house for the *wie-sien-ons*. I probably have never had that much to drink before or since, and that is saying something, considering my nights at Rodney's parties.

The *wie-sien-ons* is meant to be a proper party. You're meant to sit down and tell good, funny stories about the person who has just passed on. You're meant to take off your jackets and ties, sit in a circle and drink, reminiscing on the good times. I thought about how it might look to people that their doctor was sloshed out of his mind one day and back feeling their pulses the next, but even I could see that this was practiced paranoia. No one cared a lick what I did with myself the day I had just buried my father.

I spoke of my father giving me a hiding when I was a little boy for stealing mangoes next door. Someone had a story about getting an injection from him for the first time. He had lollies for us when we were small that helped our throats feel better. It was soothing—and so were the drinks, donated by Trunka and his family. Then things took a turn. Lelo was telling a story which was funny and we laughed at first, but then it got uncomfortable. It was about the way my father deferred to my mother on everything, and Base was saying something about how he wouldn't do that with his wife when he got married. But then Lelo was drunk and a drunk Lelo is always a ticking time bomb. He opens his mouth and people scatter because their secrets have just come out and are now lying scattered in the middle of the circle for all to watch and prod.

"But that's old stuff," he was saying after an incoherent sentence. "Aus' Tselane might know a little more."

"*Jo*, shut up!" Trunka yelled at him.

"Do you want to leave?" Sediba mouthed the words to me from where he was sitting, across the circle. I nodded and started to stand, but Lelo held me down.

"Eish . . . *askies*, *Jo*. *Askies* man. *Eish*. We all have our secrets . . . don't go."

I panicked. The bottle of beer in my hand was still half full so I brought it up to my mouth and gulped without stopping, emptying the contents before sitting down under the persistent force of Lelo's hand.

All around me I felt their eyes bore through me. I saw them all seeing the things I'd hidden, not my father's secrets. I saw my home— my flat in Durban—blown wide open and all eyes looking into my life. I stood up again and this time Sediba, throwing caution to the dogs, caught my arm and said, "I'll take him home. I'm not drunk."

I started to push him off, my mind saying, "No! They'll see!" But my body gave in and I let him take me to his car.

Once settled in the passenger seat I said, "You know you might have just told on us."

He said, "It's not school. Adults don't talk about telling on each other."

I forced a bitter chuckle.

I slept in a t-shirt and my pants were nicely folded on the chair. When I woke up I couldn't remember when Sediba had left. I remembered him pulling of my shoes and pants and vaguely remembered him stroking my forehead gently, but I must have faded really quickly because that was all I could recall.

At work I fumbled my way through the day, drinking water and feeling terribly ashamed of being at my father's work like this—barely competent.

I had been at the surgery only about an hour, grateful that it appeared not to be the busiest day. My head was throbbing from a nasty hangover and I was counting the hours until I could go back to sleep. Then Thuli came in. I didn't know Thuli very well because her family was one of the ones that had moved to our location after I had gone to varsity. She was studying engineering at the technikon and had been friends with Sediba for years, so I had heard about her from time to time. I had not been formally introduced to her though, but I knew her face very well. She is one of those people who are so ridiculously pretty that they're hard to miss.

So when she walked into the surgery I recognized her instantly. She wore a navy blue dress with a white belt and her hair was held back in a small ponytail. She has big, beautiful round eyes, long black eyelashes, and round full lips that rarely stretch into a smile.

I stood up when she walked in and shook her hand to greet her. She looked me right in the eye, one hand on her belly and said, "Your father was my doctor."

I nodded and showed her to the examining table.

I really didn't have much of an exchange with her beyond the necessary: How was she feeling? When was she due? The doctor-patient standard back-and-forth.

So I didn't think much of her saying, "So Sediba says you're back to stay."

I said, "Yes," but that was all. I thought she and Sediba must have been closer than I had realized. Still, there was something *knowing*, about the way she had looked at me. It was as if she had been told something or had simply worked out that I was gay. Her gaze was personal—familiar in a way that I couldn't easily explain.

I decided to walk to Sediba's house after work, remembering that he had said, before my father's funeral, that we needed to talk. I had held on to that moment, that brief moment in my bedroom when we had sat next to each other and life had seemed peaceful for a short while. But I was unprepared for what he was about to tell me.

Arriving at his house I saw that he was not home yet. It was easy to remember why I had loved his backyard so much the first time I had been there: the flowers lined against the shrubs that made up the fence, the two large trees standing at each end of the yard, and the beautiful, nicely cut grass. It was peaceful—as calming as it had been on my first visit there.

My back against the wide trunk of the larger tree, I took off my shoes and closed my eyes.

Then I was back at the hospital, holding Sizwe's hand listening to his wheezing. I knew he had very little time left and that I had to let go, but then he was sitting up and saying, "Every day, every day you say I love you."

"To whom?"

"To me. Say I love you to me."

"But I don't—"

I was shaking my head and he reached out and put his hand on my shoulder and started shaking it.

"Kabz? Kabz?" I was wondering why he was now starting to call me by my first name when I woke up and it was Sediba crouching next to me, calling my name. I ran my hand over my face. It was getting darker now, the sun setting. My eyes adjusted and I was staring at him, not saying anything.

He looked concerned and picked my bag off the ground. "Bad dream?" He offered me his hand.

I stood up and followed him into the house. "Yah. Bad dream," I mumbled. There was that wave of sadness. I rubbed my eyes and straightened up as if shaking it off.

"Come in and sit," Sediba said.

His house looked very much the same except it seemed freshly painted. I pulled up the first chair at the table and sat, leaning against the wall. He stood with his back against the fridge and looked out through the window across the room.

"Do you have a lot of bad dreams?" he said without looking at me.

"Since my mother died and . . . Yah, I do."

"You dream of your mother?"

I nodded. "And my patients. And you."

He walked over to the cabinet and took out a glass, filled it with water and came to hand it to me. I took a sip before putting it down, fearing that something was wrong, sensing that he was more distant than he had been the morning of my father's funeral.

He said, "You saw Thuli today."

It was odd, the way he said it, like it was so important when I myself had thought nothing of it, and it sent me into a dizzying panic and I closed my eyes.

"She's really nice," I said but Sediba didn't say anything back.

I sat up and asked, "Why do you ask?"

The room was darker now and he walked over to the wall near the fridge to switch the light on. He said, his voice heavy and dragging, like he was being forced to perform an act that went against his nature, "I'm marrying her."

My stomach turned and I was about to vomit all the beer I had had the night before. I leaned forward, started to stand up but decided against it.

"What do you mean?"

I was aware of my voice rising, my body feeling cold. My legs were trembling and I pressed down on my knees with the heels of my palms.

Sediba remained calm. He looked at me with maddening patience, as if I were just learning a language he had long ago mastered, but he was willing to help me along.

"I can't let her down now. I've already agreed to it."

"You've been sleeping with . . . a woman? Jeez, Sediba, I know it was a terrible break up, but what the hell? You've been sleeping with Thuli?"

"No! Of course not. It's just, Tshepo died and she's been miserable, not wanting to face raising the baby alone. I said I would help."

"No one thinks it's your baby though, do they?"

I noted that I had not heard anyone mention it.

He folded his arms, his chest rising.

"No one expects you to marry her!" I said and went to stand in front of him.

He blinked when he saw me come. I could see him getting ready for a defense but his heart was not in it, his voice was tired. He said, "Look, you know I've always wanted a marriage and a family—"

"Like this? This is like Lelo."

"Don't say that Kabz. Don't say that. It's not like Lelo. It's more—"

"More what? It's not more fucking honest, that's for sure."

"I wanted you. I wanted to marry you and you didn't want me. You have no leg to stand on, telling me what's honest."

I put both my hands on his arms and took a deep breath.

"I did—I *do* want you. I always have."

He turned his head to the side and moved out of my embrace and out of my reach. I followed him to the fridge, where he resumed his previous, distant pose.

"Look," he said, his voice calmer now. "It's an arrangement. It's not some love story. The man she loves is dead."

"And the man you love is not," I said. I felt bolder now. I had swum deep in the depths of loneliness and fear all my life and I had come up having learnt a new language.

He looked me up and down, shaking his head like he was seeing me for the first time since I had walked into his house. I saw his shoulders slump, his body being held up by the fridge he was leaning against.

"Diba," I whispered to him, reaching for his hand.

He kept shaking his head. "We couldn't anyway. You were right. We couldn't be together here, with everyone." His arm swept the air. His voice cracked.

I stepped closer to him. "I think we can," I told him and surprised us both. "I think you're the one who was right."

"We can't . . . not here. What do you think those guys will say? Trunka? Lelo? Can you see them looking at us as a couple? Taking us seriously? Come on, *Jo*. The things you said to me in Cape Town about living in a different world from Scott . . . it's true."

"This is what I was saying in Durban when you told me to fuck off and stormed off!" I reminded him bitterly, but he only shook his head. "That was something else. You can't bring that life here," he said stabbing the air with his finger. "You can't. Not here. Believe me,

I've lived here longer, I hear what the guys say. You wouldn't want to hear it."

"You know what's fucked up? I was always the one who was more afraid. I was always saying: Not here. Don't hold my hand here, people will know. Let's not do this, we'll be found out. Then just before you left you said something about it not being a *game*, and that really stayed with me." I paused to collect myself. "The thing is, I really did make a mess of things. I know I did. But I always assumed you were the brave one. I mean, I have never ever been brave. When we were growing up I was the one surrounded by girls, while you, you were not trying so hard. I was a mess in Cape Town, always hiding . . . doing things in the dark, running from my friends. I was miserable."

He looked at me and I could see that he was remembering Scott's wedding, my meeting Rod again.

"Then Durban was a different kind of misery, but you came and it was . . . it was the most . . . *peaceful* time of my life."

Sediba closed his eyes.

"Then you left . . . and I was alone again and I was so sorry—so sorry that I had thrown you out just so that my life could remain a secret because I didn't want anyone else looking at me the way my mother did, saying, '*Sies*' when they found out I was gay. Then I met this boy. This sixteen-year-old boy who told me about how he had loved someone and loved her until the end. I don't want to be that guy who comes home to no one and then goes out to clubs and parties looking to find something."

We stared at each other, nothing moving. I pressed my hands against the countertop and refocused. "But here I am now and I'm saying fuck it *Jo*, let's do this. Let's be together. Now you are the one who is afraid. Because your old comrades are here and you don't want them losing respect for you."

I knew that that part about "your comrades" would hurt and I was not sure how sorry I was to have said it.

He went to sit down.

"Say something," I begged. His drew in his shoulders as though he was cold and stared at the floor. There was no noise except the occasional car and a barking dog.

Finally he said, "I promised."

"She can't expect you to marry her, she knows about me. That's what was a little odd about seeing her. I thought she knew something. She knows about me."

He stood up and came to me, his eyes uncharacteristically shifty. He said, "Of course she knows. But——"

"Then she won't marry you, now that I'm back. She won't, will she?"

"I promised her. She's like a sister to me."

"Listen to yourself, Diba. Listen to yourself."

He looked down at his palms and then brought them up to cover his face. I waited for him to speak, to give me something to hold on to. He stared down at his feet before his eyes came back up to me:

"You come and go. You want me and then you don't. You want to come to the township but then you don't plan for it. I waited and waited and then one day you were saying we couldn't. Now——"

"Now I'm here."

He turned sharply on his heel and went to open the door. "I need to think," he told me.

"About what?"

"I don't just go back on my word and break promises. I said I'd marry her and now I need . . . I need to think."

"I'm leaving!" I said, sounding overly dramatic. I picked up my back, slung it over my shoulder and stormed out.

Behind me I heard him say: "Wait . . . "

I paused, then marched back in. He was sitting at his table, wiping his eyes.

"Do what you want," I said. "It's up to you. But I won't be here to watch."

"What does that mean?"

"It means I will leave. Sell the surgery and go somewhere else. I won't stay here and watch you live that life."

I wanted to go to him and hold him, but I turned my back and marched off.

I passed the next few days on the fuel of my rage. You can get a lot accomplished while running on anger. It is easier and not as debilitating as sadness. I hated my mother for her suicide. I hated my father for betraying my mother and I really hated Sediba for leaving me now, when I thought we finally could be together. So I refused to speak to him. He phoned and left me messages.

And yet every night when I returned home I needed to speak to him. There was not a part of me that didn't ache for his warmth, his comfort. The house felt empty and Aus' Tselane still had not come back.

If it had been at all possible—if I had had no memories of growing up in the place and didn't see the clean white walls behind the softer, cream ones, or if I didn't still expect to see neat rows of white roses every time I stepped out of the house instead of the tall overgrown flowers I couldn't name—I might have seriously considered staying in my childhood home. It was large and beautiful and only a short walk to and from work.

It would have made sense for another man to stay, not me. Neither the township nor the house was for me. The place was spitting me out every day, in spite of my desire to stay and serve the people and make it work. It seemed I had to pack up and find a new home.

At the surgery I found that my patients' illnesses were getting less and less varied. After the first wave of the older people coming to pay their respects, there was an influx of younger patients. I think that the older people had liked coming to have a chat with my father and their visits were really only visits in the traditional sense. Every now and then a grandmother or grandfather would come in and say, "Kabelo, give me something for my knees, *tu!*" "Your father used to give me this pill that was red and round. Give me that one." And I would have to look through their file to see what medicine they were on. They would stay and chat about the weather, about how schools were getting smaller because children were sick and not attending. They would point in the direction of a house I was meant to remember from child-hood, that used to be the home of someone I was supposed to have played with, and they would say: "Remember Tshepo (or Thuso or Phenyo)? Mmm. Him too."

But mainly I was seeing younger patients. Neo, my father's sec-retary and now mine, told me that the surgery had hardly ever been that full in my father's last few years, confirming what I had begun to suspect: I was running a very different practice from the one my father had run. I was grateful to be busy, on the one hand, on the other hand it was desperately sad to watch my old township slowly become something like a ghost town. I realized that in a few years most of the people I had grown up with would not be around anymore.

The illness was coming quickly and it was coming for my friends.

When Base came in I admit that I was unprepared. We didn't make appointments for people, which had also been my father's policy. When cell phones became popular, I remember my mother saying that he should now tell people to make appointments so that he ran what she called "a proper business," but he refused. He said it would always be his policy that whoever got up in the morning needing to see a doctor should see the doctor before the sun went down. It was challenging, but there were trees all around the yard and I had gone out and bought extra chairs so that people could sit in the shade while they waited. I asked Neo to have a jug of water ready every day. I paid a local boy who sold water in the squatter camps to sell me several litres a day, and paid two teenagers to come and pour water for waiting patients. I couldn't help how long the lines were. A few times I even worked on Sundays.

There was a long-standing camaraderie and strong cooperation between the township doctors that I quite appreciated. Although there were not many who were young—most people my age had opted for hospital or city jobs. But still, I could send my patients to other people and they did the same.

When Base decided to seek help from me, I had not seen my friends much because of the work. He came in looking frail, using a walking stick. His eyes were yellow, his skin ashen. Neo had asked him to come straight in while I was away on call, and on returning I picked up his near-empty file. My heart raced when I saw it, but I composed myself before walking in, all cheerful, like I had no idea what might be wrong with him. But Base was not fooled.: "You know, *Jo*, I saw you look at me that day when you came back. I know you know."

He was sitting in the leather armchair in the corner instead of the exam table. I suspected that was because he couldn't climb onto it.

I sat down and clasped my hands. I could see he was looking for a friend and not a doctor and this was very new for me. It was clearer now, at this moment, that Durban would have been much easier. I didn't have dying childhood friends there.

"*Eish, Jo . . .* " I started and stumbled.

Base held up his hand. "*O sa wara, Jo.* That's life."

"Did you see my father?"

He coughed. "Yoh! No man. The old man would have been good to me, but you know how it is. He was like a father to us. We get this thing from being bad. You can't go and tell your father you got stung being bad."

At least he was acknowledging that he knew what he had. HIV/ AIDS was never spoken of outright around here. Pronouncing the words was like speaking ill of the dead: it was not done. People came up with imagined causes of death: cancer, high blood, stroke. Never the right thing. It carried too much shame.

I nodded and sat up straight, looking out the window, fully aware that it was unprofessional to *want* to cry about a patient's illness, but this was not just a patient. This was a boy I had played marbles and top with. This was a guy who had swum in his underwear in my swimming pool and pulled a thorn out of my heel when I had stepped barefoot in a side bush.

"We all have it," he said, sweeping the air with his arm. "You'll see."

I wept when he left. I sat at my chair while patients waited outside for their doctor and wept into my sleeve before rolling it back up and going out to see more of them.

That afternoon I decided that I wanted to go to Morula City—which people called Central because of its proximity to the central point for taxis coming and going from different townships. Neo said we needed some things—toilet paper and hand soap—and I told her that I would go instead because there were fewer patients and I could see them before going out for lunch. She was confused and surprised because I never did go out for lunch. But that day I decided that I would do so because I needed desperately to get a glimpse of Sediba.

Central is on a road that connects two townships and across the street from the African Sun Hotel, a hotel and casino that attracts a large number of tourists to the location. People joke that the hotel is the only place to see white people in the township. There is another road, one that runs perpendicular to the township connector road. It had been built very much in the same way that roads were built under apartheid: skillfully, with brilliant engineering and, most importantly, to separate one place from another, one kind of people from another. If you were driving from town and you were looking for the African Sun Hotel, you would not have to see the realities of the location. You could drive straight down, passing undeveloped land that is green and lush in the summer so that it feels like you are passing the beautiful countryside, and then go right into the luxury of the hotel and resort with its sprawling golf course and casino that sits near a man-made lake.

I drove from the surgery to Central and parked my car in the large and clean parking lot, where women and men in overalls swept away empty cigarette packets and picked up soft-drink cans and offered to watch or wash your car for a few rand. I checked myself in the mirror before walking through to Chilly's, the café and food shop that stood across the courtyard from Sediba's salon.

Chilly is a man about ten years older than I am. His place used to be one of the location's most beloved tuck shops, a small spaza that he ran out of his house. He sold the best atchaar and Morning Meal, a special township dish with atchaar, *boere worst* and beans. It moved to a tin house, which he built behind his main house until he was making enough money to build a brick garage and put up a big sign with a red chilly as the apostrophe in Chilly's. It was sometime during my second year a UCT, I think, that my mother told me that he had moved on to the mall and was now a medium-sized restaurant with tables and chairs for patrons. He was a large man with no hair on his head and a finely tapered beard, which he got shaped every week at Sediba's salon. I had a great fondness for Bra Chilly, the man with a warm grin that missed a right canine, and a belly that jiggled up and down when he laughed.

Making my way through the sea of shoppers, I ducked into the food courtyard where there was less commotion. My heart raced at the sight of the large red and white sign that read SEDIBA'S SALON AND BARBER. Sediba's mother had named her hairdressing business after her only child and now he was her partner. I wasn't sure if I'd be able to get a glimpse of him, but didn't want to be seen peeking, so I darted across to Chilly's and stood in line to order my food. Still, I knew how things went: someone would spot me and news would spread around the mall: "There's Kabelo Mosala."

"Dr Mosala?"

"*Yah.* Still unmarried?"

"Still unmarried."

Sediba would know I was around before I saw him.

Bra Chilly spotted me from the back of the shop where he was giving orders. He raised his hand, signaling me to come around to the back. I nodded and went past the line towards him. An older woman yelled: "*Haai, wena!* We were here first."

Bra Chilly retorted, "*Heh, Mma!* This is doctor Mosala. He's the man taking care of your cousin over there while you stand here. Let's help him get back to work."

I heard the woman suck her teeth and mumble some profanity that I chose not to hear. I was embarrassed by Bra Chilly's special treatment but also a little pleased to feel so at home here. He shook my hand as always, asked how I was doing without my parents, and said how much he missed both of them, how my mother loved for him to bring her a special dish of Morning Meal every Friday.

"Every Friday, I ran over. I brought it over myself. Just me. I never sent anyone else." I nodded with a big smile. I had known my mother's love for spicy food very well. He worked as he spoke, preparing my morning meal and *pap*, remembering what I used to order. I was in the mood for bread but was so touched at entering a place where they believed they knew what I liked to eat that I didn't dare correct him.

I paid him a little extra before walking out into the sun, going to the Pick 'n Pay for the surgery supplies. Coming out of Pick 'n Pay I walked towards the salon. At the door I saw his mother walking a customer out—a woman about her age. I knew that it would be terribly rude of me to wave and not go over, so I crossed the courtyard and headed towards her. As I approached her I saw that Sediba was inside, shaving a young guy's head. I smiled politely at his mother, feeling genuinely happy to see her. She exclaimed, "*Ao, bathong*! Kabi!" and put her arms around me. Returning her embrace, I looked over at Sediba holding his clippers midair, looking at me with surprise.

My eyes turned now to his mother who held my hand and asked, "How are you, really, my child?" She was truly the bearer of her name. Everything about her was gentle and calm. She didn't let go of my hand from the moment we started talking to the moment that I told her I had to run.

"I must get back to work, I'm sure they're waiting," I told her as I started to go.

"Yes, yes! I heard you're so busy. I'm happy you're back, my child. Truly. We need you here."

She gave no sign of knowing about Sediba and me except for a brief glance at Sediba to see his reaction when I waved to him.

I said, "*Heita!*" like I was speaking to a casual acquaintance, before running off.

In my car I put my head on my steering wheel for a minute to compose myself before starting. I had wanted to go and ask how he was. I had liked seeing him at work—as I had never done before. The place was beautiful, I wanted to say. It had him written all over it: clean, white walls, long and large black mirrors. I had only ever heard about it from him.

I missed him more in that minute in the car than I had ever thought was possible.

But I had to go. I was going to have to learn to live without him because he was getting married and it was not to me. I would have to learn, at some point, not to create opportunities to get a glimpse of him.

At the end of that day I told Neo not to wait for me, that I would lock the doors after she left. I sat at my desk going over the day: it had been painful to see Base. He said that he had ignored "it," meaning the symptoms he had seen. "A girl I was seeing phoned to tell me she had had it two years ago. Said I should get tested. I had had sex with her so many times that I didn't even think it was possible that I would not have it. You know how we are, *Jo*. Skin to skin. I got this fever even before she died. I knew what was happening but I kept saying: Not me. I'll beat this. I'll be the one to beat it.'"

Then, he said, he couldn't bring himself to accept that he was dying.

"And then that day when you came back I saw you see me. I saw you see it. After that I've just been thinking it was time I spoke to you. Anyway . . . "

He'd been exhausted by the effort that the day had required: getting up and dressed, walking over to the surgery and speaking to me. In Durban when people had AIDS I couldn't picture who they had been before I met them. Now I saw the younger, more robust and athletic Base kicking a ball with the force of a bull. I saw us running behind a house and hearing his thunderous voice count to ten before coming to find us. I barely recognized the rapidly aging, fading man in my office.

I sat thinking about going to find Sediba and regretted that I had not gone over to say a proper hello. It was childish and I knew it would irritate him, but it had been awkward to do anything more than give a passing greeting because I felt his mother watching me and I wondered if anyone else in the salon knew about us. I had been silly, and it was just the kind of behaviour that he detested. Still, I was a little bit

pleased at the thought of him possibly being angry with me. I wanted
to make him feel something that would maybe lead to an exchange
between us. He seemed to have given up sending me phone messages.

I was sitting there mulling over this, when the door to my office
swung open.

Sediba stood against the doorframe with a confused look on his
face.

"So we're really not speaking now? You come by my work and you
can't even speak to me?"

I feigned nonchalance and reclined in my chair.

"I just went to get some food, I didn't have time to stop by and
chat."

He was about to say something but then his expression changed as
he decided against it. He shut his eyes and sighed.

I said, "Do you want to sit down? You look tired."

He smiled. "Come with me. I left my car at work. We can walk."

I felt that familiar jolt of pleasure but I pretended to be confused
instead.

"You walked all the way from the salon?"

"No. I got a lift. Come with me." He had his arm stretched out
towards me like he was waiting for me to take his hand, only I was too
far across the room.

"Where are we going?"

"Let's have a beer at my house. We'll sit in the backyard and talk,
because we really should, and I promise not to try anything."

I laughed at the personal joke. "OK," I said. The thought of being
in his backyard was like the thought of guava ice block in the heat of
December. I would have done anything for it. I stood up and walked
towards the door, peeling my coat off. "Come in a little, I have to hang
this behind the door," I told him. I could smell the triple X mints on
his breath as he came closer and I hung my coat behind the door and
picked up my bag. I chewed on my lower lip as I put the stethoscope in
the bag, trying to stop myself from pulling him to me. He stood really
close, so that I had the idea he knew what he was doing. He knew the

effect he still had on me.

It made me wonder if he had seen me and panicked, thinking that the quick wave I had given him that afternoon would from now on be the extent of our exchanges. I moved quickly across the door and he followed me through the surgery, going out into the fading afternoon light. We had never walked together before—not in the township. We had never been seen together, since we used to come find each other in our backyards, in the dark.

I stopped to lock the doors. We had three keys for three locks. I said something inane like, "You have to be so careful with the medicines in there." We locked it behind us. I think we both realized what was happening because we stood, hands in our pockets, staring at each other like teammates about to go out on the field for the final, crucial minutes of a big game. We laughed at each other's expressions.

"You could have driven," I said.

He nodded. "But I think we should do this."

It was a sentence with layers of meaning and I think we were both slightly terrified at what it meant. His house was not far—only about five minutes—but now it suddenly felt like we were about to trek all the way across the world.

To get to Sediba's house you had to turn left from the surgery and go from the fifty fours down towards the lower forties and into the higher thirties. The way there was also a straight line. But if we did that we would walk past Lelo's house, where he was sure to be standing outside watering his garden or chatting to a neighbour.

"Which way?" Sediba asked. I pointed towards the other road, circuitous to be sure, but he nodded right away. We started walking.

We went onto the newly paved road, occasionally stepping onto the dusty sides to avoid a car. I remembered that first evening in Durban when he had come to fetch me for our first date; how nervous and excited I had been and how quickly we had gone into conversation about home.

I said, "Your salon looks nice," and he smiled back at me. "Thanks *Jo*. I like how it turned out."

He looked my way now, hands still in his pockets, and asked, "How have you been?"

"It's been a hard day," I said. "I suspect I'll have many more of those."

"Base told me he was coming to see you."

It was tricky, working in a place where you knew everyone personally. My father had managed merely through having a quiet demeanour. He didn't have a lot of friends so I think speaking of his patients was never a problem. I had wondered what I would say about Base to Sediba and thought it best to be quiet, but now that he had brought it up, it seemed easier to just talk about it.

I said, "*Eish, Jo*," and shook my head.

"I know. I think we've all pretended it wasn't happening until now. He's been saying he's going to see you since you came back, so finally today he came."

"It's a lot of people. It's going to be a long road."

"People can't admit it and when they do, it's too late," he said. We were standing at the main road now, waiting at the stop sign. You had to be careful at township stop crossings because most drivers took a stop sign as a mere suggestion and not a hard and fast rule. It was also rush hour for taxis. When we finally crossed, we were on a dusty road, in Block A. The houses here were of less affluent families than the ones on Block B. Many immigrant workers lived here in rows of rented tin houses. I vaguely remembered Aus' Tselane leaving our house to come and live here with people who were from the same village as hers, but that had been so long ago that it was a passing memory.

"Even if people acknowledged it, at this time the medicine is not readily available. It's not affordable."

He nodded, listening attentively the way he always could.

"You asked me once why I was not angry about us—about the things we couldn't do. I think I'm always feeling furious about things having to do with my work, about this. People dying here when there are places in the world where medicine is more affordable. I reserve my anger for that, I suppose."

"But that doesn't mean you're not angry about the things we can't do." He was looking up, at the cloudless sky.

"No. It doesn't. It's just that I think I can do something about people being sick. But I can't do much about people hating who I am, making jokes about it, casting me out."

"But last time you were saying . . . it was like you decided you could do something."

I thought back to the last time I had been in his house.

"Isn't that what you were saying?"

A woman with a load of brooms balanced on her head walked past us, her toes poking holes through her shoes. We turned left towards a large and ornately decorated building, the location's only Catholic Church. We passed a wall with a crucifix. Jesus was the colour of dry desert sand, below the large silver bell.

"I was saying let's try. I wasn't saying people will accept it."

He looked at me and then ahead at the road, like he was separating one thing from the other, trying to understand me.

I said, "But you were saying 'no', so . . . "

"You know, Kabz. It's just not the kind of thing you can do alone around here. I mean, when we were in Durban, I wanted you to come back and I wanted to think we could do it. Together, maybe. But alone, once I came back here and I knew you were staying in Durban, I just couldn't."

We crossed the main road again and Mma Mathibe was standing at her gate. I've always had the idea that if anyone saw me next to Sediba they would immediately know that I loved him. It sent me into a panic several times when we walked together in Durban, because I thought we might be attacked, but we had been lucky. Now I looked at Mma Mathibe and imagined that I saw us through her eyes.

She waved us over and we walked to her. She said: "Kabi, my child. My back is killing me. Why don't you come in tomorrow after work and take a look?"

I nodded and said that I would.

"I finished my medicine—the one your father had given me. I'm finished. Come with some of it, please? It used to help me a lot. Now you see how I'm standing?"

She was leaning against her gate and I could see that her weight was fully on it. She looked at Sediba and said, "*Ao*, Diba but you are so handsome! I never see you. My granddaughter is always saying: I'm going to Sediba, I'm going to Sediba. I hear you are so busy!"

Sediba smiled and said, "I am."

"And, *mara* you are helping your mother. You know, you are a good boy. Truly. Children who help their parents, neh? You really are good boys. I wish your father were here to see you, Kabi" She took out a handkerchief and dabbed the corners of her eyes.

We were nodding and saying: "Yes, Mma," until she turned and started walking towards her house, her hands on her lower back.

"Let me go and check on the rice, my children. It shouldn't burn."

Further down two young girls still wearing their school uniform greeted Sediba with broad grins. "Sedibaaaa," they sang.

We crossed another street and we were closer to his house, when someone called him from behind. It was a young woman I had never seen before. She had her dreadlocks in a neat bun on her head and was waving wildly at us.

"Sediba! Sediba! Thank you so much!"

"How did it go?" he called back at her.

She held up two thumbs and he smiled and waved back.

"How did what go?" I asked.

"She had a job interview and came to fix her locks. She was nervous about her hair looking professional."

We walked into his house and I put my bag down on the first chair at the table. He went to take two beers out of the fridge, but as soon as he handed me one his phone rang. He went to answer it.

I took my shoes off and rolled up my pants, then stepped out onto the backyard. The grass was soft against my feet, the beer cold in my hand. I looked up at the swaying branches, leaves rustling in the cooling breeze. This house felt like a home to me. Every time I had been here I had wanted to stay.

I walked back and forth between the trees, savouring the feeling of the soft grass on my bare soles. I sensed that Sediba was standing at the window, watching me, resisting coming out.

It was hard to get used to the idea of leaving here, going back to the strange and empty house up on the hill. It was harder still to get used to being with Sediba and not be close to him, walk into his bedroom like it was mine.

I think we were both dreading the end of our time together. The walk had felt easy, comfortable and even somewhat sensuous. The proximity of our bodies, going back to speaking the way we always had, and resisting the temptation to touch was like another time. But now I went in because it was getting darker, and he was not coming outside, and I couldn't put it off any longer.

He was standing at the kitchen sink when I walked back in, his hands in his pockets. I stood near the door, thinking I'd put on my shoes but not quite able to. Then suddenly I started to tell him about Sizwe. I had been meaning to do this for so long that when I started, the words came flowing out of me. I wanted desperately for him to know where I had been while we were apart. He listened, nodding, understanding.

"Something about the way he looked at me," I told him. "Just something about him. Like he knew about me and he was fine with it."

"Are you fine with it?" Sediba asked.

"What do you mean?"

"Who you are, who you want to be with. Are you fine with it now?"

I didn't speak.

I left my shoes at the door and came up to him. "I'm fine with it."

"Because your parents aren't here."

"Because I want more than this. I want more than hiding and lying and going home alone staring at the walls. I want you."

"I still want—"

"I know, Diba. I know. A life. A house, a child. Marriage. I know."

He shut his eyes. "Kabza . . . I miss you. I miss us, Durban. I miss you. Every day."

I stepped forward, slipped my hands under his t-shirt and put both my palms on his stomach, feeling his rigid muscles.

He took my face in his hands and I tasted sweets on his warm breath.

It was like finally coming home. A slow kind of lovemaking, reminiscent of our lazy, easy, blissful Durban days. My body made sense again. All of me made sense again.

I now understand this about loving and being loved: it's the making sense that's the point. It's not the weak knees and the times you can't get someone off your mind. It's when the life you live makes sense, feels whole, that's the point.

In the night, in his bedroom, I felt at first like I had swum to shore and then later, when he was asleep, terrified that this might be the last time. His breathing had fallen into a slow and steady rhythm but my body would not settle down. I sat up and swung both my feet onto the floor and faced the open windows. There was a street light just outside that was so bright that it faded the night and made the place feel like it was still engulfed in daylight. These lights were all over the township, meant to deter thieves and robbers. I thought about how sometimes the township makes every man feel like a criminal.

I stood, gathered my things and started to leave. I reckoned that since Sediba had always been a deep sleeper he wouldn't notice me walking out, but I was wrong.

As I slowly pulled the door open he said, "Are you leaving?"

Startled, I turned back went to sit on the bed beside him.

"I didn't want to wake you. I have to go home so I can have fresh clothes tomorrow."

Sediba sat up and pressed his fingers against his eyelids.

"You should stay. You can borrow my clothes tomorrow."

"Someone will see me walking out . . . "

He kissed my bare shoulder and then leaned his cheek against it.

"If we're to do this, you can't walk out in the middle of the night like we're teenagers sneaking in and out of each other's houses. If we're to do this, you'll have to stay."

"And Thuli?"

He let out a faint and tired laugh. "Look at me. Look at me begging you to stay like . . . well, like a young man in love, really. You think I'm going to be able to wake up next to anyone else in the future?"

I kissed his clean-shaven head.

He moved over and made room for me.

I slipped back in, excited and afraid. Morning would come and I would have to walk out with him, with all his neighbours there.

It's hard to say that I slept at all with the usual township night sounds keeping me up. Sediba, for his part, held on to me through his sleep, pulling me closer every time I started to move. All night long I thought about how we could do it and by the time the cock crowed I had decided one thing: I would work here but I would not live here.

We went about with our familiar routine the next morning, me borrowing his clothes, Sediba making me tea and being his old attentive self, sliding his hand up and down my back, kissing my neck.

In the midst of getting ready he stopped and looked at me, his eyes dancing with relief:

"I really missed you," he said.

I kissed him: "I love you."

The knock on the door jolted us back to reality. I nearly dropped my cup of tea and I started to move, getting ready to leave the room, to go and hide in the bedroom, but Sediba shook his head and motioned for me to stay. My throat was dry, my shirt felt too tight. I adjusted my belt. He put his hands in mine and squeezed before going to open the door. I fiddled with my keys and waited.

When he opened the door, and Thuli stood there, her eyes moving from Sediba to me. It took all the courage in me not to look away. Sediba seemed so unsure of himself that I didn't know if I was imagining it, but I thought I was losing him all over again.

Epilogue
A New Kind of Home

IN A FEW MINUTES I will have to go and lock the doors and put up the Re Tswaletse / Closed sign. This afternoon it's my turn to go and fetch her from school. The biggest challenge is getting through the last patient's visit. People always come with more than they admit at first. You think you're seeing someone for a headache and you find out the headache is because of trauma suffered a few weeks ago, so you have to sit, talk, make time. There's always more. I've come to understand now why my father's work took so long, why he left at sunrise and didn't close until long after supper time. I understand, also, my mother's resentment of the job and I'm lucky that I am with someone whose job sometimes requires late working hours, who also thinks people are there for one thing but they always bring in so much more of their lives.

So I've learnt, on the days that I have to drive into town to fetch her, that I must put someone whom I know well as the last patient on the schedule. It has to be a patient whose health concerns are more familiar to me—preferably someone I've seen very recently.

The road to town is not as long as it used to seem when I was growing up and being driven to school. Things—places—always seem much larger in the eyes of a child. I feel more and more tightly wound, and as is my way, I am fidgeting, patting my pockets looking for keys when I should know that I've put them in my bag. I feel giddy with anticipation because this is the best part of my week.

I pick up my jersey now and put it on. It is a rather stylish v-neck pullover, with leather trims around the openings of the sleeves. Of course I didn't buy it myself. I place my father's stethoscope in my father's old leather bag and sling it over my shoulder, wondering what he would say if he saw me now, taking over big parts of his life but not at all being the man he thought I was.

Outside my window I see there might be a storm on its way, clouds are gathering in the distance, white, grey, red. My thoughts turn to where I am going: there is a girl waiting for me and I must hurry before the storm lands.

Days after we bought the house, I stood at my gate and watched a scene from my childhood and one of my earliest memories repeat itself:

A large lorry, white as a sunny day's cloud, came to a standstill in front of my house. Sediba's father jumped out from the driver's seat as cheerfully as he had done when I was eleven years old. Again he rubbed his hands with the excitement of a child, his overalls as large and paint-stained as they had been on that day long ago. I wondered if they were the same pair.

Sediba's mother, as impeccably dressed as ever, stepped out and smoothed down her blue polka dot dress, her handbag slung over the crook of her arm. The boy who once wore a blue and white scarf around his neck was, this time, the man standing at my side, nervously fiddling with the keys in his pocket.

"Hallo boys!" His mother called out cheerfully, her easy chuckle reassuring us both. I stepped aside as she came towards us, one arm flying out and landing around her son's neck, lips landing on his cheek, her other arm stretched out beckoning me to her. Working to clear the lump in my throat, I moved in for the hug, felt lips moist with dark brown lipstick brush against my cheek.

The man called out: "*A re eng banna!*"

We quickly moved to help, unloading the truck. Bits of our old lives—chairs, tables, came out of the lorry, and we carried them into our new home.

Now I know what Sediba meant when he said his mother didn't ask questions, but she knew. Once a month or so his parents come in, groceries in hand, to join us for a meal. His father walks around tinkering with screws and handles, whistling all the time. He then sits with his son on our porch and they share beers while I walk around the garden with his mother, talking about plants, gardening, and nothing else. I have a bit of my own mother in me, it seems, because I'm quite happy to spend time in the garden. We eat together and they seem almost to not have noticed that there is one large bed and we both sleep in it.

After the meal they go next door through the adjoining back yard, because they are in love with the little girl.

Her name is Reitumetse and we call her Itu, Nana, Setsana, Ma-Itus, and Tutu. She has big round eyes with long eyelashes. Her skin is a smooth dark brown, darker than either one of us. Sometimes when I stand at the gate to the school see her come running up to me, school bag heavy on her back, her jersey in one hand and a flask in the other, I marvel at her beauty and at the sight of someone who looks at me like she loves me more than anything—like she just wants to fall into my arms.

I scoop her off her feet—school bag and all. She giggles on the good days or her head flops onto my shoulder on the hard days. No matter what kind of day she's had, she throws her arms around me and cries, "Papa Kabelo, can we get ice cream?"

Thuli always tells me, "Stop, don't feed her ice-cream *every time*. Not every time. Sometimes, once a week, is fine but not every time." Sometimes I smile and shrug away her concerns, other times I say: "OK, I'll try," but I never promise because if there is a way to refuse the child anything I swear I haven't found it yet.

From school we drive to the ice-cream place in Sunnyside, the one that claims to have "the best Danish ice cream." She says, "Can we go to Denmark someday, since they seem to have the best ice cream?"

I tell her, "Of course," and then I spend hours after she has gone to sleep in her room or next door to her mother's house, thinking and looking for ways the three of us can go overseas together, until

Sediba comes up and puts his arm around me and says, "Leave it to her mother, don't offer it."

I am very good about respecting her mother's wishes. I try never to do or say anything to suggest that she is mine—but at home, in private, I don't know how to fully let her be someone else's. I don't think of her as her mother's until Sediba reminds me. Until he says, "We agreed, remember?" and I shut my eyes and make myself remember that I have a child who is not mine.

I know he feels the same way because we talk about it when we're alone. Just the other day he had to phone me in the middle of the day from the salon. There he was making his customers wait because Itu had begged him to relax her hair and he faced a dilemma. He was short of breath when I picked up the phone, so that I had to ask, "Were you running?"

He explained the problem and said, "What's the harm, really?"

It was only after I had explained what the harm was, the thing about it not being our decision, though it would be cute, that he said, I could just blow dry it very straight. It would be the same thing to her but not to Thuli, right?"

"Still . . . " I started.

"Yah, still . . . "

She is ours but she is not ours. She lives mainly next door and moves freely between the houses with no fence in the backyard. She calls me Papa and she calls Sediba Papa but only softly, quietly, because she knows that it's not allowed—because one day she had spoken referred to me as her Papa to her grandmother and to this day she can still remember the tongue-lashing she received for it.

So, this is the way it is: when there are other people around, she speaks to us as if we're people with no names. No "uncle" or "papa" or even our first names. In public she only has a mother, in private we are a family.

People talk and stare but we have never said anything, not officially anyway. We are in the same house, in the same bed every night and Thuli and Itu live next door. Sometimes she sleeps at our house. When

Thuli works late or has a guest she doesn't want her to see, we take her out to the movies or out for supper and she comes to sleep here, in her own room with her own things.

We are not a family but we are. To us this is a family: separate houses; some lies or refusal to correct that misunderstanding that we're her uncles and to each other we are friends. We live with stories woven out of fear and the details tangling, tangling more with each passing year.

We have chosen to live in the suburbs, surrounded by people we don't know, even while we are still very committed to our jobs in Kasi. My parents' old house is Aus' Tselane's. I never go a whole week without visiting. I suppose at this point she is the only one left from my family of origin and as Sediba pointed out, if she lived there with my father and changed the house then the house is rightfully hers.

Sometimes when Sediba and I are planning something, when we are about to have a guest or to go and see people, we look at each other and ask, "Do they know?" and proceed, based on the answer.

You let go of people and places because of where you are. You choose to forget people you once wanted in your life because they don't know and you need them not to know. You have fewer family members because you're afraid of what might happen if they found out. Your loving happens when shadows fall and behind closed doors because that is the only way for it to survive. But here we are in spite of everything. Here we are, a family.

Our friends are the toughest part. There's a silence around us, around our being together. They're too close and too smart not to have noticed, of course. They no longer ask us about finding wives and they adore Itu, but no one ever says anything to suggest that they think we're a family—but I also think that it's kind they never suggest that we're not. We still have beers with them, still have parties with them, but always in the township and never at our home.

A lot has happened there. Base died before Itu was born. I know who is probably next, but I won't let myself think it. Who Sediba and I are to each other is hard for our township friends, but what is going on with them, the fact of losing each other, looking at houses going empty when everyone in them is still young: that is much harder.

Sometimes I do catch a scornful look or a disgusted comment from someone on the street. A patient comes in and says something believing that it's cryptic, but I recognize it as thinly veiled curiosity about me and Sediba, about why neither of us ever got married, or why Thuli's child sometimes comes and plays at the surgery and other times at the hair salon. I say nothing and reveal nothing. In the end I think people may be angry and disapproving—they may feel that we've betrayed them in some way because they trusted us to be the men they raised us to be, but as Sediba often tells me, people need good doctors and great hairdressers and that is all we have to be to them.

Glossary of Setswana, Afrikaans and Township Slang Words

A re eng banna! – (Setswana) "Let's go, men!"

Ao – (Setswana) pleasant surprise

Askies – (Afrikaans) "I'm sorry"

Aus' – (Setswana) Sister

Braai – (Afrikaans) barbecue

Eish! – Urgh!

Eng – (Setswana) a very polite Yes

Haai – (Slang) No!

Hao! – (Setswana) similar to "Oh, no!" showing surprise

Heita – (slang) for Hi

Howzit – How's it going?

Jo – a friendly nickname used between friends

Ke – (Setswana) It is

Lenyalo – (Setswana) wedding

Lobola – (isiZulu) Dowry

Mara – (Slang, derived from Afrikaans word *maar*) but/however.

Mfana – (isiZulu) young boy

Molweni – (formal, polite isiXhosa) hallo.

Monna – (Setswana/Sesotho) for Man

Na? – (Setswana) Is it?

Neh? – (Afrikaans) Right?

O right? – Are you alright?

O sa wara – (Slang) Don't worry

Ou' – (Afrikaans) old

Sies! – (Afrikaans) Gross!

Tjo! – (slang) shows surprise, usually for something unwelcome

Wie-Sien-Ons – (Afrikaans) A funeral after-party, to celebrate the life of the deceased

Zol – South African slang for marijuana

Acknowledgements

Jude Dibia, who breathed new love and life into this book. Martin Reesink and Anyes Babillon for loving the book and loving me more. David Austin for the 5 a.m. phone calls and ever-present love. Adrian Harewood for the many phone messages reminding me you were there. Amma Asante, for refusing to let me give up. Chris Abani for your love and time when I most needed it. Zukiswa Wanner and Thando Mgqolozana for reading and insisting it really was that good. My sister Lopang, for making me laugh when I thought I no longer had it in me. My sister Tumelo, for the 2 a.m. phone calls, the words of wisdom, the trips to come and be by my side, the relentless love.

Motsumi and Siamela for beautiful, overwhelming, glorious, frightening, endless love.

KAGISO LESEGO MOLOPE was born and educated in South Africa. Her first novel, *Dancing in the Dust* (Mawenzi House) was on the IBBY (International Board on Books for Young People) Honour List for 2006. Her second novel, *The Mending Season*, was chosen to be on the school curriculum in South Africa. Her third novel, *This Book Betrays My Brother*, was awarded the Percy Fitzpatrick Prize by the English Academy of Southern Africa, where it was first published. She lives in Ottawa.